his dying patients, but also wrestles with his wife's emotional state, and her COVID illness. He grapples with the scientific workings of his superior and fellow doctors, his best friend's infidelities, and the speculative treatment of the new variant causing Amnestic Brain Fog; notwithstanding, his determination to unravel the mystery surrounding the Pi variant. In all of this, he suffers the denunciations of his superior as he ferociously attempts to demystify his own beliefs. Although the fictional Pi variant rendered the patients into a human bog, Gomes fictional creativity enables the Pi variant to invade the emotional brain centers ameliorating his wife's dysfunctional personality and killing his friend's sexual appetite. As we approach the final chapter we wonder whether Jeff's determination to save lives and unearth the mystery of the Pi variant, will kill him too! As a thriller, Gomes gets the reader involved in his characters private and professional lives as they battle to alleviate the suffering of the struggling humanity.

—Linda Thorson, Honors Graduate of the Royal Academy of Dramatic Art, London, UK; starred as Tara King in the British TV series *The Avengers*; *The Other Sister* with Diane Keaton, *Sweet Liberty* with Michael Caine & Michelle Pfeiffer; *Valentino* with Rudolph Nureyev; on Broadway, *Noises Off*, *City of Angels*. Recipient of the Drama Desk Award, BAFTA Award UK, Theatre World Award, and The Le Prix Triumph.

BY ANTÓNIO GOMES

MEDICINE (AS J. ANTHONY GOMES)

Signal Averaged Electrocardiography:
Concepts, Methods and Applications

Heart Rhythm Disorders:
History, Mechanisms, and Management Perspectives

Rhythms of Broken Hearts

POETRY

Visions from Grymes Hill

Mirrored Reflections

NOVELS

The Sting of Peppercorns

Nas Garras Do Destino

Have A Heart

Love in the Shadow of Death

This powerful novel, set in the pandemic years, brings us close to the mystery of love in a time of destruction and death. It tells the story of lovers caught in the grips of mortality; their luminous, ebullient lives misted over in a world subject to rapid change. Beautiful and profoundly moving, it is emotionally accurate, and wise. Gomes' creation of the Pi variant causing Amnestic Brain Fog, is imaginatively immense.

—Grace Schulman, author of seven exclaimed books of poetry including, *New and Selected Poems*, and winner of the Frost Award for Lifetime Achievement in American Poetry. She is currently Distinguished Professor Emerita of English, Baruch College, C.U.N.Y.

Everyone in the world of this novel is threatened by the presence of Covid, each one's fate an uncertainty. It is all seen through the eyes of a physician, Jeff Anderson, an infectious disease specialist with a central role in fighting the challenges of the pandemic, accentuated by the personal dilemma of finding the people he loves most transformed into patients he is committed to cure. Again and again, love and friendship face an urgency. For Jeff, what would have been a medical challenge if his cases had been strangers becomes an emotional crisis when those in danger are the people who make his life worth living. In this novel, Gomes through his characters and his creation of a new Pi variant speaks directly to his readers, aware each of us must cope with the vulnerabilities of a new, and constantly mutating, unfamiliar virus.

—Walter Cummins, author of more than 10 books including *Knowing Writers*. He is an Emeritus Professor of English Literature at Fairleigh Dickinson University.

Love in the Shadow of Death, by António Gomes is a powerful and haunting story of love and loss set in the background of the most devastating pandemic of our lifetime. This remarkable novel accurately reflects the oppressive darkness of the disease and the extraordinary toll that it took on patients and health professionals in our hospitals and ICUs. At the same time, one experiences humanity's resilience and adaptability in the face of unprecedented adversity. Gomes creatively and masterfully uses the rapid mutation of the Corona virus to fictionally create the Pi variant that selectively affects the brain causing Amnestic Brain Fog in his friend Jacques, the playboy intervention cardiologist and several other patients. "The scene looked like a human bog with some patients floating around as they circled their beds aimlessly in an awkward maze-like formation staring into nothingness, zombie-like, while others lay on their beds, heads bobbing, all attired in the same blue scrubs." Gomes is a masterful storyteller in the vein of Gabriel Garcia Marquez.

—Umesh K. Gidwani, MD, MS, FCCM, FACC, FCCP, FSCAI, Professor of Medicine Icahn School of Medicine at Mount Sinai, Chief, Cardiac Critical Care, Zena and Michael A. Wiener Cardiovascular Institute; Director, Cardiac ICU, Mount Sinai Hospital and System Director, ICCM Patient Safety and Quality.

Love in the Shadow of Death, by António Gomes takes us into COVID-19's outbreak through the eyes of Jeff, an infectious disease physician. "My usual inwardness was now thrust outward, as if the essence of my soul had uncoiled in preparation of my life's work." Manhattan is at the beginning of a pandemic that now seems ancient as the plagues of Rome. A sense of the dystopic pervades the text as we enter the ICUs of breathing machines and deathbed separations of families, a world where Code Blues are no longer called as the death toll mounts. Gomes, a cardiologist as well as an author, writes masterfully of human physicality and psychology under pressure. "I held a leucospermum flower in my hand, marveling at its globe like shape with radiant red spikes." We meet Fleur, Jeff's wife, beautiful, rich, and haunted by the sexual molestation and kidnapping that lie in her past, and his lover, Antonina, an Italian physician. A new variant causing Amnestic Brain Fog invades the high stakes world of Jeff's mentor Jacques, the playboy heart specialist, that strips him of memory and self. The variant begins to spread, and suspicions surround the Center designed to study it. A thriller, a passion play, a poetry of disease, Gomes' prose is supple enough to illuminate the scientific as well as the metaphorical. His imagery is often stunning. "As their vines opened my mouth wide the alliums with their long stems entered my throat and went down my windpipe." Gomes has written an impassioned and essential novel about a turning point in our history. "A frothy crimson blood with floating corona flowers."

—Stephanie Dickinson, author of more than 9 books and *Harlow/Smith Postcards: Icons in Black & White*. She is the founding editor of Rain-Mountain Press.

Novels are intriguing and valuable tools in the hands of the imaginative writer. In *Love in the Shadow of Death*, António Gomes does not spare his imagination to penetrate the distant interiors and the complexities of the evolving Coronavirus that devastated NY and the world at large. In the novel Love and relationships constantly compete with Death. "And man was being finally defeated by an unseen microorganism...." Gomes brilliantly uses his medical mind and fascinating imagination to scrutinize the multi-sector intersection of human ecology. As much as the Pi Variant and Amnestic Brain Fog are fictional developments in the imagination of the author, they represent evolving, elusive and challenging new domains of viruses in anticipation what may be inevitable in the future. In this novel, Gomes shows us his expansive knowledge of medicine and boundless understanding of the socio-anthropological, economic and political complexity of our society when faced with a catastrophic pandemic.

—Basilio G. Monteiro, PhD. Professor, St. John's University, NY, USA, author of *Humanizing Artificial Intelligence: The agonizing relationship between anthropomorphism of the machine and the mechanomorphism of the human.*

Love in the Shadow of Death, by António Gomes, is a breathtaking story of man's moral timber in the face of unprecedented calamity brought about by the Coronavirus pandemic. We encounter the main protagonist Jeff, a dedicated infectious diseases specialist, a sleuth with a compassionate heart, who not only struggles carrying for

Love In The Shadow Of Death

António Gomes

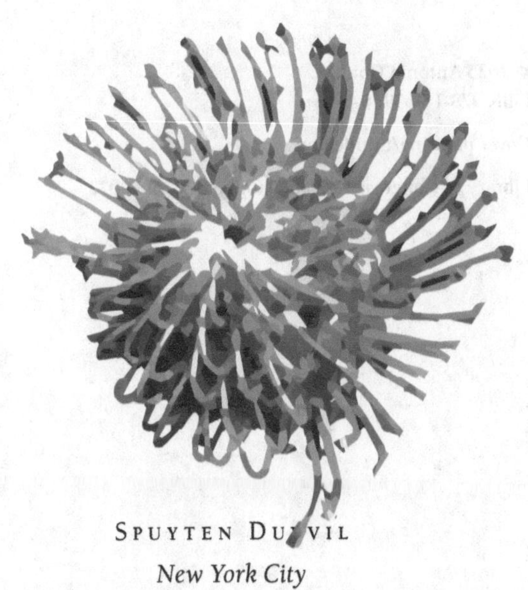

SPUYTEN DUYVIL

New York City

This book is dedicated to the doctors
and paramedical personnel in New York
who worked ceaselessly even without
appropriate protective equipment
to care for COVID-19 patients.
And to those who ultimately succumbed to the virus.

In 2020, a pandemic caused by COVID-19 devastated New York. This is a historical fact; otherwise, this book is entirely fictional. The characters and incidents described in this book are the creation of the author's imagination. The introduction of the Pi variant that produced Amnestic Brain Fog, is to add to the plot. And it, too, is a product of the author's imagination.

Contents

Part 1
Chapter 1: When Jeff Met Fleur
Chapter 2: Dinner At Jean-Georges
Chapter 3: Fleur's Stint In Saudi Arabia
Chapter 4: Jeff's Story
Chapter 5: Fleur's Miscarriage
Chapter 6: At The Leonardo Da Vinci-Fiumicino Airport
Chapter 7: Back To Work

Part 2
Chapter 8: The Pandemic Blows Into New York
Chapter 9: The Birthday Party
Chapter 10: The Chaos In The Intensive Care Unit
Chapter 11: Fleur's Loneliness
Chapter 12: At The Lincoln Center: The End Of Music

Part 3
Chapter 13: Love Smeared Corona Spheres And Spikes
Chapter 14: Wine, Jazz And Sex

Part 4
Chapter 15: Deaths From Neglect
Chapter 16: The Pandemic Comes Home To Roost
Chapter 17: Montauk
Chapter 18: It's An Upside-Down-Sideways World
Chapter 19: Fleur's Slow Recovery
Chapter 20: Life Lost, Life Regained, Lost Again
Chapter 21: Streaks Of Sunshine

Part 5
Chapter 22: The Amnestic Brain Fog
Chapter 23: The Saint Dymphna Brain Fog Center
Chapter 24: The Human Bog
Chapter 25: Housekeeping
Chapter 26: The Speculative Treatments
Chapter 27: The Lighting Bolt
Chapter 28: All For One And One For All?

Chapter 29: The Case Of Jacques Charpentier (#1)
Chapter 30: The Aftermath
Chapter 31: The Revelations
Chapter 32: A Doctored Covid Virus?
Chapter 33: The Road To Recovery

PART 6
Chapter 34: The First Plot
Chapter 35: The Execution Of The Plots
Chapter 36: The Picnic In Central Park
Chapter 37: The Reckoning

Epilogue
Glossary
Acknowledgements
About The Author

PART I

*Our greatest joy and our greatest pain comes in our
relationships with others*
—Stephen R. Covey

CHAPTER 1

WHEN JEFF MET FLEUR

It was eleven o'clock in the morning on a hot, steamy day in August, the year 2018. I was sitting in my small, windowless, gloomy office going over my messages and emails when the phone rang.

"Hi Jeff," said Jacques. "I'm sending you a female friend who has come down with a fever and bad sore throat."

"Why don't you see her yourself?" I said.

"I'm in San Francisco and won't be back for another four days. Moreover, you are the right man—an excellent internist, my friend. By the way, she is an absolute knockout."

After completing my residency training in medicine at Columbia hospital, I started a solo private practice in New York City. Since adolescence when my close friend David—my pastor's son—died of viral encephalitis after a missionary visit with his parents to Soweto, South Africa, I wanted to specialize in infectious diseases and virology, but the large college and medical school loans had gotten in the way. I was advised that general practice in the city was a tough bet, with the many medical schools and their affiliates and their multistoried campuses and high technology with computerized charts and innumerable internists, specialists, and super-specialists. Nonetheless, I decided to take a chance.

It was a little more than two years since starting the practice and what with the high apartment rent in mid-town Manhattan—where I preferred to live—the malpractice premium, the office rent, payments to a part time secretary and a part time nurse, I was barely able to survive. I moved to a cheaper large studio apartment on Broadway and 110th Street and gave up the car and mostly walked to work. My office was on 105th Street and 5th Avenue across the park, which I shared with other internists. This wasn't what I envisioned in med school. I expected to work in a major medical center, teaching house staff and doing research instead of working in a damp, dreary shared office in East Harlem.

My practice consisted mostly of patients with Medicare and Medicaid, unlike the high-powered practice of my friend Jacques who catered to the rich and famous of New York City. But I didn't mind it at all—doctoring was a mission like Evangelism, not a profession to make loads of money.

Many of my patients suffered from diabetes, high blood pressure and obesity and with it came sleep apnea, anxiety, insomnia, sexual dysfunction, and the premature cancers perhaps brought on by the carbohydrates and chemicals in their food obtained with food stamps from cheap convenience stores and supermarkets. This was the city where the poor were obese, and the rich were slim and dandy.

My life would take an unexpected turn when on that day, at about two o'clock in the afternoon, Jacques' referral, Fleur Boucher showed up in the office.

As I walked into the examining room with nurse Jacinta, I couldn't help but notice Fleur's beauty. Jacques was right.

"Can you open your mouth wide, Ms. Boucher?" I said, with a subtle smile.

After examining Fleur's throat and sending a throat swab for culture, I listened to her heart and lungs. I myself felt a skipped beat seeing her beautifully carved body under the blue- bliss hospital gown. I sensed a rush of adrenaline fearful of the rapid heartbeat diagnosed as Supraventricular Tachycardia. It was time to pay a visit to my heart rhythm expert.

I held my breath and the feeling of an oncoming palpitation ceased.

"Can you take in deep breaths through your mouth, Miss?"

"Sure, Doc."

"Your throat is fiery red and there is a white film on your tonsils," I said. "Are you in contact with children?"

"Yes," she said. "I was babysitting a five and a two-year old."

"I think you have a strep throat. I'm going to write you a prescription for penicillin. I'll call you with the results of the throat swab. And for now, stay away from the kids."

She listened to me attentively; her eyebrows pulled up and together.

"Is it serious Doc," she said, as her eyebrows twitched.

"Not at all. The penicillin will take care of it."

"Thank you, Doc." She smiled.

After she left, I couldn't get her out of my mind. She was about five-feet nine-inches tall, with a disarming childish face with high cheek bones, a fine Greek nose and a receding forehead with ample curly red hair and dark green eyes like that of Siamese cats. She looked years younger than her thirty-four. The other women I had met at recent parties after my wife's death— and admired for their stature, complexion, body line—paled in front of Fleur. My friend Jacques was right after all. Why not ask her out when I see her next time? It is just a strep throat— and I wouldn't be dating my patient. After the next visit, she wouldn't be my patient at all.

That evening I called the office of Dr. Grimes for an appointment, and because of a cancellation, the secretary informed me that he would see me the following morning. My palpitations had started a few years ago after the death of my wife Martha; however, they were sporadically occurring once every six months to a year.

After a thorough examination, Grimes told me that I likely have a Supraventricular Tachycardia, what the doctors call SVT.

"It's a benign condition but can be highly bothersome," he said. "Since the episodes are so infrequent, I'm going to prescribe a betablocker to slow the heart rate. It's to be used only when you get the episode and cannot break it by straining or pressing the artery in the neck or immersing your face in ice-cold water…We do have an ablative curative procedure, but it can wait for now."

Rather reassured, I proceeded to my office.

Fleur's throat swab came back positive for strep throat. I called to inform her that the culture was positive and emphasized that she should take the Penicillin religiously for the full ten days.

"Should I make a follow-up appointment?" she asked.

"I'll see you after you finish the course of the antibiotic."

Ten days later she was in the office. The examination was unremarkable and without beating around the bush I asked her out for dinner. She readily accepted. I was thrilled.

I called Jacques to tell him that I had a dinner date with Fleur.

"If you want to impress her—a worldly woman who has travelled the globe—take her to Jean-Georges in the Trump Tower, 1 Central Park West," he said.

"How do you know her?" I asked.

"I took care of her father many years ago," he said.

On my way home, I wondered whether Jacques was

having an affair with Fleur. However, he would have surely told me so and wouldn't have encouraged me to ask her out even suggesting where to take her. Although Jacques was married and had a three-year-old daughter, he was flying high with a three-bedroom apartment on Central Park West, a house in Montauk and a Lamborghini in the driveway. A much sought after cardiac interventionalist stenting the coronary arteries of New York celebrities and millionaires and billionaires, I was well aware of his extramarital forays. But as a heart interventionalist he was famous for his speed, his daring, his boldness, his inventiveness, and his calm under duress.

CHAPTER 2

DINNER AT JEAN-GEORGES

I could not take my eyes off Fleur when I went to pick her up. She was wearing a dark yellow above-the-knee dress that hung loosely over her body, and a pendant with a large smoky topaz and diamonds all around sparkled against her bare neck, accentuating her ginger hair.

"My God, you look stunning," I said. Her body emitted a rose fragrance with a woody and spicy undertone.

"You look sharp in that turtleneck and blue blazer. They match your sea-blue probing eyes," she said. "Your six-foot athletic frame looks younger than your approaching thirty-nine."

"How do you know my age?"

"I googled you and checked you out on LinkedIn."

I couldn't help laughing. "Everyone knows everything about each other nowadays. There are no more secrets left."

As the waiter seated us at an elegantly laid table over-looking a large window with shrubs in the background, we smiled at each other, and I commented on the opulence of the place: the hanging chandelier, the sedate lighting, and the comfortable, beige-colored seats.

"Would you like a cocktail?" I asked.

"Yes, a frozen Margarita."

"One frozen Margarita for the lady and a straight up

Martini with olives for me. Grey Goose please," I said to the waiter.

"I'm anxious to see the menu," said Fleur.

"I believe it's a prix fixe menu," I said.

"Before the waiter returns, I want to hear about you, Jeff," she said.

"Well...I was born on a farm in Ohio of Evangelical Christian parents, of meager means, but a strong Midwestern work ethic. I graduated from Case Western and went to med school at the Cleveland Clinic. For pastime, I listen to jazz, watch movies and shows, jog in Central Park and do long-distance cycling...but my life had been an unadventurous straight line until I met our common friend Jacques Charpentier during internship at the Cleveland Clinic."

"How so?"

"Well, Jacques introduced me to fun and booze after our hard working twenty-four hour on-call internship off days."

"That figures," she said.

"After I landed in New York for a residency in medicine, I was too busy doctoring and did not have time to attend church services. Unlike my parents, I was a 'doubting Tom,' who went along with the rigors of the Christian faith not from conviction but more so to keep in tow with my deeply religious parents. But after the death of my wife, Martha, I sort of realigned to my faith. I sometimes pray before bedtime, but I don't attend services at all." She looked at me with furrowed eyebrows. I wondered whether she resented my Evangelical background.

"So, are you religious?" she asked with a subtle, forced smile.

"No! Not in an organized sense. I...I don't attend services." The waiter had arrived with our drinks. I took a mouthful of the Martini.

"When did you meet your wife?" she asked as she licked the salt of her full lips.

"When I was in med school, and she in nursing. We married about a year after I moved to New York."

"I'm so sorry about your wife. Someday hopefully, you'll tell me details."

"Yes, sure…What about you Fleur?"

"I'm French in origin," she said with a flourish. My father was an oil executive. I lived with him in Saudi Arabia, Venezuela and Houston, and travelled the world with him. Ultimately my father retired in New York with his Russian second wife, Victoria. I was adopted at the age of five and followed my father after my mother passed away from breast cancer, when I was eight years old."

"I'm so sorry. We both seem to have had our share of death."

"I grew up without a mother," she said, lowering her eyebrows and squeezing her eyes. I could sense her hurt in her expression.

"Moving from one place to another, I turned out to be a rolling stone except for a stint at modelling, a chef's school, and some recent acting in commercial advertising…I had a terrible experience once. I was nearly raped in Saudi

Arabia."

"Oh God, I am so sorry." I squeezed her hand in sympathy.

"I don't want to talk about it now. Let's enjoy the dinner."

"What about religion?" I asked.

"I was baptized a Catholic. But I don't practice and I do not believe in religions. Does it bother you?"

"Not at all."

"I'm not American and not religious! Doesn't that trouble you?"

"No! Variety is the spice of life. And this is New York," I said. "Did you know that nearly 40% of New York City residents are foreign born? I'm sure I have a lot to learn from you…culturally speaking."

"Really? You think so?" she asked with a smile.

I shook my head. "I'm surprised you are single. With your looks, any man would grab you."

"Moving from one place to another, it was hard to develop a permanent relationship. But I did have a steady boyfriend in Caracas, Venezuela, which could have resulted in marriage. But after the kidnapping, I did not want to live there, and my boyfriend—who had a brewery—was unwilling to move to the States."

"Kidnapping?"

"That's another story. Some other time." Fascinating woman with a lot of stories, I thought to myself. Will she be a handful? But her beauty: the face with high cheek bones, the proportional nose, the feline eyes, the red, shiny, curly hair. I cannot wait to kiss her full lips.

"You are staring at me," she said.

"You are beautiful. I cannot take my eyes off you." She gave a hearty laugh.

We ate a prix fixe menu with wine pairing. She: Meyer Lemon Gelée, Caviar, and Crème Fraîche for appetizer; and for the main course, Butter Poached Lobster, Fall Vegetable Tapioca, with Gewurztraminer, and Passion Fruit. I: Warm Glazed Potatoes with Caviar, Tapioca and Herbs for appetizer, and Black Sea Bass Crusted with Nuts and Seeds, Sweet and Sour Jus for the main course. For dessert she opted for Bittersweet Chocolate and Passion Fruit, and I chose Pistachio Financier, Strawberry Sorbet accompanied by Cappuccino and Quinta das Carvalhas— Vintage Port, her choice. After all the wine, she hardly talked, but laughed a lot. Her laughter was addictive. Again, I felt an urge to kiss her full red lips. Was I falling in love with her? No doubt I was infatuated.

The dinner was expensive, but exquisite—I could barely afford. Fleur was worth the price. I could sense that she was impressed.

"Thanks for the dinner—the food and the ambiance were great," she said. "And the company." She stretched her hand and touched mine. It was electrical.

"Yeah…you are most welcome. The place is highly rated with two Michelin stars."

We were quite high from the wine and Port when we left the restaurant. She invited me to her apartment, and I kissed her as soon as we entered the elevator. When we stepped into the apartment we pawed each other hungrily, and had sex standing, half-clothed. We fell asleep as soon as we hit the bed.

After I woke up at ten in the morning, I checked my messages and email on my iPhone, after which I roamed around her spacious two-bedroom apartment.

She woke up at eleven and cooked a Pomodoro omelet. We ate it and gulped down a half-bottle of Moet and went back to bed again. We both ravished each other's bodies; I, prodded by her moans as I tongued her erogenous zones; and she took the initiative to caress, to lip and tongue my body, in places I had never experienced before. Lying naked on the bed she looked like an Raphaelesque putto. I was ecstatic at the sex act. Perhaps it was the champagne that had copiously aroused our pheromones. I had read somewhere that the sight of beauty extols Eros into our lives, even if for a short time, and that sex with a beautiful woman apotheosizes us somehow.

Suddenly, she jumped off the bed and began singing:

L'amour est un oiseau rebelle
Que nul ne peut apprivoiser,
Et c'est bien en vain qu'on l'appelle,
S'il lui convient de refuser...
L'amour! L'amour! L'amour! L'amour!

"Wow, you have a great voice. *L'amour*—Love! Love! Love! Love! You should have been an opera singer," I said.

"Yes, a wasted talent. Maybe I should take singing

classes." We finished the bottle of Moet.

"I love you Fleur," I said, spontaneously and perhaps thoughtlessly. "I love you too," she said and began laughing hilariously. I too laughed along. I knew that it was too fast to swear love —after all we were not teenagers— but then, we were both high on champagne. And both seemed to be tickled by the love chemicals in the brain. She was the real deal. Flawless. Born with taste. Elegance. *Balenciaga. Dior.* It was the best date I ever had.

After a short nap, I dressed and got ready to leave. "Where are you going?" she asked. "Why don't you stay here? *Mi casa es su casa.*" I knew what that meant. After all, many of my patients were Latinos. She told me that she spoke several languages: English, French, Spanish and even some Italian and Arabic.

She insisted on showing me the apartment with its glass walls and high ceilings. She went over the curios and the paintings relating where she had purchased each of them: "The blue plates are antique Cantonese porcelain bought in Macau; the Vase is an antique Ming—a gift from my father; the rug is an antique Persian; the paintings are by Venezuelan, Cuban and Peruvian avant-garde artists…"

"This is a great, comfortable apartment, meticulously put together, with taste. I'm impressed."

Suddenly, it was as if I saw the future ahead. This was the opportunity I had to take: a rich beautiful young wife—how common was that? I can give up the practice and go back to specialize, get into a fellowship program and join the ranks of Jacques as an academician. I felt rather guilty at the thought. Was I being selfish? Was I euphoric and irrational? Am I taking advantage of her? I decided to take it easy, give it sometime. I wasn't running the Kentucky Derby.

"What do you do for a living, Fleur," I asked to make conversation, to kill my selfish thoughts.

"Odds and ends to kill time and for pocket money if I'm up to it," she said. "I'm well provided for. My father made a Living Trust for my protection just before he re-married and transferred this apartment to me. I don't have to work really. I would love to model, but I'm not tall enough and not slim enough for modelling. The competition is stiff. But I need something—a niche to hang on to."

"You have the luxury to do whatever you wish... Do you see your father often?"

"Yes, I do. He has an apartment on the East Side. We are very close, but I avoid him when Victoria is around."

"Why so?"

"She's jealous of me. Thinks I'm a spoiled brat."

"Are you?"

"No, not at all."

"What about your adopted mother? Do you remember her?"

"I only have a vague memory."

"What about your biological mother?"

"She is French. I have an inner desire now to meet her,

and my dad is helping me out. We are looking for a private detective to locate her."

"I really hope you meet her. One needs closure of such an important event in one's life."

"Do you have a girlfriend?"

"I just started dating women. No, I don't have a girlfriend."

She told me that the constant move from one country to another, and the constant loss of her friends, had had a negative impact. "I was losing friends as fast as I was making them," she said. "Besides, I was traumatized by the loss of my adopted mother Adrianne, and my father Allain wanted me to be with him and took me around the globe."

"You were very young when your mother died. Who really cared for you?"

"I lived with my grandparents in Paris initially. I had a nanny who cared for me. That changed when we moved from one country to another."

"It must have been exciting living in all those foreign countries," I said.

"Well, yes and no," she said. "I had a bad experience in Saudi Arabia, and I was kidnapped for ransom in Venezuela. I don't want to talk about it now. It's a long story. A painful story. Someday, I will tell you."

"Oh my God. I'm so sorry." I saw her eyes flush with tears. I went and hugged her.

"I appreciate your concern… I got over it. Time is often the best healer."

"Yes, time is the best healer." I could read anxiety and trepidation across her face as she became serious and one of her eye lids began twitching.

"It is traumatic to rehash bad times," I said.

She suddenly began to cry. I took her in my arms and held her tight.

CHAPTER 3

FLEUR'S STINT IN SAUDI ARABIA

One evening when Fleur invited me for dinner after work, I found her cooking her favorite Daube, a hearty Provençal stew consisting of lamb simmered low and slow in wine with various vegetables and seasonings of cinnamon, cloves, thyme, bay leaves, and peppercorns. She had all the ingredients meticulously arranged on the kitchen counter. I watched the time-consuming process in which the ingredients were added in layers, with the meat on the bottom and the spices and vegetables on top. It confirmed my impression that she is a multi-talented classy type unlike the couple of nurses I had dated and had dinner in their apartment who ordered out.

"Where did you learn to cook?" I asked.

"With my grandmother in Paris," she said. "This was one of her favorite recipes. Besides, I took cooking classes after I came to New York. I wanted to become a chef."

We sat for a candlelight dinner relishing the Daube with a bottle of Châteauneuf-du-Pape. Her knowledge of French wines was impressive as well, and I was learning fast.

"I have been meaning to ask you: How do you know my friend Jacques?" I asked.

"I met him after he placed stents in my father's three coronary arteries," she said. "It was magical. My father's cardiologist had recommended open heart surgery. A friend asked him to see Dr. Jacques Charpentier, and it made all the difference. He fixed his arteries in two sittings one week apart and he was home the next day."

"He is a great technician, and a flamboyant character. Did you have an affair with him? I hope you don't mind the question."

"Yes, a short fling. We remain good friends now."

I was reassured and felt a sense of admiration for her honesty. After all she was of French stock, and they take *le amour* and sex with a *laissez-faire* attitude.

"Did you live in Paris with your grandparents after your mother died?"

"I lived on and off with my grandparents in Paris until the age of fourteen. I was an adventurous spirit during my teenage years, totally out of control. After the hormonal changes of puberty, I began having episodes of depression followed by an unruly high phase when I ran away with my crush and stayed away for an entire night. It was then that I lost my virginity."

"How old were you?" I asked.

"Fourteen. What about you?"

"You'll make fun of me if I tell you. I grew up in an Evangelical Christian family, and I was taught that sex should happen only after marriage. But I broke the vow. I lost my virginity during my internship with a nursing student. I was twenty."

"My grandparents were alarmed after I stayed away from home. They were old and couldn't manage the situation. My father came back to Paris and took me to Saudi Arabia where he was stationed at the time."

"In Saudi Arabia, we lived in the Aramco compound known as the Dhahran Camp —a gated residential community in the Saudi Eastern Province close to the world's largest oil reserve. The compound was a replica of a California settlement, right down to its way of life. For non-Saudi residents there were schools, a medical clinic, movie theaters that screened the latest Hollywood blockbusters, bars, golf ranges, tennis courts, a baseball field, and Christmas decorations in December."

"What was your life like in Saudi Arabia?" I asked. I sensed she was in the mood to get it off her chest.

"For the Americans living in the compound the arrangement was great, but for me, a Parisian it felt too artificial, too manicured, too uncultured," she said. "We were advised not to venture out of the camp alone, and without wearing the *abaya*—the ankle-length black dress and head scarf. I made friends with some American girls, but I didn't fit in. The Arab and other Asian workers kept staring at me. At first it was sort of a novelty, but the men gazed at me as if they were stripping me naked. They stared at all the white girls, but I felt that they stared at me in a rather naughty, dirty way."

"I was told by a friend of mine that in South Asia it is common to stare at white women."

"One day my father and I joined a Saudi friend, a coworker with a high position like my father's in the oil company. He showed us around the city outside the camp after which he invited us for dinner at his home. He had a daughter Ayesha, my age, and a son, Saad who was nineteen. Ayesha and I became close friends. At home they lived a posh life dressed in western clothes and watched western movies, but outside the house it was a different story. Both Ayesha and her mother, Abida, wore the abaya and a hijab.

"What's the difference?" I asked.

"Hijab is a headscarf that covers only the upper parts, the head and shoulders, of the women; abaya is a long robe covering the woman's body."

I poured two glasses of Cabernet Sauvignon and handed a glass to Fleur. "Please continue," I said.

"Right from the day I met Saad, he kept staring at me," she said. "In the beginning, I didn't think much of it…his stares were flattering and at the same time embarrassing. One day I asked Ayesha why her brother keeps staring at me like all the other Asian men."

"'It is your red hair,' said Ayesha. 'They wonder what it's like down there—is the flower red too?'"

"I just couldn't stop laughing," she said. "But it was no laughing matter."

"How so?" I asked.

"It was a Sunday afternoon when my father and Ayesha's father had left for Riyadh for a company meeting. I had made plans to visit Ayesha at her home at about five in the evening. The chauffer of the company car had some errands to perform and dropped me early. Ayesha phoned telling me that she had gone shopping with her mother and would be a bit late. She told me that her brother and the servants would be there to let me in. She asked me to put on the VCR and watch whatever movie I wanted to watch. She would take me to a recently opened French restaurant in town for dinner. Her mother would chaperone us. I was excited to eat a French meal at a posh new restaurant.

"Saad opened the door when I knocked. I was surprised at the smell of alcohol on his breath. Alcohol was not served in their home…I wondered where he got it from. I went to Ayesha's room and put on the VCR and inserted *Lord of the Rings*. As I was midway into the movie, suddenly and unexpectedly, Saad burst into the room.

"'I got to show you something,'" he said. "'It's a surprise. Come hurry up.'"

"As soon as we entered his room, he pushed me onto the bed. He came on top of me and started licking my face like a poodle. I giggled and told him to stop it and tried to push him away. But he was a heavy-set kid. Before I knew what was happening, he lifted my skirt and tore my panties away and had his mouth on my crotch. I tried to push him away. He began licking and biting me there. It was then that I mustered all the strength and managed to untangle my right foot from his hold and kicked him hard on the face with my healed shoe. The kick ended up breaking his nose. He was in agony as I broke loose. At that moment I heard footsteps, and both his mother and Ayesha were in the room."

Fleur went to the bathroom and came back with a lit cigarette. She then continued telling her story.

"He tried to rape me. I shouted. I kicked him hard on his stomach as he was writhing in agony." Fleur puffed on the cigarette and inhaled deeply.

"'I was only checking if the flower was red like your hair,' he said amid sobs."

I felt uncomfortable and to some extent angry. I clenched my fist tight, and the fine Czechoslovakian crystal glass of wine cracked and slipped out of my hand and as I let go of the broken glass it came crashing on the parquet floor. I went to the kitchen for a broom and paper towels and cleaned the mess on the floor. There was a small cut on the palm of my hand. Fleur washed it with peroxide and applied a strip of band aid.

"Please continue. I'm sorry for the mess. I simply cannot tolerate sexual abuse," I said.

"You wait till I tell my father," I said to Saad. "You are going to jail. I began to cry. Ayesha cuddled me and took me to her room. Her mother remained in Saad's room wailing, not knowing what to do. She did not speak much English and did not understand what I said but obviously surmised that her son had attacked me.

"Oh God…you poor thing," I said.

"I asked Ayesha to request their chauffer to take me home right away," Fleur continued. "In the evening I received a call from Saad's uncle to keep whatever happened a secret and not even tell my father because the consequences for me would be more serious than for Saad if my father pressed charges. I could be accused of seduction. I was furious. I could hear Saad's mother talking in Arabic and the uncle translating what she was saying. He told me that Saad was taken to the hospital to fix his broken nose and that they had mentioned that he slipped and fell on his face."

I poured myself some wine and asked Fleur if she wanted a refill.

"No thanks," she said. "The next day I dyed my hair black. My father was surprised to see the sudden change. He loved my curly red hair. He asked me why I had dyed it. I told him that red hair provoked stares from Saudi, Indian and Pakistani men working in the compound. I was tired of their stares.

"I stopped going to Ayesha's house and my dad kept on asking me why. I told him that I was bored of their place, of Aisha and her family. All we do is watch movies. I want to go to Paris for the summer holidays."

"I'm not at all surprised by your reaction," I said.

"Ayesha had come to visit me one evening when my father was travelling in South America. She again asked me to bottle up the events of that evening, and at the same time she expressed great satisfaction for standing up to Saad."

"What did you say?" I asked.

"I did not respond."

"Ayesha then told me that Saudi women wouldn't have

the courage to confront a man even if they were raped. She told me that he messed around with one of the servants—a Filippina, and we had to let her go. Sometimes, he comes to my room when I'm asleep. Once I saw him smelling my panties and masturbating."

"I asked Ayesha whether Saad was messing with her. She said an emphatic 'no'. But I didn't believe her. I felt she was hiding something. They are very secretive about these things."

"I understand," I said. "Sexual abuse is not talked about in such cultures."

"As time went by, I fell into a mortal depression to the extent that I refused to go to school," Fleur said. "I remained in bed all day eating Swiss and Belgian chocolates and gained considerable amount of weight. Finally, my father exasperated took me to see a psychiatrist in the medical clinic in the compound. He was an Indian doctor, a very genteel person who opined that my depression was hormonal and placed me on a mood elevating pill I don't remember the name. I perked up with the pill, but ultimately stopped it because of palpitations."

"It must be Elavil," I said. "Did you confide in the Indian doctor about the sexual abuse?"

"No, absolutely not. When summer arrived, my father agreed to send me to Paris, and my mood improved. I promised to behave and not to trouble the old folks. Hardly was I in Paris for a month or so, when my father called to tell me that he had accepted the job as vice-president of the National Venezuelan Oil Company in

Caracas, Venezuela and that he was leaving Saudi Arabia. He said he would call for me once he got settled."

"That was very brave of you," I said. I embraced her and held her close and cupped her face in the palms of my hands. My eyes were moist and teary. I poured myself a stiff brandy and pored one for Fleur.

"I had nightmares for a long time. I saw him on top of me. What would happen if I hadn't kicked him? Would he have raped me? The very thought sent shivers down my spine." We both fell silent.

"I guess social restrains make them what they are," I said, to break the silence.

"Yes, with no sexual outlet, they become sexual hot potatoes; but most are restrained by their Islamic faith," she said. "They blame the women accusing them of seduction."

"That is simply intolerable…an afront to a woman's dignity," I said.

She told the story calmly and unemotionally; but then suddenly she began sobbing uncontrollably. "Now you know what my exotic life was like," she said.

"I'm so sorry Fleur," I said.

"It was hard for me after the incident with Saad. I couldn't stand men. It took me a long time to start dating when in Venezuela."

"Yes, memories stir up other memories reopening old scars turning them into fresh wounds," I said.

I embraced her and tears began running down my face, something I hadn't felt since my wife's sudden unexpected death, and her story rekindled my suppressed emotions. I was consumed with guilt for my own protected life right from childhood when my parents were there to shield and safeguard me from bullies in school and God from evil, until tragedy struck unexpectedly later in life.

"I will protect you, my Fleur, my flower, from now on," I said, and held her in my arms, and the crying gradually stopped.

She went to the bathroom and came back with another lighted cigarette and pored herself a generous refill of the wine.

"Just this one cigarette," she said. "I ran out of weed. It's way more relaxing."

It was obvious to me that her story was anxiety provoking. She badly lacked a mother to confide in, to protect her.

"Did you tell this story to your father? I asked.

"Not right then. Many years later. He sobbed. I had never seen him cry."

"You poor thing. You had no one for support. It must have been hard."

"I told you my story," she said. "What's yours?" I met her question with a sly smile and silence. I was not yet ready to open up. Besides, I did not want to dilute her story with mine.

We saw each other often and in about six weeks or so I moved in with Fleur. I soon noticed her mood swings just before her menstrual cycle, and the weed habit, but her beauty, her charm and sexuality drowned all.

CHAPTER 4

JEFF'S STORY

Several weeks later, Fleur and I had a dinner date at an Asian fusion restaurant in Manhattan—her treat. I was supposed to meet her at her apartment at about six o'clock and the reservations at the restaurant were at seven. I called her at five-thirty in the evening.

"I'm sorry honey, you'll have to cancel the reservation," I said. "I am busy attending to a patient's family. I will explain when I get home." I expected Fleur to understand— the life of a doctor is often plagued by emergencies.

I arrived at about seven-thirty all dejected and mentioned to her that a young patient of mine blacked out on the street and died in the ER. "It was so sudden and unexpected," I said. "I had seen her a week ago. She had complained of palpitations, and I had ordered a heart monitor. In the emergency room she went into the lethal rhythm, called ventricular fibrillation, a heart rhythm incompatible with life. She did not respond to resuscitative measures and electrical shocks. She was barely twenty-one years old, an undergraduate student at Columbia University who lived in Harlem and was raised by a single mother. She was a lively person with a joyful contagious smile and great potential. She wanted to become a doctor. I was simply crushed. She reminded me of Martha's sudden unexpected death."

Fleur hugged me and held me tight.

"I'm so sorry Jeff. Please tell me what happened to Martha," she said. "It's time you get it off your chest." She offered me a shot of my favorite single malt.

After a stiff shot of Glenmorangie, I began relating my story.

"I had met Martha in my last year of med school when she was a nursing student. It was common for med students to date nursing students. Both of us coming from the same religious and cultural backgrounds, *first love* seeped rapidly into our hearts. She was a slim five-feet-eight blonde with regular features, and a roundish face.

Was she beautiful?" asked Fleur.

"She was a rather plain woman. Not particularly beautiful. But what attracted me to her was her captivating smile and her happy disposition. She was the fifth of six children: three girls and three boys. Two of her siblings, one sister and one brother, had passed away at the age of three and four before she was born. She was told that their deaths were a divine act, God's call so to say! Martha was very religious and prayed for her dead siblings to intercede on her behalf whenever she encountered any misfortune." I stopped talking to catch my breath and take a long draught of the single malt.

"Please go on Jeff," said Fleur. She was listening to my story attentively.

"Misfortune had recently tumbled upon the family. Her mother had died in a car accident when she was a nursing student and apparently had blacked out once before the accident. Her father was an Evangelical Christian Pastor—a flamboyant good looking grey-haired middle-aged man. Pastor Edward Johnson's sermons delivered in a sharp, cutting tenor voice were of fire and brimstone. He admonished gays and gay marriage. An avid anti-homosexual and anti-gay marriage preacher, he was partly responsible for motivating the Christian right in Ohio to vote for George W. Bush when gay marriage was on the ballot orchestrated by Karl Rove.

"Who's that?" asked Fleur.

"Senior advisor and Deputy Chief of Staff for President Bush…Well, to continue…the pastor, Martha's father was reported to be soliciting men in airport and nightclub bathrooms and having gay sex with a male prostitute. He had initially denied it all, but pleaded *Mea Culpa, Mea Maxima Culpa* when the male prostitute threatened to go public with revealing photos. He repented and prayed for forgiveness and overnight proclaimed himself a born-again Christian. He was forgiven and readily accepted by his congregation.

"I sympathized with Martha's pain and did not appreciate the double standard and the hypocrisy in the Evangelical Christian community. Martha loved and highly regarded her father and was awfully let down. She felt betrayed. She ultimately broke with him and left the church. I admired her courage and fortitude under the circumstances.

"For Thanksgiving when I brought Martha home, and when my father William came to know that his only son was dating Pastor Edward Johnson's daughter he was simply elated and saw salvation for his faith-wavering son-soon-to-be-a-doctor. What he did not know was that Martha had lost her faith all together, and so had I."

"What did your father think of Pastor Johnson?" she asked.

"He didn't say much. I gather he was forgiven."

"Forgiveness is an important part of Christianity," said Fleur.

"When I started my internship at the Cleveland Clinic, Martha began working as an ER nurse in a community hospital in Columbus, Ohio, and intended within a year to join me at the Cleveland Clinic to do her master's in nursing.

"That winter, Martha and I went to St. Martin for a holiday. On the very day we arrived in sunny St. Martin, while making love she passed out. When she came out of it, for a brief moment she was confused and rather confounded for soiling the bed. It was as if sadness crushed her under its weight and I held her naked body gently as if to repress a deep-seated wound."

"Why did she pass out?" asked Fleur.

"I thought it was likely a vasovagal attack—a common faint," I said. "I asked her if I'd hurt her. She shook her head."

"Sorry for the interruption."

"The next day, while swimming in the ocean, in shallow water, she passed out again, and again I thought she had fainted. I made her drink lots of water and pickled her with plenty of salt."

"We got married about a year after I moved to New York City—for my residency training in medicine—and Martha began her post-graduate studies in nursing while working parttime in the ER. She became pregnant but had a miscarriage and once again after an argument with a rowdy patient in the ER she passed out. Finally, at the recommendation of Jacques I took her to see Dr. Grimes who found an abnormality, a slightly prolonged QT interval on her ECG."

"What's that?"

"The QT interval on the electrocardiogram reflects relaxation of the heart before it contracts. He also performed a Tilt Test where she was tilted head-up for twenty minutes, but the test was negative. He sent her blood for genetic testing suspecting the possibility of a genetic abnormality—the Long QT Syndrome that can result in sudden death. He discussed the possibility of inserting a defibrillator in view of the death of two of her siblings, history of her mother's car accident possibly due to a blackout at the wheel, and Martha's history of recurrent blackout spells and a miscarriage. The defibrillator was a major undertaking for Martha and we both decided to wait for the results of the genetic test. Moreover, a monitor she wore for forty-eight hours did not show any rhythm disturbance."

"It seems you made the right decision," said Fleur. "A defibrillator is a major undertaking, I was told. Doctors wanted to put one in my father after his heart attack, but decided against it after his heart function improved on medications."

"A week or so later as we were crossing the street in midtown Manhattan, a car made a sudden turn from a side street and honked at us—a shrill and loud honk that startled us. Martha collapsed and was pulseless. I administered CPR. The paramedics gave it all to no avail."

"Oh my God. How awful. And you witnessed it all," she said.

"The results of the genetic test would confirm that Martha had the dreaded Long QT Syndrome—a genetic abnormality that most likely felled her siblings and her mother. Dr. Grimes mentioned that she had the variety that triggers a heart arrhythmia during emotional stress: a loud noise such as the honk of a car or a sudden thunderclap and even an alarm clock going off during sleep."

"My Lord, what a catastrophe," she said. "I never knew these things can happen to young people. Sudden death I was told occurs in old people with coronary disease. My grandfather died suddenly at the age of seventy-two from heart disease."

"That's correct. But it can occur in the young, even in athletes due to genetic abnormalities in the heart's rhythm *a la* Dr. Grimes."

"How did you cope, Jeff?"

"I was devastated. I was no cardiologist or heart rhythm expert, yet I couldn't accept that I badly erred in her diagnosis, repeatedly misdiagnosing her condition as a common faint. It was a gross mistake to hold off on the defibrillator. If she had the defibrillator she might have survived."

"I fully understand," she said. You poor thing."

I fell silent in contemplation. I thought of a loved one's death, the very idea, impossible for a young person to latch on to, to permeate the mind, that one's time on earth, one's life, is a short flimsy thing, a mere gust of wind.

"When I think about my mother's cancer appearing out of the blue, and how she was gone in barely six months' time—" said Fleur, as if to break the silence. "Life can be so fleeting! How did you handle all of this?"

"Her death and her burial in Columbus, Ohio officiated by her father with her siblings and cousins in attendance would remain my private wound. I was crushed and despaired blaming myself for her death that I even contemplated leaving medicine altogether. My listlessness and gradual loss of interest in life spelled of depression. I immersed into a solitude that grew in heaviness day by day, and it crushed me into a shadow. I locked myself up in the on-call room. It was then that I developed a rapid heartbeat and had to be taken to the ER where a diagnosis of Supraventricular Tachycardia was made and terminat ed with an intravenous medication. Finally, the head of the residency program at the hospital acted. I was admitted to the psychiatry ward and medicated, and over the course of several weeks I began taking control of my senses. My friend Jacques came to my aid. He convinced me to keep going, to keep busy, to plunge into medicine wholeheartedly—that's what Martha would want for me—to serve the suffering humanity—a noble undertaking—for her sake. I owe Jacques a lot. He visited me several times a week.

"Yes, Jacques is a good and helpful friend."

"Ultimately, I swallowed the fact that overall, we have very little control of our lives. Sheer luck and serendipity have shaped some, if not most of it. Our birth parents are a matter of chance, as are the wealth or poverty we are born into, the country of our birth, and more often than not, even our marriage partner. And as far as disease is concerned our genetic makeup. All we can do is to go on living and hope for the best."

"How did you recover from depression? It took me a long time to get over it."

"With medications and psychotherapy. Over a course of a couple of months I snapped back and finally acquiesced to that reality like a fish in a shallow pond. I took some time off from the residency and went back to Ohio."

It was obvious to me that when Fleur heard my story, and I hers, black and grey drafts of our lives, we were crushed, she perhaps more than me by the weight of sadness, and it triggered in her a long sobbing fit. She held me hard as if stanching a deep wound and our tears intermingled like blue blood comingling with the red in a cocoon. It was then that we both realized that we had suffered enough and that we were meant for each other. It was time for us to find happiness.

I continued living with Fleur, but marriage remained on the back burner for both of us. In the meantime, I sold my practice to the Uptown Medical Center and was accepted for a fast-track fellowship in infectious diseases. My previous research on viruses at Chapel Hill and a strong recommendation from the influential Jacques added up. The chairman of infectious diseases Dr. Welch accepted me for a one-year fellowship at the Uptown Medical Center and commitment for a full-time faculty position. I was in seventh heaven. My dream was being fulfilled.

A few months later, an unexpected pregnancy came our way and we decided to tie the knot.

CHAPTER 5

FLEUR'S MISCARRIAGE

The hormonal changes associated with Fleur's pregnancy brought her mood disorder to the forefront. Any minor argument or setback triggered strong emotions characterized by bouts of crying and sometimes anger directed at me and her physicians. The total abstinence from cigarettes, weed, and wine due to the pregnancy seemed to have aggravated the problem.

While I was on rounds, I got a call from Fleur's obstetrician, a good friend and a highly regarded doctor.

"I just wanted to give you a head's up," he said, "Fleur had a bit of a meltdown when I recommended amniocentesis. She left here very angry and upset. She began to cry and said that I don't know what I am talking about."

"I'm so sorry," I said.

"You are in your thirties and this is your first pregnancy, I told her," said Max, her obstetrician. "I informed her that there is a small risk of Down's syndrome in the baby, about 1 in 400 at age thirty-five. She stormed out of the OB office."

"I will speak to her. She will come around, Max." I said.

When Fleur got home, she called me on the phone. "I don't want to have the amniocentesis," she said.

"It is a standard procedure. There is nothing to worry about."

"It's my body and it's my life, and I will have to care for the baby. That obstetrician is smart, but rough at the edges. No bedside manners. Besides, what do men know of women's inner feelings? I told you that I wanted to see a female obstetrician."

"Dr. Max Davis is the best obstetrician at the medical center with high ratings and extensive experience. If you want to see a female obstetrician for a second opinion, I can look for one." Momentarily, her tone of voice changed. She calmed down.

When I arrived home, she was anxious, irritable, and jittery. I went to hold her in my arms, but she pushed me away.

"You don't love me," she said. "I would rather die than have them poke my uterus. It is the Holy Grail of the female body." And she began sobbing. After the heavy crying episode, she finally calmed down. I inched close to her on the sofa and hugged her. "Trust me," I said, "everything will work out. I will find you a good female obstetrician."

Dr. Nisha Desai was a sweet, young, soft spoken and considerate female obstetrician with excellent bedside manners. After speaking with me, she understood that she would be dealing with a highly emotional and edgy, pregnant, doctor's wife. After examining Fleur, she spoke at length with us in a soft and sonorous tone explaining the risks and advantages of the procedure, and like Max Davis advised amniocentesis. However, Dr. Desai's assurances did not allay Fleur's anxiety and fears. In fact, they heighten her apprehension and dread of the procedure. Two days after seeing Dr. Desai, she had a miscarriage.

The miscarriage had a dramatic effect on her psyche. She stopped eating, smoked like a chimney, and drank a bottle of wine every day. This continued for nearly a week, and then all of a sudden, she stopped talking. She lay on the bed the entire day: lethargic, listless, a catatonic state marked by immobility, sporadic agitation, a far off alarming blank stare, and total lack of communication. I sponge bathed her and changed her nightgown every day without any reaction from her. I brought her food, but she wouldn't touch it. I tried feeding her; her mouth was clenched tight. It was as if she had fallen out of life altogether.

I was totally thrown out of balance. Momentarily, I moved into a tunnel of blackness, afraid that I might remain there, chained in despair. Having gone through depression after the death of Martha, I felt paralyzed physically and emotionally without an escape. Ultimately, I called Fleur's father Allain who came over and attempted a conversation with her but to no avail. Fleur did not react. He confirmed that a somewhat similar situation had occurred once before in Saudi Arabia. He assured me that she would get better with medications. Both Jacques and his wife Alex came for a visit, and they likewise were devastated seeing Fleur's morbid depression. I could no longer concentrate on my work at the hospital. It was difficult to deal with disease on both fronts. I took some time off and stayed with Fleur.

Finally, I together with Allain and Jacques took her to the hospital. She was admitted to the psychiatry service. Her condition was severe enough that she was started on medications for acute depression. Even electroconvulsive treatment was considered, if there was no response to the drugs.

I remained devastated fearful of a relapse. I started back on anti-depressive medication on the advice of my psychiatrist.

Over a course of two weeks in the hospital, Fleur improved significantly with medication and psychotherapy and began talking and eating and was discharged from the hospital after a three week stay. Gradually, over a couple of months, she reverted back to her baseline state.

Ultimately, I finished the fellowship and took a staff position in the medical center.

After her complete recovery from depression several months later, I decided to take her on a holiday to Rome. She was simply thrilled, and it elevated her mood. A few days later when I came home from work, she mentioned that the private detective she had hired had located her biological mother.

"Can we go to Paris before Rome?" she asked.

"Yes, sure," I said. "But are you psychologically prepared to meet your biological mother?"

"Oh yes, what could go wrong?" she responded. She was ebullient and happy. Dom Perignon was already chilling in the bucket.

CHAPTER 6

AT THE LEONARDO DA VINCI -FIUMICINO AIRPORT

Fleur and I were on our return flight to Newark after a brief visit to Paris and a one-week holiday in Rome. In Paris Fleur was supposed to meet with her biological mother, a deep inner desire common in adopted children, and I readily supported her in her quest. However, I felt she was psychologically unprepared for the encounter. What if her expectations were dashed? But ultimately, I went along with it. After half a year of monthly retainers, the private investigator claimed to have found her mother. Fleur was brimming with confidence, wondering what her mother would look like and whether she acquired her good looks from her mother or her father.

"I'm anxious to know about my father and what happened to him," she said. "I hope she has a picture of him."

"You can certainly ask her about your father," I said. "But in the beginning focus on your mother and see where the conversation leads."

"I wonder whether it was a one-night stand!"

"I wouldn't go there. You can ask her if you have siblings."

The meeting was due to occur in a café near the Eiffel Tower. The detective was supposed to accompany her, and after the introduction, he would leave. I anxiously and expectantly waited in the hotel.

Her mother never showed up. The detective called several times after waiting for over an hour. There was no answer, and the voicemail was full.

We left for Rome and our friends Jacques and Alex were supposed to join us there. Two days before their arrival Jacques called saying that they had changed their flight plans because of the spreading COVID-19 epidemic in the Lombardo region and cases were being detected in Rome. We cut short our stay in Rome and headed for the airport.

There was an altercation at the check-in when Fleur found that we were not sitting next to each other. She went on and on with the check-in clerk of how she had reserved seats together several weeks back and she couldn't understand the separate seating arrangements. "Your airline is incompetent. I'll never fly with you again!" she shouted amidst tears.

"I'm sorry Ms….but you changed your original flight plans."

"It's okay Fleur," I said. "I don't care where we sit. I just want to get home." Fleur started crying and abruptly walked away. It did not entirely surprise me. It was her usual modus-operandi. A small altercation in a tired, stressed mind was the trigger for her irrational outburst.

Besides, Paris was a big flop!

"Go ahead and please issue the boarding passes," I said to the check-in clerk. Once the boarding passes were issued, I ran looking for Fleur. As soon as I caught up to her, she cursed me.

"You don't love me. You are insensitive. I'm just your fuck-baby—your trophy wife. You don't want to sit with me!"

"What are you saying? What the hell did I do wrong? We changed the original flight plans because of the spreading epidemic." I went to hug her, hoping she would calm down. She pushed me away. I handed her the boarding pass.

In Paris she had a meltdown in the bathroom after she returned to the hotel sobbing. There was the sound of plastic slapping tile. She was hurling things.

"You don't love me!" she had shouted through the door.

"Of course, I love you, my darling," I said to the door. "I'm here with you… to support you."

There was a long silence. "You don't care that I did not find my mother! That the woman was an imposter, a fraud, a *phon-ee*."

"Of course, I care! I'm outraged! But there's nothing we can do about it. It's obvious she got cold feet. It's not entirely uncommon in mothers who have given their children for adoption. They often don't want to face the past. You should have been prepared for this outcome."

"I'm going to kill myself."

The smell of cigarettes wafted through the bathroom door.

"Please come out. We'll meet up with Alex and Jacques in Rome…"

I walked away from the door hoping that the cigarettes would calm her down. They usually did. I poured myself a bourbon from the well-stocked bar cart and waited for her to emerge, impeccable and ravishing, as always. As if nothing had happened. She finally did come out and drank a whole bottle of wine and went to sleep.

The detective had tried calling her mother again the following morning. The phone was disconnected.

I had hoped that the trip back home would be smooth. But it was not to be.

"It's over between us," she said. "I want a divorce." She had said that over and over again whenever we fought during some imaginary banal happening that triggered the dark space in her brain. During these moments, I was just an afterthought in her scheme of things. It was as if she sliced through our lives like a knife through butter and bread. Her shades of life were dark grey and black; mine were blank on a screen. I leaned on the wall and covered my eyes with my hands. When will this torture end? I asked myself. I had to pay a steep price for her ravishing beauty. When she was in a good mood, she was talkative, charming and highly engaging. She was excessively sensitive and equally idealistic, and sometimes when in a down mood, expressed that she was not made for this world. "It would be better for all if I died," she said. During these irrational conflicts, I sometimes thought of my dead wife. How peaceful and dignified our relationship had been. We protected each other from each other's idiosyncrasies. I prayed to God to somehow bring closure to this madness. At my coaxing, she had seen a psychiatrist who had diagnosed a borderline personality disorder and placed her on medications which she was in the habit of discontinuing claiming that they didn't help.

Fleur's borderline personality related mental contortions were unsettling. Often, I had to walk carefully, as if on frozen ground. I wondered why I had to take all this load on my chest. Was marrying Fleur a mistake? I had thought of divorce several times but realized that whatever she said and did during the emotional outbursts, she didn't mean it; besides they were temporary, only lasting for a few days. She was entirely governed by her emotional brain during these times, but I loved her. In hindsight, I pitied her too and her intense suffering during the sudden uncontrollable expressions of emotions; it was as if she was just a girl in a woman's body, who otherwise, had a lot to offer. I just couldn't abandon her. It was not a part of my makeup, my Christianity, my very soul. I had gone to therapy to understand her mind, and how to cope with it and it had helped somewhat.

But now, we had to get back home to New York. I had heard that Italy had suspended flights to China after two cases of the Coronavirus were confirmed in Rome. I had mentioned it to Fleur, but during these explosions, Fleur was in her own concocted bubble.

"Please Fleur, be reasonable, calm down, we are in a foreign country possibly teaming with the Coronavirus. There is no sense in making a scene at the airport," I said, and immediately realized it was a wrong choice of words. But when was it the right choice of words during these irrational explosions?

"You can go back to New York by yourself. I'm staying here," she said, and sat on the floor like a child having a tantrum. I too sat on the floor, tired, leaning on the wall.

In about ten minutes or so, I saw her leave. I followed behind to see where she was going. I always lost control during these situations. She was in total command. I sort of felt humiliated, and my manliness shredded to pieces. And yet, I loved her, and I knew that she loved me. She wasn't doing any of this on purpose. It was an illness—chemicals in the brain gone awry. And I was a doctor who hoped and hoped and reconciled to these facts. When she was at her best, she was loving and caring of me and held me in high esteem.

I found her sitting on the counter stool of a coffee shop with a Cappuccino and a croissant. I felt reassured, but stayed far behind, eying her next move. I followed her and caught up to her as we entered the security check. We walked together in silence, and I knew that the flare-up was probably over or tempered down. At least for now. Another reality had taken shape—the sudden transition from darkness to dawn. I always wondered whether the flare up that induced profuse tears and anger towards me somehow served to replenish the depleted serotonins in her brain receptors.

On the plane she was sitting next to a young, tall, lean and handsome man and they were deep in conversation when I passed by the aisle to go to the bathroom.

"How are you doing," I had asked of Fleur.

"I'm doing great," she had said with a broad smile.

I felt reassured that the episode at the airport had lifted like the fog but knew that the separation could last for a couple of days during which there would be no affection and certainly no sex.

I was taken by surprise to see Dr. Antonina Bucco sitting next to me in the window seat. She was to join the fellowship program in the infectious diseases department in my hospital.

Introductions made, I asked her about the epidemic situation in Italy.

"The first documented cases of COVID-19 were seen at the Alzano Hospital," said Antonina. "By then, the virus had sickened thousands of people, many of whom went to the Emergency Room of the referral ASST–Papa Giovanni XXIII hospital. These patients soon overwhelmed the hospital."

"How did they manage?"

"There was a major reorganization led by a crisis team."

"What treatment are the patients getting?" I asked.

"Just symptomatic, I believe. If you'd like to speak with the chief of infectious diseases at ASST–Papa Giovanni XXIII Hospital, I can put you in contact," said Antonina. "He is my cousin."

"Sure," I said. "It might be important to learn from their experience once the virus lands in New York, so that we don't make the same mistakes."

In the Uber on our trip to Manhattan from Liberty Newark Airport, I finally broke the ice: "How was the flight?" I asked Fleur.

"Okay, I guess. The premium seats were fine. The chicken was horrible, like eating wood. But the company was great—a young handsome model from Milan."

"Aren't most male models gay?"

"We talked about my one stint with Yves St. Laurent and Prada years ago. He is here for an audition with Calvin Klein. And, by the way, not all male models are gay." I wondered whether the man had made a pass at her. Who in his right mind wouldn't?

"What about you? How was your flight?"

"The pasta was good. And the company was even better. A female doctor from Rome, Antonina Bucco who is about to start a fellowship in infectious diseases in our hospital. We talked a lot of what's going on in the Lombardo region with the Coronavirus. In Wuhan thousands are infected and many are dying. It won't be long before the virus makes its appearance here."

Fleur did not react. She seemed in her own distant world.

"The doctor from Rome—is she attractive?" she suddenly asked. "Will she be working with you?"

"Yes," I said. That was good enough to make any wife jealous. But Fleur was not the jealous type. She was confident of her beauty like the single red rose in display in a bud vase.

Once we reached the apartment on 74th and West End Avenue, after unpacking, she told me that she was going to her father's apartment on the East Side.

"He'll be back late Sunday, and I'll have two days for myself."

"Why don't you go tomorrow?"

"I can see that I exhausted you with my horrible mood at the airport. You need to sleep… I want to be by myself." She sounded normal and considerate. The flare-up some hours ago was forgotten.

I kept silent. I knew from experience that it was best for her to be by herself. I then remembered that we had tickets for the opera the coming Wednesday. When I mentioned it to her, she immediately responded, "I haven't forgotten. I'm looking forward to it. Are you?"

"Sure. Jacques and Alex are going to join us. It's his first opera. I'm dying to see his reaction."

CHAPTER 7

BACK TO WORK

On Monday, I returned to work at the Uptown Medical Center at seven in the morning. Sitting in my academic office I went over the recent articles in *The New England Journal of Medicine* and the *Journal of Infectious Diseases* as well as scanned the news items on Yahoo, Google and *The New York Times* for any information on the Coronavirus epidemic raging in Wuhan, China. I learned that Wuhan was placed under quarantine. A good idea, I thought. Having written and published a review article on the impact of the SARS epidemic that spread to over 8,000 people worldwide and killed almost 800 before it was contained, I wondered about the impact of the current epidemic and whether the new type of Coronavirus the Chinese identified as nCoV-2 would have the same or worse impact than the SARS virus. I remembered an article published in *Nature Medicine* in 2015, from the Department of Epidemiology, University of North Carolina at Chapel Hill, where I had spent two years before med school as a research assistant working on viruses. They reported that they had taken the spike protein from a bat virus and implanted it into the spine of a mouse-adapted SARS-CoV backbone creating a chimera virus that revealed poor efficacy both for monoclonal antibody and vaccine approaches. The study suggested a potential risk of SARS-CoV re-emergence from viruses currently circulating in bat populations. I re-read the article, and it sent a shiver down my spine. Could it be possible that the *chimera* virus escaped from one of the biological labs? What I found of interest was that the study was supported by grants from the National Institutes of Health (NIH) and by the National Natural Science Foundation of China. I also read that President Obama had stopped the funding of such *gain-of-function* research involving genetical alteration of the virus to enhance its biological function making it more lethal, more infectious, more resistant to vaccines. Subsequently, the research was outsourced to Wuhan, China.

At one time after finishing my training in infectious diseases, I was considering a research faculty position at the Department of Epidemiology, University of North Carolina at Chapel Hill, but Fleur wouldn't hear of it. She had no intention of leaving New York City and moving to the South. Besides, I had already committed to joining the fulltime faculty at the Uptown Medical Center.

Fleur called me at about eight forty-five to say that she was on her way home, and that her father had returned last night from Texas after the Board meeting. She sounded chipper. I was relieved.

At about nine I met my fellows Andy Sommer and Antonina Bucco, both specializing in infectious diseases, and we began morning rounds on patients with pneumonia, infections of the heart valves and several wound infections including a nasty infection of the breastbone in an elderly eighty-four-year-old patient who underwent coronary bypass surgery and valve replacement.

"I wonder why surgeons operate on these elderly patients," I said to my two fellows. "It is important to consider quality of life issues versus survival in old age. Do you agree?" They both shook their heads.

"In general, in Italy, we wouldn't operate on such elderly patients," said Antonina.

"It's not the age that really matters. It's the physical and mental condition of the patient that is paramount," said Andy.

Finally, late in the evening I was called to see a Chinese patient, Gao Yang from Queens, who had pneumonia and low oxygen levels. He gave a history of visiting his daughter and Italian son-in-law in Milan just a week ago. I was puzzled at the extent of lung involvement. I advised broad spectrum intravenous antibiotics and requested Andy to arrange for an immediate medical intensive care unit (ICU) transfer for possible placement of a breathing tube.

As I was on my way home, I received a call from Andy saying that as the resident was waiting for the anesthesiologist, the patient went into a cardio-pulmonary arrest and died. I wondered whether this was the first case of Coronavirus in New York City. Unfortunately, the family refused an autopsy.

When I arrived home at about seven o'clock in the evening, I found Fleur sound asleep. There was a Bolognese pasta she had cooked sitting on the stove. After our marriage, Fleur had taken up cooking and singing lessons. She had become a gourmet cook and an amateur Mezzo-soprano. There was no question in my mind that Fleur had the potential of becoming a professional opera singer had she taken singing classes in her childhood. I marveled when she sang the part of Mimi, in *La bohème* and was happy that she had found a niche. It had also affected her psyche for the better.

She woke up at about nine o'clock in good spirits, but tired and jet lagged. We had dinner together, when she mentioned that the Milanese, Patrizio Columbo had called.

"What did your talk about?" I asked.

"He was jet-lagged and seemed very tired and sort of in a hurry to go back to sleep. He is leaving for Florida for a month's holiday. The audition with Calvin Klein has been postponed."

"At this juncture he is better off in Florida than in Italy."

"I was glad to see my father who returned from Texas after the Board meeting at Texaco. He plans to spend the summer at the French Riviera."

"That's great. Do you want to join him?"

"Wouldn't it be wonderful if we both went? she said.

"It will be a nice holiday and I'm sure if you are there it won't incite Victoria."

"Well, sure. Let me think about it and look at my schedule. I haven't been to the French Riviera...and they say it's a fun place."

"I really want you to come. It will be fun."

"I expect things to get a bit dicey at the hospital if the COVID situation suddenly explodes. If things get worse, I may not be able to come home, so that I don't pass it on to you if I get infected."

"Where will you stay?"

"In a hotel."

"I have an idea. You stay here, and I'll stay with my dad."

I sensed she was in a good mood. It was sex-time. And there might not be sex for a long, long time.

"Darling, are you up to some loving tonight?"

"Sure honey," she said. It was a more than a year that we were married, and more recently our sex act had changed dramatically. She seemed to have lost interest in foreplay, and the sexual activity reverted back to penetration—the bam-bam in the ham, not uncommon in married couples.

PART II

Thick darkness has gathered over our squares, our streets, and our cities. It has taken over our lives, filling everything with a deafening silence and a distressing void that stops everything as it passes by; we feel it in the air...We find ourselves afraid and lost...:

—Pope Francis

CHAPTER 8

THE PANDEMIC BLOWS INTO NEW YORK

Suddenly, the winds of change crashed into New York City gathering hurricane force, while cruise ships became floating test tubes of COVID-19. It started with the New Rochelle outbreak when patient zero tested positive for COVID-19. His was considered the first case of community spread. Over the next week, the virus spread rapidly to more than fifty cases linked to patient zero and included his family members. The state took drastic measures to create a containment zone.

The Uptown Medical Center in New York City swung into action. The hospital president and chief operating officer, in collaboration with the Institute of Critical Care and various departmental heads moved forward in devising a game plan for the pandemic. A task force was formed with the appointment of the intensivist, Dr. Umesh Mukherjee, and me as co-chairs. We immediately instituted protocols for isolation, negative pressurization of rooms, and donning and doffing of Personal Protective Equipment (PPE). It was felt that transmission of the virus was by droplet and that N95 masks were not needed; they were not available anyway. All elective procedures were cancelled, and all paramedical personnel were recruited for several teams for breathing-tube insertion, respiratory ther-

apy, tracheostomy, and so on. Cardiopulmonary resuscitation was not offered for high-risk elderly patients—a policy unheard of in the past. Treatment
protocols were established and reviewed on a daily
basis, but there was no proven drug available to kill
the virus. Every morning Umesh and I held a Zoom
conference attended by doctors and paramedical personnel to report on the hospital statistics, the death
rate and current evolving treatment approaches.

Expecting a possible avalanche of patients, most of
the floors were converted to handle COVID-19 patients
and sicker patients with difficulty breathing. Those in
shock who required a breathing tube and circulatory
support were sent to the ICUs and all units in the
hospital were converted into COVID-ICUs. The rooms
in the Coronary Care Unit—that temple for heart attack
victims where modern medicine works its miracles—
was also converted to a COVID-19 ICU. In these ICUs,
the angel of death would unapologetically hover with a
vengeance.

In less than a week we were ready to deal with the
deluge of patients. I was assigned to one of the COVID-
ICUs and my team was co-led by the intensivist Dr.
Umesh Mukherjee and consisted of Karen Brown, a
nurse practitioner, and several nurses and medical
residents including my infectious disease fellows, Dr.
Antonina Bucco who I had recently met on the flight from
Rome to New York, and Dr. Andy Sommer. We worked
the day shift from seven in the morning to seven in the

evening.

In the meantime, I was consulted on a few patients with fever, dry cough and difficulty breathing who appeared in the hospital's ER. I suspected COVID-19 and in those with low oxygenation, I advised transfer to the ICU and recommended supportive care and a breathing tube with connection to the respirator machine. Those who had mild symptoms and good oxygen levels were sent to COVID floors.

After morning rounds, I held a meeting to discuss the use of Personal Protective Equipment (PPE).

"Are we absolutely sure that the virus is transmitted by droplet?" With a blank stare this is the first question Karen asked.

"That is indeed a most important question," I said.

"At this time, it is felt that the transmission is by droplet," Umesh said.

"What about masks?" Karen asked with an arched brow.

"Masks would be an additional precaution, if we could get them, but the protocols aren't calling for them at this point," said Umesh.

"We should all wear surgical masks however at all times when dealing with COVID patients," I said. Karen exhaled in relief.

"There is a lack of proper attire for the medical and paramedical personnel," said Karen with a tight-lipped smile of concern.

"You are absolutely right. There is a pervasive lack

of PPE such as N95 masks, gloves, face shields, and other patient equipment such as ventilators," I said.

"There was enough warning to prepare for the pandemic but precious time was wasted in denial rather than in preparedness," said Umesh with a scowl.

"I agree," I said. "It is a shame that one of the richest cities in the world, and soon the whole country with vast military and economic power would ultimately be on its knees as the virus spreads."

"For lack of proper attire, some medical and paramedical personnel in some boroughs of the city have resorted to wearing ponchos if they could get hold of them," said Karen, cocking an eyebrow.

"I was told that the richer hospitals in Manhattan, including ours are in the process of increasing bed capacity, ramping up testing and acquiring protective gear, due to their political and financial clout," said Umesh.

"Please, I want all the medical and paramedical personnel to be properly attired. This in an order!" I said. "If, by chance, there is the possibility of aerosol transmission a race to procure N95 masks from China will begin."

"This morning I was informed that Warren Buffett's planes will be heading to China to procure N95 masks for our hospital," said Umesh.

"That's good news," said Andy Sommer.

"I am really anxious," said Karen. "I heard that doctors and nurses are dying in Wuhan and in the Lombardo region." Droplets of sweat gathered around her brow.

"You are right Karen," I said. "The death toll among the doctors and paramedical personnel in the Lombardi region in Italy has been rising. I'm concerned as much as you. We need to be extremely careful."

"There is a new policy in place forbidding family members to visit their relatives to even say their good-byes to the dying patients," said Umesh.

"Yes, that's correct," I said.

"This policy is unheard of in modern day medicine in the US and elsewhere," said Andy Sommer.

"Agree," said Umesh. "We have no choice. The directive went into effect in all of New York's hospitals."

"One more thing: how do we handle the patients' relatives?" asked Karen. "They keep on calling."

"Karen and Antonina, I want you to come up with a daily time slot to call the patients relatives unless it's an emergency or a death."

"Will do," said Karen and Antonina simultaneously.

"One more directive," I said. "Following our shifts, we need to keep away from our spouses and children. Hotels nearby are offering free rooms. You guys should take advantage and stay at nearby hotels."

"I wonder when the shadow of death will appear among us," said Antonina.

"That's the very reason we have to be careful," I said. "I remember the words of the poet Grace Schulman:

Around us death: the numbers spin the mind.
Fever dreams. The last breath held, alone..."

There was fear, anxiety, and trepidation on our faces as we broke the meeting to surge ahead to care for our COVID patients.

During lunch I called Fleur to tell her that I would stay in a hotel. "I'll come this evening to pick up my things."

"No," she said. "Absolutely not. You stay in the apartment; I'll stay with my dad. Victoria is still stuck in Russia."

I was relieved. I was a poor sleeper and preferred my own bed.

In the late afternoon, I received a stat call from the ER. My patient the seventy-five-year-old Rabbi Isaac Cohen who I had treated for asthma and pneumonia was brought by Hatzalah with symptoms of COVID. He had a cough and fever for days, but thinking it was a flu, stayed home fearful of acquiring COVID-19 in the hospital. Finally, after his condition worsened due to a rapid heartbeat and difficulty breathing, he agreed to go to the hospital. He was accompanied by his wife, several sons and daughters and many members of the Orthodox Jewish community who insisted on accompanying the Rabbi to the ER but were turned off at the entrance.

After examining the Rabbi, I immediately requested the anesthesiologist to place a breathing tube and the Rabbi was transferred to the ICU. There, he went into a rapid heart rhythm—the atrial fibrillation—and required an electrical shock to his chest to get him out of the rhythm that was putting him into heart failure. He was started on the antimalarial drug Hydroxychloroquine and the antibiotic Azithromycin, and a drug to control his heart's rhythm. He had diabetes, obesity, hypertension, and previous heart bypass surgery and I felt that his prognosis was guarded.

When I left the hospital rather tired and anxious not knowing what to expect over the next few weeks, the Rabbi was stable and heavily sedated on the ventilator. He lay in lassos of tubing, his face somewhat swollen, his long beard—a lump of snow white around his mouth. I talked on the phone with family members and mentioned that the Rabbi was stable and that we were doing our best. The wife felt somewhat reassured. I had been his doctor and had cared for him and got him out of difficult medical situations over the years.

CHAPTER 9

THE BIRTHDAY PARTY

A bash for Jacques fortieth birthday at Monarch Rooftop booked several months in advance was cancelled in view of the spreading pandemic. A party at his apartment on 75th and Central Park South with only the closest of friends was scheduled with one caveat: the invitees had to be tested negative for COVID-19 forty-eight hours before.

In addition to Fleur and myself, her father Allain, a patient of Jacques was also invited. And so was another friend and patient, the conservative columnist and editor of Ziegbart magazine, Tom Branigan. A couple of Jacques fellows and his associates—the wiseacre Dr. Vinod Swami and the heart rhythm experts Drs. Jonathan Levy and Tony Grimes were also invited. The dinner party was set for seven in the evening.

At the suggestion of Swami, Jacques mentioned that the greeting should be the Indian "Namaste" rather than a handshake or a hug or kisses on both cheeks *a la* European or the recently introduced elbow knock. However, both Fleur and I were the first guests to arrive and ended up hugging and kissing the hosts, but Swami, dressed in Indian garb insisted on the Namaste. All came wearing masks, but ultimately some discarded them, others had them wrapped around their necks. Moreover, it was not possible to strictly maintain the six-feet distance.

To us at the medical center, Jacques and Alex were a sort of power couple. He was a prime cut New York Heart Internationalist, and she had moved on from being a rep in a drug company to being the manager of a heart device company for the Northeast USA. They both travelled extensively on business and entertained in their home in the Hamptons and in the city.

The guests walked around the large living cum dining area with a view of Central Park and the lit towers on the East Side and Central Park South sipping champagne, red and white wine, and vodka and apple martinis, peppered with small talk about the oncoming COVID pandemic. I sauntered sipping a vodka martini hallowing my doctor colleagues from the medical center.

I saw Alex, the longhaired brunette, dressed in a multicolored Moroccan kaftan gathering the women in one corner of the living room chatting about the dire situation with the quarantine, the isolation in one's apartment, the imminent escape to the Hamptons and other locales around New York City. I joined the conversation.

"For the Manhattanites, Europe is out of the question this summer," said Fleur. "I feel depressed locked up in my father's apartment."

"Fleur, my dear, you should come home," I said. "It's better I move to the hotel and visit you as often as I can."

"I am going to the Hamptons day after tomorrow and you are most welcome to join," said Alex to Fleur. "I feel cooped up here. Besides, with elective procedures cancelled, there is no action in the device industry."

"Sure, I may take you up on it. There is nothing to do in the city. It is getting deserted," Fleur responded. "At this rate with restaurants closed, no movies, Broadway and Lincoln Center shut down, New York City is dead."

"So is Europe," said Alex.

"It's a great idea. Why don't you join Alex in the Hamptons at least for a few days?" I interjected.

"I am driving to Virginia to my sisters and taking my two kids with me," said Swami's wife, Jigna.

"I'm afraid for you Jeff. You are in the thick of things. I'm terrified," said Fleur hugging me. And out of the blue she began crying. Alex hugged the two of us and gradually Fleur calmed down. I left their company to go to the bar for a glass of wine.

As I was coming out of the bathroom, I met Alex in the corridor. "Alex baby," I said, "you look great in the Moroccan kaftan." I briefly kissed her on the cheek. I was a bit tipsy after the vodka martini on an empty stomach and the wine.

"You do know that my mother was Moroccan," said Alex.

"Yes, I remember you saying so when I first met you in the Moroccan desert atop a camel, and again in Fez," I said, laughing. "And we danced to the Barbers singing and beating of drums in a desert tent."

"And we watched the desert sunset and sunrise. It was marvelous. I want to go back after this pandemic is over. I want to take Belinda to meet the Moroccan side of my family even if Jacques doesn't come."

"Can we come with you?"

"Sure, you and Fleur are most welcome."

When I met Alex, she was a representative of a drug company. After her return to New York from Morocco, she had visited me in my office to peddle the anticoagulant drug Pradaxa, just approved by the FDA. Since the first time I saw her, I was attracted to her and was planning to ask her out. A few days later, when Jacques and I were waiting at the bar to be seated for dinner in a restaurant, I had seen Alex accompanied by an entourage of doctors she had invited for dinner at the company's expense. She had approached me, and I had introduced her to Jacques. "This is the famous heart interventionalist, Jacques Charpentier—you have to peddle your new drug to him," I had said.

They had exchanged professional cards. After she left, Jacques had commented: "She is a fine-looking woman. Not particularly beautiful but has a knockout body. Is she single?"

"When I met her in Morocco, she was with a man, an Australian photographer, but I guess it was a short holiday fling," I said.

Jacques, unlike me, did not waste time. When she went to see him in the hospital the very next day, Jacques asked her on a date. And I was the best man for their destination wedding in Hawaii. I had cursed my instincts; I was a slow-mo. Alex could have been my wife. I liked her happy disposition, and the fact that she too was in the medical field was another plus. Whenever I saw her, I sometimes wondered what it would be like to make love to her. Even now with an alluring, glamorous, Fleur for a wife, I sometimes fantasized about Alex. Why do men fantasize about some women and not others? Why does the forbidden fruit tempt us? I wondered as I went to the bar to refill my glass of wine.

"The buffet dinner is served," said Alex. "For fish we have Poisson d' Avril and baked salmon with dill. For meat, we have Steak tartare and Coq au vin. For the vegetarians we have creamy onion pasta and an assortment of braised vegetables, chickpea curry and vegetable biryani. To accompany the fish, we have Louis Latour Pouilly Fuisse, and to accompany the meats we have Napa Valley Pinot Noir 1990. All the food is prepared in our kitchen by Chef Antoine Allard of Le Coucou. Please give him a hand."

We all clapped generously, and the chef, in his typical attire of a toque blanche, white double-breasted jacket, pants in a black-and-white houndstooth pattern and apron took a generous bow like that of an opera singer.

We barely started eating, when there appeared Dr. Andrew Muster, the chairman of cardiology and Jacques' boss, wearing a surgical mask. "I'm sorry for being late. Unfortunately, I have to leave for an important Board meeting regarding the hospital's response to the pandemic. I'd like to say a few words," he said.

"Champagne to raise a toast?" asked Jacques and handed him a champagne flute.

"Jacques, Alexandra and friends," said Muster—the Master. "I would like to raise a toast to New York's best coronary interventionalist—Jacques Charpentier and wish him a most wonderful birthday. We are going through difficult times with the pandemic, but I'm sure we will overcome. Jacques has been a great asset to our department and the hospital, and I owe him a lot for our robust finances. By the way, I have to congratulate Jeff Anderson for doing a great job assembling the task force."

"Thanks," I said. "By the way, any news about the N95 masks?"

"I was informed that they are on the way from China. They will be available for all doctors and paramedical personnel taking care of COVID patients."

"That's swell news," I said.

"Have a great party, my friends," said Muster. He elbowed Jacques and Alex and left unceremoniously, rather typical of Muster. He barely had a sip of champagne.

The dinner over, the guests retreated to the study, and Jacques introduced Tom Branigan. Pointing to me he mentioned that Tom wanted to interview me for Box news for a special program on the pandemic.

"Well, let me explain," said the middle-aged, portly, red-meat-complexioned Tom with a cigar in his mouth, and a vodka martini in his hand. "I'm going to host a TV program entitled: *The Plot Against America*. Several prominent personalities are going to posit that the pandemic is a Communist plot against the government's hardline position on China."

"*The Plot Against America* a la Phillip Roth?" asked Grimes.

"Oh, no. That was fiction. This is real!" said Tom.

"You mean a counterplot to kill the plot?" said Swami. "The 'plot' to 'destroy' the Chinese economy with tariffs?"

"That's way farfetched," said Jacques. "The tariffs wouldn't even dent the Chinese economy."

"It's all a show," said Grimes.

"We just want to even the score," said Tom.

"I feel confident that the virus that I'm going to call the Communist virus that originated in the Wuhan Laboratory was released to cause chaos in the American economy."

"You have no evidence for such an assumption," I said. "How come the virus was released in Wuhan to begin with?"

"Well…releasing it in Wuhan was just a masquerade. The aim was the USA."

"That's a possibility," said Levy.

"Anyway, where do I come in?" I asked.

"You are an infectious disease specialist working in a major medical center, right? Are you using the drug hydroxychloroquine to treat your COVID patients?"

"Yes, we are…since we have nothing better at this time."

"I would like you to confirm its efficacy to treat COVID patients," said Tom. "We think the drug is a genuine game changer."

"I can confirm that we are using the drug. But I cannot say that the drug works. The evidence is entirely anecdotal."

"Well, lots of doctors think it works."

"I agree with Jeff," said Grimes. "Dr. Anthony Fauci mentioned that there is no scientific evidence of its efficacy. Anyway, what is your interest for peddling the drug? Is it because the government is stockpiling it? Is money the issue here?"

"Well, Anthony Fauci is a scientist," said Tom. "He is no God. Lots of doctors I know think it works. We need a drug for COVID-19—pronto!"

"You cannot take these antimalarials lightly," said Jacques. The heart rhythm experts—can you guys give an opinion on this?"

"Sure," said Grimes. "The drug can cause a blackout spell due to a dangerous rhythm we call ventricular tachycardia and sudden death in susceptible individuals."

"I agree," said Levy.

"Tom, you need to point out that America First—a country with unmatched hard and soft power—doesn't have enough cotton swabs, N95 masks, gloves, face shields, ventilators, special lab chemicals and enough ICU beds," said Jacques.

"What is most distressing is that our paramedical and medical personnel have to work with inadequate protection at the very risk of their own lives," I said. "I got to level with you Tom. Many of us on the frontline are frightened for our lives and that of our families."

"I have seen doctors in Brooklyn and Queens turned into beggars with hands outstretched for ponchos because they couldn't get proper medical gowns," said Swami.

"I see anxiety and trepidation on the faces of doctors and nurses as they surge ahead to care for COVID patients," I said. "Following my shift, I keep away from my wife, who has been living with her father. Several doctors I know live in their apartments in New York City caring for COVID patients, while their wives and children have moved with their in-laws or relatives away from the city and some have even left for other states. This Mr. Branigan is the norm of the day for paramedical and medical personnel, rather than the exception."

"I agree with Jacques and Jeff. However, I really think you guys are missing the big picture," said Swami. "Who cares if it's a Communist virus or a Capitalist one? It's here and spreading all over the world. The issue is 'meat' my friends. I repeat—M-E-A-T! I would like to come to your program and vouch for vegetarianism to kill the scourge of animal viruses and climate change."

"Great idea," said Jacques. "But I can't stay away from meat. And America is a meat-eating nation."

"True," said Swami. "But a lot of young people are staying away from meat—Beyond Meat is the future. Vegetarianism is the solution. You guys think like old farts!"

I could see frustration on Tom's face. He obviously did not expect the discussion to take an awkward turn.

"You academic docs are a complicated lot," he said. "I need another martini." He left for the makeshift bar.

At about midnight, Fleur and I left the party to make our way home. "What happened to your dad? I thought he was looking forward to the party?" I asked.

"He looked a little tired when I left," said Fleur. "He told me he'd come by at about nine. Perhaps he fell asleep."

Clinging to each other we walked on 75th Street going west. The street was empty. Our world was a vacant lot. We passed a silver maple, a naked cherry tree about to bloom and bicycles waiting to be ridden. Soon, around us would be death in large numbers never seen before.

"Let's take a short walk through Central Park," said Fleur. We walked back towards Central Park South. We entered the park at the Columbus Circle entrance. There were no vendors. There were no people. Columbus Circle was empty. An occasional taxi, a sporadic car passed by. American elms lined the street where once people walked and foreign tourists babbled in different tongues as they sauntered by lazily. We entered a large open field surrounded by tall lighted buildings, half-empty giants towering toward the sky. Suddenly, a flock of birds appeared singing wildly, as if celebrating their freedom. They flew over us, unafraid, undeterred. We saw a red fox. Several white-tailed deer. They owned the Park now. Will it be theirs for keeps? It felt as if they were winning the battle between man and beast. And man was being finally defeated by an unseen microorganism, at least for now. Our great military industrial complex: the F-16's, the Tomahawk missiles were no match. We walked out of the Park and went down 74th Street toward West End Avenue. We remembered the good old days: we would stop at a café and order an espresso. From the window seats we would watch the nightlife of this colorful busy world: men and women casually dressed, happily sauntering on Columbus Circle, entering and exiting shops, chatting away as they made their way out of Lincoln Center after watching a ballet, an opera, or a concert. This city never slept. The human patina present and thriving just a few months back had all but disappeared. When will life return?

As we walked back to the apartment, we saw a homeless man at the corner of Amsterdam Avenue smoking a cigarette and drinking from a paper bag oblivious of his surroundings. I took out a five-dollar bill. It fell in the cup of his hand.

Fleur started crying, but this time it was a different cry: a cry of fear, a cry of desolation, of impending doom. I held her close.

"I love you," she said. "I worry about you. I miss you at nights."

"I love you too," I said. "Don't worry baby, I will stay safe."

"I can't stay at my father's any longer. Besides, Victoria is on her way back."

"Sure. I understand. Why don't you stay in the apartment? I will stay at one of the hotels nearby. I promise to visit if not every day at least every other day."

That night we made love, as if it was the last time. After the lovemaking I sensed an element of foreboding in her look as if she knew that something was wrong, that tomorrow would bring catastrophe. I felt she was entering the depressive phase. I felt sorry for her. I felt sorry for myself. How will we cope?

I embraced her and tried to assure her: "We'll be okay Fleur. The pandemic will pass away soon. It's best you go to the Hamptons with Alex. It's lonely being here all by yourself."

She didn't respond but she was wide awake. I gave her an Ambien and took one myself. Tomorrow while leaving for work, I would ask her to go back on the Paxil. We both fell asleep in unison—the Ambien bond.

CHAPTER 10

THE CHAOS IN THE INTENSIVE CARE UNIT

Suddenly, but not unexpectedly, there was an avalanche of very sick people in the hospital, and soon all ICUs were filled. It was as if everyone had the virus and heart disease and cancer had disappeared like extinct species. Within a couple of days all hell broke loose, and organized medicine fell into chaos.

"What are we going to do?" asked Karen. "How do we treat these patients? They are dying like flies."

"Maintain them as best as we can," I said. "We have no other option."

"There is no drug to kill the virus," said Umesh. "And I don't foresee anything in the near future."

"Dr. Mukherjee, any idea when this killer virus pandemic will end?" asked Andy Sommer.

"I'll defer the answer to this question to our expert Dr. Jeff Anderson."

"I have no idea. Viruses are known to mutate. It could get worse before it gets better," I said. "Antonina, can you connect me to the head of infectious diseases at the Papa Giovanni XXIII Hospital in Bergamo, Italy?"

"Sure will. Maybe they have something up their sleeve now," said Antonina.

"In the meanwhile, I will contact the Huoshenshan Hospital in Wuhan," said Umesh.

Late that evening we had some answers. The Italians mentioned the use of the antimalarial drugs chloroquine or hydroxychloroquine and the antibiotic azithromycin. This information was not new, however. We were already using these drugs without proven evidence that they were beneficial. The Chinese mentioned extracorporeal membrane oxygenation in which blood is pumped into the heart-lung machine that sends oxygen-filled blood to tissues in the body for the sickest of patients.

On the overhead paging system, the code: Team 700 was called more times than one could keep track of for patients who had stopped breathing, or the heart had stopped beating. It became an all too familiar calling like a death knell of a church bell in a Western movie. However, it became evident that calling codes on the very critical patients was a futile exercise, and so Umesh and I decided in advance not to call a code in such patients and a "do not resuscitate" order was placed in the chart after discussion with a family member.

Zoom cameras were installed in the ICUs so that family members could have a peek at their loved ones to see that they were there, struggling, but still alive. It was heartbreaking to see patients all alone among masked individuals moving like robots. It was as if they were suddenly marauded on a piece of island in a hostile environment to face death by themselves. However, it was impossible to know what was going on in their minds. Devoid of adequate oxygenation and once heavily sedated on the respirator, the mind was in a state of oblivion in the living dead.

Antonina and Karen Brown were assigned to take phone calls in turn, and if they were too busy, then Umesh and I filled in. In the absence of a personal touch, it was hard to comfort a loved one: a husband or wife, a daughter or son or even a close friend. To save time and not to belabor a lengthy discussion of a patient's condition, I instructed the staff to give brief answers, often finding silence at the other end. At other times, sobs, a loud moan and then sobbing again. But rarely did anyone express anger. Death was all over the TV screen and relatives knew what to expect in the best and worst of situations.

It was almost three weeks that Rabbi Isaac Cohen was waxing and waning on the respirator. At times the erratic heart rhythm reappeared, and the blood pressure plummeted, and he required electrical shocks. He lay there with tubes entering and exiting his swollen body: the puffed-up face, eyes taped shut, a bearded blob waiting to die. As I was about to finish the shift, the Rabbi had a cardiac arrest. A code was called since the family was unwilling to permit a 'do not resuscitate order.' Within ten minutes of chest compressions, injections of stimulants into the heart and electrical shocks to the chest, the code was called off—the Rabbi was pronounced dead.

I called the Rabbi's son first and informed him of his passing away, and subsequently I spoke to the daughter. They took the news in silence.

The realization was not late in coming. The demoralizing effect on medical personnel to deal with death at such a large scale—almost one death on the hour. Thus, to prevent acute depression among medical and para-medical personnel, recharge rooms were established in each ICU with dim candlelight, soft music, and lounge chairs. After every few hours, the ICU staff took turns to spend some time in the recharge rooms. Often, Karen and Antonina and other nurses were crying, and both Umesh and I tried to console them, sometimes embracing them, at other times listening to their overwhelming emotional upheavals. I was concerned for Antonina's precarious mental state. She cried often thinking of her five-year old daughter who was in Rome with her grandparents. Besides, she was a single mother and had no family in New York.

"Why don't we go for a drink after our shift is over?" I said to Antonina.

"I'd love that," she responded. "There is a bar in the hotel."

After our shift was over, rather exhausted, we walked

to the hotel and sat at the hotel bar and ordered beers over shots of Jack Daniels. After wearing the same mask for hours, we lowered them wrapping them around our necks. The hotel lobby was empty, desolate, and silent. Normally, there would be a piano man or woman playing soft music. There was none that day. We sat on bar stools staring at each other and slowly sipping the golden yellow liquid. Then suddenly, Antonina spoke.

"Five patients I was involved with died today," she said.

"Yes, I know. It was horrible," I said.

"Among them was a forty-year-old Hispanic man, Ricardo, with a wife and two children." Antonina continued: "I had taken his history when he arrived in the ICU. He was a technician working for a telephone company. He was healthy, well-built, and muscular with no risk factors except for asthma. One week ago, was his daughter's fifth birthday. He couldn't taste or smell the cake. He did not know why—he just let it pass. The next day he went for his daily two-mile jog. Over the next few days, he felt short of breath while jogging. He thought it was the asthma and used an inhaler. The day he came to the ER he was short of breath at rest and had a blackout spell. His oxygen level was low. He showed me the picture of his wife and two kids just before he was tubed. One day after his admission to the ICU he had a heart attack and died."

Antonina started sobbing. I held her close and wiped her tears with my soiled handkerchief.

"I remember—I shocked him with electricity several times. Dr. Grimes was on attendance at the code, and we gave all we had because he was so young."

Amid tears she continued recounting: "I called his wife. Words I had prepared just stuck in my mouth. I began to sob. His wife began to sob. She understood her husband was dead. We stood there sobbing. Finally, I pronounced the words in-between the sobs: "Ricardo passed away. I'm so sorry."

I heard children crying in the background: "I want my Papy."

"I remembered my daughter. If I have COVID and die, what will happen to her?"

I again hugged her, and she cried in my arms. In surgical scrubs, we remained hugging each other for a long time. "Now, now, we'll see that you are adequately protected. No harm will come to you," I said. But was I being realistic?

"I can't take it Jeff," she said. "I think of my daughter who is with my parents in Rome. What if they get COVID? What will happen to my five-year-old daughter? COVID is all over Italy."

"What's your daughter's name?"

"Violetta."

"Do you have her picture?" She opened her wallet and showed me her picture.

"Wow, she is beautiful like the flower Lavender. Don't think of it for now. Just take one day at a time," I said. "Please call your parents when you get to the room and speak to your daughter."

"It's too late now. I'll call them in the morning."

"Yeah, it must be three in the morning in Italy."

"Do you think loss of taste and smell are the early signs of COVID?" she asked after she calmed down.

"I have no idea Antonina, but why don't you make a note of it. If we have enough patients, you can report it."

We finished the beers and stood up to leave. More doctors and paramedical personnel arrived. The barman refused to accept money for the drinks. We took the elevator and Antonina, teary eyed, hugged me again before entering our respective rooms, which were side by side. I felt that she did not want to untangle the embrace. In surgical scrubs, we remained hugging each other for a long time—with masks on. At that moment a bond developed between us as if we were bound by the protein spikes of the virus.

I suddenly felt the fragility and the dwindling of life, a life out of balance, of a world in flux: the thunder of creation in one hand, the flame of destruction in the other; that we live for now, for this instant, that tomorrow may never come.

Our masked lips found each other—masks that unceremoniously we shed away, and soft wet flesh met soft wet flesh. I felt an urge to ask her to my room but resisted when I remembered that Fleur was in the apartment all by herself.

As soon as I entered the hotel room, I thanked the stars for not falling into temptation. I called Fleur and briefly related the events of the day. Her concern for me was palpable in her faltering voice. "I'm...I'm afraid for you," she kept on saying.

"I'll be fine. I'm taking precautions; we all are," I said.

"I'll pray for you. You must be exhausted. Go to sleep. Call me tomorrow," she said.

I had never seen her pray. In sickness, she was always considerate and compassionate. Some other parts of her brain seemed active; the angry irritable brain cells bathed in dopamine surges seemed depleted. She confirmed she had started back on the Paxil. I felt somewhat reassured. But her praying, her concern for me was unsettling. I decided to go to the apartment before work to see how she was doing.

I lay on the bed waiting for sleep from sheer exhaustion, but the images from the ICU, the buzzing sounds of ventilators kept ringing in my ears making sleep impossible. I thought of Antonina, her precarious state of mind. In the morning, I planned to tell her to take the day off, that I would speak to Dr. Mukherjee. It was then that my mind's eye saw the contour of Antonina's lips, her bra-less ample breasts. I couldn't fathom my own body's reaction amidst all this tragedy, all the death and suffering. I wanted to shut these thoughts out of my mind. I took an Ambien pill from the bottle resting on the side table. The mental stores, the synapses, their electrical transmission ceased and gradually I fell into an Ambien induced coma.

I found myself walking in Riverside Park. Attracted by the overpowering beauty and powerful scent of abundant alliums and leucospermums, I entered a garden. As I held a leucospermum flower in my hand, marveling at its globe like shape with radiant red spikes, I saw people walking around plucking flowers and eating them and new flowers appeared instantly. I saw a red-haired woman walking like a drunk, oblivious to her surroundings. Was it Fleur? I called out to her, but she kept on walking. I saw countless ravens sweeping down like drones to eat the flowers; some chasing the woman and pecking at her head attracted by the red color of her hair. Soon the people themselves turned to plants from which sprouted countless flowers. I couldn't see the woman any longer as the plants grew taller and taller. They surrounded me and their vines opened my mouth wide and the alliums with their long stems entered my throat and went down the windpipe as I retched. I began to choke. I started fighting the vines with my hands and legs until I was overpowered and fell to the ground. The vines attained giant sizes, and they lifted me up into space and rocked me side to side—the ravens followed the swinging pecking into my torn flesh.

Then suddenly I tumbled down the sky. It was then that I saw Antonina flying toward me and I woke up drenched in sweat, my heart pounding away. Was it the Supraventricular Tachycardia? I felt a chill and wondered whether I had a temperature from the alliums infiltrating my lungs. I was still in the post-dream state, semi-asleep. I felt as if my lungs were flooded like in "pulmonary edema"—a soup bowl of lung tissue and frothy crimson blood with floating corona flowers—an exotic oriental soup—a witch's brew.

Finally, fully awake, I staggered into the kitchenette of the suite and inserted the thermometer in my mouth. Was I coming down with COVID? The temperature was 97.4 degrees Fahrenheit. I felt reassured and splashed ice-cold water on my face and strained hard to break the Supraventricular Tachycardia. I took hold of the scotch bottle resting on the counter and gulped some mouthfuls and drank a whole can of ice-cold sprite from the fridge and rushed to bed. What sort of a nightmare was this? What were Fleur and Antonina doing in my dream? And the alliums and leucospermums—symbolic of the Coronavirus— millions of stars in the Corona galaxy! Did this dream have any significance at all? Was this a warning of things to come? Will the Coronavirus take over my lungs?

CHAPTER 11

FLEUR'S LONELINESS

I arrived at the apartment at about eight a.m. On my way I called Umesh to inform him that I'd be late for work. All alone for several days, it was obvious to me that Fleur was lonely and depressed. She was awake but reluctant to get off the bed and dress up. After stirring up a breakfast of scrambled eggs and coffee, I finally managed to coax her to come with me jogging in Riverside Park. The park itself was desolate unlike in the near past when there were people jogging and cycling and taking yoga class, like the one she had attended in the open-air ground with the Hudson in the background. But yet, absorbing the materiality of the park: the fresh air, the sunshine, the waters of the Hudson flowing toward the Atlantic, the glassy skyline of the Westside, it seemed to me she felt rewired, more cheerful. When we walked back to the apartment, the emptiness of the streets, the loneliness in the apartment again consumed her like the desolation of a graveyard at nightfall. It was then that she remembered Caracas, Venezuela when she was kidnapped, blindfolded, and chained to the bed in a shack in the mountains.

"How did I manage then?" she asked. "Every minute was a slow tortoise pace; every hour was a reckless, heedless falling...every day was a frightening frozen day, like cattle at the gateway of a slaughterhouse."

"Was it the loneliness, or the fear of an unpredictable outcome?" I asked. She did not respond.

"I feel tired…I'm going to take a nap," she said. "Are you going to work?"

"Yes," I said. "After I eat your delicious onion soup." It was already one o'clock.

At about five in the evening, Fleur's phone rang. *"Ciao signorina, come stai?"* It was the Milanese Patrizio Columbo.

"What a surprise! Are you back in NY?"

"Yes… I overstayed my holiday in Florida. How are you?"

"Buena, ma triste e sola," said Fleur. "I was lying in bed with a glass of Chardonnay, reminiscing about my life in Venezuela."

"Solitaria e triste? Perché non vieni nel mio albergo per un drink? My audition is cancelled. I am going back to Italy tomorrow—to Roma—Milan is closed. Come let me cheer you up."

"Okay. That sounds like a great idea. I'll be there at about seven."

"Ciao signorina Fleur," said Patrizio in the lobby of the hotel as he approached unmasked. Fleur hesitated but

before she could stretch her elbow, he hugged her. "This is my cousin Enzo," he said. "He was just leaving."

"Hi Enzo, nice to meet you."

"Have fun you guys," he said. "I'm on my way home."

"Do you live here?"

"Yes, in New Jersey."

"Let's go to the Rooftop Bar and Restaurant for drinks," said Patrizio. "You'll love the spectacular view of the New York Skyline." They were seated at a table for four with a spectacular view of the Empire State building. There were half-a-dozen or so guests dining.

"You look *Bellissima*," said Patrizio. "Very chic in black pants, red tank top, Gucci bag, and the black mask. You look like an actress—like Lucrezia Lante Della Rovere."

"I don't know who that is...but thanks for the compliment."

"I am expecting a male friend for dinner," he said. "You don't mind, do you?"

"Hey, not at all."

"What would you like to drink?"

"A martini straight up with olives."

"*Per favore due martini*," he said to the waiter.

"Grey Goose, please."

"This is terrible. This *pandemia*," he said.

"Yes, life has come to a screeching halt."

"My mother has come down with the virus and is hospitalized. I have to find a way to get to Milan from Rome. I don't know whether I will be allowed to see her."

"I doubt it," she said. "My husband tells me that in

NY hospitals, visitors are not allowed…even the closest family members.”

“That’s hard on the family members.”

“Is your mother in the ICU on a respirator?”

“No, she’s not on a respirator.”

“Thank God. Hope she will recover.”

“Yes. *Si, Si…Prego che si riprenda.*

“My husband is deeply involved in caring for COVID patients. I’m afraid for him. He is staying in a hotel not to pass the virus to me if he gets infected.”

“I remember you mentioning…he is a doctor…”

“An infectious disease expert. He is in the thick of things.”

“Is he caring for COVID patients?”

“Yes… He is sleeping in a hotel… I have been lonely and depressed… I was thinking of my kidnapping in Venezuela and how I had dealt with it when you called.”

“*Mio Dio*, you were kidnapped! Tell me about it.”

“It’s a long story.”

“Per *favore*—please, *signorina Fleur.*”

“My life in Venezuela was exciting and adventure-some…until…well, it had been a welcome experience after Saudi Arabia. My father and I lived in El Rosal, one of the safest and upscale areas in the city, in a gated community in a large five-bedroom house with servant quarters. I loved Caracas. It is a city in a valley of rolling green mountains.”

“I have never been to South America. Brazil is my next destination,” said Patrizio.

"What attracted me the most were the mountains and rain forest all around the city where I often went hiking. I was captivated by the passionflower. This was a real country not the artificial Dharam Camp in Saudi Arabia where we lived before we moved to Venezuela."

"You seem very fond of nature."

"Yes…But Caracas was a dangerous place with a lot of crime and kidnappings. The area we lived in was safer than other areas…But, whenever we went out, the chauffer kept in radio contact with the security people in the complex giving the location as we went from one street to the other, one avenue to the next. Local gangs kidnapped rich people, people in high positions for ransom."

"Really? That is *terribile*."

"My father and I had already lived there for several years. He was seriously considering moving to the US and working for Texaco."

"Would you like a refill?"

"Yes, please."

"For the first time in my life, I had made friends and we often went to *LeClub*, dancing. It was here that I met my boyfriend, the son of one of the Venezuelan breweries."

"What did you do in Caracas?"

"I worked as an administrative assistant in the same company as my father."

"Please go on. Sorry for the interruption."

"It was my birthday celebration and my father who had just returned from the US the night before, gave me permission to stay late at the club. My boyfriend was away in the US on business. We drank a lot and even tried some uppers. *LeClub* was crowded and I became detached from my friends some of whom were probably on the floor dancing. While sitting at the bar I met a handsome friendly boy who offered me a drink and asked for a dance. By then I was pretty high. I was swaying like a leaf wavering in the wind before it hits the ground. All that I remembered was being shoved into a car. And then I lost consciousness. My drink was spiked. The handsome boy was the bait."

"*Dio mio.*"

"When I woke up the next morning, it was pitch black and the air was dense. I soon realized I was hooded, and the events of the previous night slowly flashed in front of my eyes. I tried to get up and found myself spinning in a vertigo. Trying again, I managed to stand and found my foot chained to the bed. It immediately occurred to me that I was kidnapped for ransom. I became frightened. I began screaming. When I calmed down from sheer exhaustion, I called out in Spanish repeatedly saying I needed to go to the bathroom. Two masked men appeared; one of them placed a potty in front of the bed and removed the hood. I assured them that I wouldn't shout or resist, but to please keep me unhooded and my hands untied. The men began whispering among themselves. I recognized one of the voices, but I couldn't place it at the moment. After they unhooded me, I could smell the rain, the dead wood, the moss, and I knew that I was in a shack somewhere in the mountains around Caracas. One of the men assured me that no harm would come to me as long as I did not try to escape.

"I was in captivity for seven days. It was frightening in the beginning, but over days and nights, I managed a certain degree of calmness and control over my emotions. They treated me rather well, except for one altercation when one of the masked men pressed his body against mine and squeezed my breasts. I screamed so loud that the second masked man appeared and slapped him and kicked him out of the room.

"The living conditions in the mountain shack were bad: there was no bathroom nor a kitchen. I hated to do it in the pail. And the food was horrible: mostly soggy sandwiches. My fear was somewhat allayed because I was sure that my father would arrange the ransom money. But during one of these kidnappings anything could go wrong. A son of a diplomat was killed."

"How did you manage?"

"I survived because they gave me plenty of *maté de coca* to drink and pot to smoke. I was high and slept most of the time. A cocaine producing camp was close by. Sometimes I heard machine gun fire in the distance."

"Weren't you frightened?"

"Oh yes in the first three days of my captivity. After that I guess I was stoned. Some five days into solitary confinement, in the late evening they took me for a walk through the forested path. Perhaps they themselves were tired of sitting around and needed some physical exercise. They had guns—there was no point in me trying to escape. During these walks through a meadow,

I was high enjoying the sweet smell of Lupine flowers popular with butterflies and bumblebees. Venezuela was known for its orchids with strong scents. The kidnappers were surprised when I identified the national flower—the orchid *Cattleya mossiae*, known as *flor de Mayo*—May flower. In our rented home in Caracas, there was a large terrarium, an orchid garden built by the owner who now lived in Miami, Florida.

"What was the ransom?"

"The kidnappers sought one million dollars."

"That's a lot of money in Venezuela. Did your father go to the police?"

"No, my father did not approach the police since often they too were involved in the kidnapping racket. Though an American friend, my father approached a CIA operative in Caracas, a man named Gus Bradley. What tipped my father and Gus and my boyfriend—who had returned from the US—was that one of the male servants, a young man named, Ademir Rojas had not appeared for work the day after the kidnapping. His wife called saying that he was sick. Gus's local contacts and my boyfriend who knew the terrain, shadowed his shack on the hilly barrio surrounding Caracas. They found that he would leave in the morning and come back late in the evening. They followed him to the shack in the mountain. In the meantime, my father agreed to pay the ransom and the drop site was arranged at a remote road at the base of the El Avila Mountain, after a video was delivered showing that I was alive and well. He was told that a black SUV driven by a man named Carlos was to pick him up in front of the Lidotel Hotel, and that he would be hooded all the way to the pickup. They warned that if the police were notified or the SUV was followed the drop off would be cancelled. I was hooded and driven by the captors. The car was parked some distance away. We went on foot to the drop site.

"The mutual delivery was made. We were ordered to remove the hood only at the direction of Carlos. As soon as I was seated in the back seat, hooded, my father and I embraced each other and cried in each other's arms."

"Is that the end of the story?"

"No, the best part is yet to come." The waiter came with caviar on eggs, raw oysters, and artichokes a la Roma as appetizers.

As they were relishing the appetizers, Patrizio's friend appeared—a shorter older man named David, dressed in slacks, a red blazer, and a Tradesy Gucci bag with a red stripe around his shoulder. They embraced and kissed each other.

"Please go on with your story," said Patrizio. He briefly summarized Fleur's story: "She was kidnapped for ransom in Caracas, Venezuela. I will fill in the remaining later."

"It's rough down there," said David. "A friend of mine was stabbed in the chest and robbed in broad daylight. He was lucky to survive."

"In the meantime, Gus and his local men had infiltrated the area around the forest the night before and had surrounded the shack where I was kept," said Fleur. "They considered attacking the shed but decided against it. My father had asked for guarantee that no harm would come to me. As the captors were tracking back to the shed with the money, Gus and his men were waiting. All four of the captors were killed in a blaze of machine gun fire. One of the captors was the servant Ademir Rojas. The marked one million dollars was secured."

"*Dio mio. Quanto sei stato fortunato.*"

"That was the end of my life in Caracas. I no longer wanted to live there. It also ruptured my relationship with Raul. I was not allowed to go out with my friends to nightclubs, cinema houses or even shopping by myself and was always accompanied by a security guard. In about a year or so, my father took the job with Texaco, and we moved to Houston."

"Wow! *Che storia*! You are a true survivor," said Patrizio, and hugged her.

"South America is a violent continent," said David.

"Your country is violent too," said Patrizio. "So many guns…school shooting…even children getting killed."

"You are right," said David. "Our country is ruled by the NRA. Our politicians are spineless."

"I better leave," Fleur said. "I need to visit a friend."

"*Ciao* signorina…you have my number. The next time you come to Italy, call me and I'll show you around. That is if I'm alive!"

When Fleur arrived home, she was surprised to see me seated on the couch half asleep.

"What a surprise! What are you doing here?" I immediately put on my mask.

"I gathered you must be lonely. I came to visit," I said. She masked herself and we hugged.

"That was very thoughtful of you. I was lonely and depressed and thinking about my captivity in Caracas and how I managed then, when Patrizio called and invited me for a drink."

"I'm glad you went."

"You were right, Patrizio is gay. I met his boyfriend. After eating the delicious appetizers—particularly the raw oysters and caviar on eggs, I took my leave—after all it was Patrizio's last day in New York City, and he and David would want to spend some time together. With the pandemic spreading like wildfire, they might never see each other again."

"Yes, that's true," I said.

On my way home, I stopped at Jose's for a load of marijuana. Like during my captivity in Venezuela it might help to get high to quench my loneliness."

"What did your talk about?"

"His mother has COVID and is hospitalized. I told him my story: the kidnapping in Venezuela."

"When you told me that story, I was impressed and felt a certain admiration for your fortitude and courage in the face of such danger. I was surprised at your pragmatism for dangerous life-threatening events."

"I'm myself flabbergasted at how my mind works. Sometimes I can be calm during difficult situations, at other times react emotionally and illogically," she said.

"It is called survival."

She did not respond. It was as if her mind was far away into the Venezuelan jungle.

"I'm going to spend the night here. Will sleep in the guest room."

"I have some good pot. It will help you relax."

"Sure. I'll try some."

Deadened after a glass of wine and weed, we fell asleep in separate rooms.

The next morning when I went to work, another unexpected event occurred. Umesh informed me that his aging father who lived in Mumbai had come down with COVID-19.

"My father lives all by himself," he said. "I'm leaving for Mumbai this evening."

"What about your mother?" I asked. "Any siblings?"

"My mother died five years ago. He hasn't been doing well since. My sister with her family live in California. She informed me yesterday that he has COVID. I agreed to go back."

"Is he at home or hospitalized?"

"He is at home. I spoke to him last night. He could barely talk. The hospitals are crowded in Mumbai. There are patients on cots in the corridors. My father said he'd rather die at home."

"You have to go my friend…good luck and please stay safe."

"Dr. Swami has agreed to cover for me. Hopefully I'll be back in a week or so."

"Please let me know how he is doing…safe journey."

CHAPTER 12

AT THE LINCOLN CENTER: THE END OF MUSIC

A few days later when I was at work, I received a call from Jacques who was at home since the cath. lab was closed for routine procedures.

"Hey Jeff, its Tom Branigan," he said with urgency in his voice. "The man has a cough and fever. He feels washed out. I think he has COVID-19. I am sending him to the ER. Can you take care of him?"

"Sure, I'll call the ER and tell them to call me as soon as he comes in."

"Thanks buddy."

"What are you up to?"

"I'm on standby for any emergency for the cath. lab. Off for a jog in Central Park. Alex is in the Hamptons. I thought Fleur was supposed to join her."

"She changed her mind. I will talk to her and try to convince her to go. She is lonely in the apartment all by herself."

"Yeah. It's depressing. The streets are empty."

"Swell, man, have a great jog. Bye, got to run. I hear a code in the ICU."

When I went to the ER to see Tom Branigan, it was overflowing with COVID patients with beds in the hallways and nurses and orderlies some adequately attired while others barely. Almost all had surgical masks on; only few were wearing N95s. Fear and anxiety were equally present on patients and paramedical personnel. Some patients had a confused expression on their faces not knowing what to expect, while others had a blank stare. The paramedical personnel rushed around nervously, some keeping their distance fearful of infection.

I found Tom sitting in a wheelchair with an oxygen mask. There was no question that his symptoms were consistent with COVID. I managed to get a bed for him on the COVID floor. He was stable enough with good oxygenation and did not need an ICU bed.

"Doc, am I going to live?" he asked. "Will you start me on Hydroxychloroquine?"

"Yes," I said. "That's the only drug we have on our hands." I could read anxiety and nervousness on his face and restlessness as he kept kneading his sweaty hands. He was a different man than the man I had met at Jacques birthday party: afraid, apprehensive, unsure of himself.

I mentioned that I wouldn't be taking care of him and introduced him to Dr. Jonathan Levy. They had met at the party and he was in charge on one of the COVID floors. But I assured him that he would be in good hands and that I would keep a close eye on him.

I went back to the ICU and continued my rounds. Antonina had taken the day off and Andy Sommer had come down with mild COVID symptoms and was quarantined. Dr. Jake Rand was substituting. It was a busy day for Swami and me and our short-handed team with three codes in the morning hours and two deaths.

It was all becoming routine—the tedium of one day followed by the next. When will it all end? Will there be new mutations?

At about six in the evening, I asked Swami whether it was okay for me to leave. "Please go ahead," he said. "Will call if we need you."

I left the hospital and decided to walk back to the apartment through Central Park. The chaos in the ER—people coughing into their masks; people short of breath as if the oxygen they were receiving was not enough; some delirious and others with fear in their glassy eyes; the toxic flotsam of the virus all around; and trucks with freezers lined outside waiting to receive the dead—all this was too much even for a doctor to absorb, to deal with, to ignore. I felt weathered and soiled longing for fresh air. As I sauntered into the park in a daze, only after walking for some fifteen minutes, the gloom that covered my sensorium lifted, and I absorbed the materiality of the surroundings: the trees in the park with tiny blazing green leaves and birds flying and singing under a blue firmament, as if trumpeting the arrival of summer. I noticed a few joggers and cyclists and decided to go on a slow jog the rest of the park from east to west. As I continued jogging, I felt refreshed and energized. On the West Side, while on my way home, I encountered homeless men peeing on the street, another masturbating and still another injecting heroin. I then realized that these men were housed in nearby hotels by the mayor because of COVID. I sped up my walking pace as I passed by the closed Lincoln Center. I felt an urge to sit by the fountain now silent, reminiscing. I remembered the last opera, *Cosi Fan Tutte,* Fleur and I had attended some weeks back.

We had opera tickets for the 2019-2020 season. At the coaxing of Fleur, we were frequent concertgoers at Lincoln Center. At first somewhat reluctant to indulge in classical music, I soon realized that the genre was highly relaxing and an excellent pastime. Moreover, I had taken up the sax when in high school and was a jazz aficionado. Before I met Fleur, I often frequented the jazz clubs in the city including the Blue Note and Jazz at Lincoln Center in the Time Warner building. Jazz excited me, while classical music felt relaxing. I took Fleur for several jazz performances; however, she wasn't taken up with contemporary jazz, but liked Brazilian Bosa Nova, the music of Eliane Elias, and Afro-Cuban jazz. Fleur, on the other hand, after introducing me to opera was rather insistent that I accompany her. I began enjoying opera, its theatrics based on dramatic stories, but when it was too long my back ached and I ended up leaving the Met after the second intermission. I was assured that *Cosi fan tutte,* wouldn't be one of the long ones and I had coaxed Jacques and Alex to attend. I had read the story in advance of the performance and was taken by surprise to learn that *Cosi fan tutte,* literally meant 'Women are like that.' Like *what* I was anxious to find out.

We had hurriedly walked from our apartment to the Metropolitan Theatre.

"Let's hurry or we'll be late," I had said, turning to Fleur.

Usually the aristocracy, the beau monde, the cultured class of New York City made their appearance for operas, and Fleur enjoyed watching the parade. But that day people seemed to be dressed casually and they seemed in a hurry. We ended up in line behind a group of German and Japanese tourists.

We had made it into the theatre a few minutes before the doors were closed and were shown to the front row center sitting by the side of Jacques and Alex who had arrived a few minutes before us. It was Jacques first opera and I hoped he wouldn't be impatient to leave before the intermission. After all, Jacques was a coronary interventionalist and they were an impatient lot anxious to balloon and stent and move on to the next adventure. Surprisingly, the house was not full, and I wondered whether it had something to do with the oncoming pandemic.

"Look, there are many empty seats. Isn't that unusual?" I had said to Fleur. She had ignored my question as the chandeliers grew dim as they rose to the ceiling, and pin-drop silence filled the theatre.

The theme of the opera was to dupe two sisters Dorabella and Fiordiligi who were vacationing with their fiancées, the soldiers Ferrando and Guglielmo. Their friend, the cynical Don Alfonso, told the two men of his doubts in the fidelity of women. He would prove that both sisters like all other women, if given the slightest chance would be unfaithful.

During the intermission, we, together with Jacques and Alex immediately rushed to the bar for four flutes of champagne.

"So, buddy, are you enjoying your first opera?" I asked.

"Yeah, but it's a bit slow for me. Its already ten o'clock. I'm tired, and tomorrow I have six complex cases. I think I'm going to head home after the champagne."

"Are you staying?" asked Fleur of Alex.

"I'd like to, but I didn't like the theme of this opera. Infidelity of women? Wow! What about the infidelity of men?" Alex said.

"The opera was composed by Wolfgang Amadeus Mozart when sexism prevailed, and women were looked down as unfaithful creatures," said Fleur. "It doesn't bother me. It's the music I'm interested in. It's just an opera." The bells tolled announcing the start of Act II.

"Ciao guys," Alex said.

We took our seats. I looked around and noticed that many had left after the intermission.

The opera over, we left the Met at twelve midnight. "What did you think of the opera? I asked.

"I loved it. The singing was great," Fleur said.

This was the last opera. Lincoln Center closed down.

The jazz clubs in New York City shut down. The doors would probably remain shut for a long, long time.

It was the end of music. It was the end of theater on Broadway.

As I scanned the desolation of the area, the fountain silent and Damrosch Park deserted, I felt a sudden pang in my chest. What had happened here? They had said it before, after 9/11. But that was different. The virus was invisible. It had killed this city's lungs. It had paralyzed its vocal cords. Immersed in the Coronavirus cocoon, I did not know when the city would find its breath, its voice anew.

In the valley of the shadow of COVID-19 you meet insecurity, the unknown, breaths become gasps, a state of confusion prevails; and the angel of death hovers above like a hawk ready to pluck and kill or a famished tiger just around the corner to tear apart.

While walking home I got a call from Umesh. "My father passed away yesterday in his sleep," he said. "He simply refused hospitalization."

"I'm so sorry Umesh," I said. "Please take as many days as you want. Swami is a great help."

"I will return to NY in two days."

On my way home I wondered what this world is coming to. COVID is everywhere and the devastation in the developing overpopulated world like India, Pakistan and Bangladesh among others will be enormous.

When I got home to find out how Fleur was faring, I found her lying in bed drunk and in a horrible mood. She got up to go to the bathroom and swayed from side-to-side banging on the wall and nearly crashed on the bathroom floor. I held her preventing the fall.

"I don't need your help. Go away," she blabbered.

I waited outside the bathroom and when she was done, I helped her to bed afraid she would fall and injure herself. This time she did not protest.

I sat on a chair by the bedside, and momentarily dozed off.

My phone rang. I woke up startled and went to the living room to pick up the call.

"We have an emergency with Mr. Tom Branigan," said the resident physician. "He is having a heart attack."

"I am on my way," I said. "Please alert Dr. Jacques Charpentier."

"He is on his way. The cath. lab was notified," said the resident physician.

As I arrived at Tom's bedside, there was a code going on. Both Jacques and Levy were co-directing the code with chest compressions, electrical shocks, and injecting stimulants into the heart. Finally, after three electrical shocks to the chest and intravenous medications they were able to control the lethal rhythm—ventricular fibrillation, a consequence of the heart attack.

Tom was rushed to the cath. lab where Jacques performed his miraculous intervention on his coronary artery which was blocked by a clot as a consequence of COVID-19. On a respirator and an intra-aortic balloon to maintain adequate blood pressure and perfusion of the coronary arteries, Tom was transferred to the ICU in critical condition.

PART 3

Its love that enslaves us...It is the play within the play, the stage on which the tragic drama of our human lives unfolds.

—Justin Cronin, The City of Mirrors

CHAPTER 13

LOVE SMEARED CORONA SPHERES AND SPIKES

After attending to Tom Branigan, I walked the deserted streets to the hotel. I called Antonina to find out how she was doing. She asked me to come over for a nightcap. She was wearing a purplish-blue silk nightgown that accentuated her black eyes and flowing black hair. A soft Italian *Ciao* burbled out of her mouth as I entered her hotel room. Surgical masks notwithstanding, we hugged each other, but this time it was as if we could not resist one another, the ebb and flow of our restless pheromones taking over.

Spontaneously, unobtrusively, our masked mouths with strap marks and a stale recycled odor gnawed at each other. In a frenzy we snatched them away and she handed me a brandy snifter. After a gargle and a long gulp of Armagnac, my flesh met hers, and our juices intermingled. Her nightgown slid easily to the floor as we lay naked on the bed my mouth ravishing her ample upturned breasts. For a moment I saw spheres of the Coronavirus—her nipples multiplying like protein spikes filling my mouth and I smelled of them a sweet musky odor, inhaling and swallowing them letting them populate my lungs and my gut.

Was this all a dream? I had dreamt of alliums and leucospermums recently. I lifted my head and shook it, absorbing the materiality of my surroundings: the sterile hotel bedroom with its white sheets, the window curtains half drawn, the air conditioner spewing cold air. I was alive, and not in a fog—that my brain cells were responding. No, this was not a dream. This was real. I was with Antonina. Her body odor of saffron mixed with cedarwood and sultry amber, aroused, and I moved down below her navel to her pubic area as she parted her legs and welcomed my lips and tongue into her sex. She pushed me away gently and kneeling down took hold of me and her lips like petals of red bromeliads circled around my penis. She stroked me as I lay by her side and then, I entered her mound through her parted legs—the dark valley of nirvana. "*Forte. Forte. Ficame Forte*, I heard her say. "*Non faccio l'amore da molto tempo*," she softly uttered. I felt her heat as she pushed herself against me. "*Più forte*, she said and asked me to suck her nipples. "Bite them," she ordered. I disengaged and sucked hard on her nipple. She moaned and came in a staccato high-pitched squeal. "*Più forte*," she said again.

I turned her around exposing the round contour of her bounteous buttocks. I rolled her onto her stomach, lifting her onto her knees, tasted her there and plunged into her. I was large and thick, and she uttered a muffled cry. She turned around and pushed me down and taking hold of me she thrust it deep inside her like a matador's sword piercing the bull's spine. Momentarily she winced with pain. She moved at a frantic pace, her mouth wide, her eyes closed, and we rode into each other like a speeding train until I spasmodically ejaculated thick gelatinous fluid that mingled with the sap of her cunt—the elixirs of life, and we both gave a loud cry as if it was our last gasp.

We went into the shower and the hot steaming water massaged our bodies, relaxing the muscles. Our mouths found each other again and she stroked me with lather, and I washed her sex with soap and both re-aroused, we went at each other again.

We lay on the bed in each other's arms for some time and then we separated as the lingering afterburn of sex evaporated into thin air. We remained silent at arms-length under the covers. It was what sex does: the mind, the body, demanding an uncoupling, a certain detachment reaffirming the physical and mental individuality that we are after all two different people, and at the same time often opening up, unclogging the fountain within, that makes us ruminate, talk about our lives, confide our secrets, the unknown unspoken past.

In flagrante delicto, but did it matter? The world was in decay, a world subject to rapid change, and the shortness and temporariness of human life made many things bearable, even guilt—one act of love in the midst of destruction and death. I remembered the painting Memory of the Halls of Mirrors in Brussels, by Otto Dix, I saw when I was attending a conference there. In the painting, Dix was able to tell the bitter realities of war that involved sex, murder, death, and torture. Sex and death will always be around, along with war and the human body, giving a greater sense of transient reality.

I was half asleep when she broke the post-coital silence. "I spoke to my daughter today," she said. "She is well, and I was happy to hear her voice. She told me that grandma has a headache and is sleeping. I am concerned for my mother."

"What about your daughter's father?" I asked. "Where is he? Can't he help caring for her?"

There was a long silence as if she was contemplating on the answer or she wished not to address the question.

"Her father is dead," she uttered suddenly, dropping it like a stone in a pond: plop; or like a sudden gust of wind, and began telling her story. I was fully awake now.

"I had met my husband, Farid, in a bar in Rome when I had gone to celebrate my graduation from med school with my friends. He was a French Muslim of Algerian descent, a student of history at the Sorbonne who was visiting Rome. He was tall and slim and handsome with dark wavy hair and a chin strapped style beard. Except for the height he looked like a lean, handsome, Sicilian, and I was physically attracted to him. He spoke French and some English and even managed a bit of Italian. He was excited about the Vatican, and I agreed to be his tour guide. I showed him the Sistine Chapel and the Apostolic Palace where the Pope lived. He marveled at Michelangelo's painted ceiling dome, a work of high Renaissance art, and his eyes flushed with tears. "I feel as if I am in the presence of God!" he said. He expressed a desire to see the Pope in person.

For me it was love at first sight.

"It seems for young lovers often it is not communication that matters much; the attraction lies in looks and great sex," I said.

"Right at the outset his interest in the Vatican surprised me and at the same time cemented my interest in him," she said. "He riled about the infighting between the Shi'a and the Sunni sects and marveled how the Protestants and the Catholics had settled their differences. His total absorption in the Vatican astonished me creating a strong bond and at the same time an engaging curiosity. At times I wondered at his sincerity. Was he a faux child, taking me on a ride? But when he mentioned that he was in the process of writing a paper on the medieval Papacy it all then made perfect sense. Sometimes when I came home after doctoring, I found him busy on his laptop, at times writing, at other times surfing the internet. He promised to have me read the manuscript after it was finished.

He often went back to La Goutte d'Or in Paris where his family lived. He told me that his father had passed away five years ago after they moved to France and that his mother was sick with diabetes and heart disease. He was the only child and felt guilty for leaving his mother alone in the care of his uncle's family. Hardly had we met, I became pregnant. I am a Roman Catholic and abortion was out of the question. Moreover, he was excited about the pregnancy and suggested marriage. We were civilly married and lived in my parents' home on the outskirts of Rome. I found him a part-time job as a cook in my cousin's restaurant. He was very respectful of my parents and often helped in household chores, cleaning dishes and cooking. He would prepare a wonderful couscous and a *Tajine zitoune*—a green olive and chicken stew—my favorite. He told me that he wanted to learn Italian first before transferring to *Sapienza Università di Roma*. Whenever I got home early after my work at the hospital, I spent time teaching him Italian. He was a quick learner. He intended to be a teacher of medieval European history and perhaps someday a professor.

My cell phone rang. It was the hospital. "Do you mind if I take this call?"

"Sure, please do," she said.

"This is Dr. Jeff Anderson. Who is this?" I asked.

"This is Dr. Robert Wang, medical resident covering the night shift. I got a call from the ER. They need an ICU bed, and all beds are taken. Mr. Singh in Bed Three is already two days post extubation, with good oxygenation. Can I transfer him to the COVID floor?"

"Please go ahead. We were planning to transfer him tomorrow."

"Thanks Doc. Sorry to bother you this late."

"No dice," I said, and hung up.

"Please continue your story, Antonina."

"Farid would go back to Paris at least once in two months and stay for several days visiting his mother and his nieces and nephews. To me he seemed a homey person: dedicated, caring, and a good and loyal husband. Several months later he was visited by a friend, Mustafa, who stayed for several days in Rome in a nearby motel and they went out together. And then suddenly when I was in the sixth month of pregnancy, Farid disappeared, and I never heard from him. I called him but the phone was disconnected. I began to worry.

On the fifth day of his disappearance, late at night, I received a call from the Italian branch of Interpol that Farid and Mustafa were shot dead during a terrorist raid in a bar in Paris. They told me that Farid was sent in advance by ISIS to plan an attack on the Vatican and to kill the Pope, but the attack was foiled—an ISIS cell with French connection was discovered in London by MI-6. They identified him as the main French ISIS contact and informed the Italian secret service that he was in Rome. He must have sensed that they were looking for him and so he fled to Paris and he and Mustafa carried their last random attack in a Paris restaurant. Apparently before he came to France he had trained in Swat, in Afghanistan. His real name was Abdelkader. His *nom-de-guerre* was Rabah Mohammed.

"One day I will have to tell my daughter that her father was an ISIS Jihadi," said Antonina.

"You never suspected his intentions?"

"Sometimes I doubted his sincerity. But that he was

ISIS? No. Never. Perhaps I was too naïve. A Papal audience was scheduled two weeks after he was killed."

"Did the secret service give you a hard time?"

"Oh yes, they searched the house, impounded my computer, but they found nothing. Finally, they were convinced that I was an innocent bystander. They told me that I was randomly selected—the bait to show him around Rome and the Vatican. This way he wouldn't raise any suspicion."

"How did you manage? You must have been devastated."

"The Pope obviously was debriefed. He asked to meet with me. He blessed me and when I couldn't stop crying, he held me in his arms and wiped my tears. He said to me that he forgave Farid, and that I shouldn't feel guilty about his intensions. It was a source of great consolation to me."

I held her close in my arms and stroked her face, dreamily. Fatigue was written all over my body. "I admire your resilience under such duress," I said.

"I'm okay, Jeff," she said. *L'ho superato.* You look terribly tired. Please go to sleep."

I got off the bed, dressed and went to my room. I was in a daze. I took a long draught of scotch and crashed on the bed. The day was coming to an end and there was much that happened, much to think about, much to digest or just forget. But I felt drained, befuddled. It was as if my mind was entering a koyaanisqatsi world—running away from the old. But this was no time to deal with what happened—the incongruous juxtaposition of images, its fleeting reality—the self-involved sophistry. Fate dealt me a hand, and I played the hand I was dealt with.

Suddenly, exhaustion came over me, a thickening shroud of fatigue like a monsoon cloud darkening the horizon; but fearful of early morning arousal, with its unending thought process, I took an Ambien pill—the god of slumber—my savior, and I floated away into the darkness of the night.

CHAPTER 14

WINE, JAZZ, AND SEX

Surprisingly, I slept soundly, an undisturbed sleep without dreams or nightmares. I wondered whether it was the result of the high-octane unexpected sexual encounter. After waking up at six in the morning, and after having breakfast in the hotel cafeteria, I left for the hospital. I intended to call Antonina but did not want to wake her up so early expecting to see her at work. There was no point in calling Fleur. She was in a sour mood soaked in alcohol and likely she wouldn't pick up the phone. I thought of calling her later in the evening.

On rounds that morning, Antonina's absence was sorely felt; additionally, the team was short of one doctor and two nurses. The nurse practitioner Karen Brown and another nurse had come down with COVID-19 and both were on a fourteen-day quarantine in their apartments. Karen had flu-like symptoms, a slight fever and cough, but had no difficulty breathing, and since her oxygenation remained good, I advised her to stay at home. Nonetheless, I was concerned for her health.

"Am I going to die?" she said.

"No! You are not going to die," I said emphatically. "Please check your oxygenation in the morning after walking for five to ten minutes in the apartment and repeat it in the afternoon and before bedtime." I was unsettled with her illness.

"Will do, Doc," she said. "Thanks for your concern."

"If the cough gets worse and or the oxygenation drops, please let me know. And call me any time."

After speaking with Karen, I joined the rounds. The ICU was full, but we had managed to take two patients off the respirator.

"I think we should transfer the two patients to the COVID floor," said Umesh.

"I entirely agree," I said. "We are terribly shorthanded. I will call the other ICUs to find out whether we can transfer one or two patients."

"That's a good idea," said Umesh. Under the circumstances we cannot provide adequate care for the patients."

After rounds, I called the residency program director informing him that we were severely shorthanded. I requested he pull a medical or any other resident or fellow from the floors and send to the ICU with urgency. I also called the nursing service, and they immediately reassigned Miss Gamboa, a nurse practitioner from the cardiac service. It was obvious that several staff members and nurses treating COVID patients in the ER, the ICUs, and the COVID floors were getting infected. It also became clear that the infection was spreading like wildfire with aerosol transmission. New instructions by our task force mandated that all personnel taking care of COVID patients had to be adequately attired with gowns, shoes and head covers, N95 masks, goggles, and face shields. Luckily, the hospital by now had received a consignment of N95 masks from China.

At about ten o'clock my cell phone rang. It was Antonina sobbing at the other end.

"My mother has COVID… She is hospitalized and in the ICU. She has bilateral pneumonia…and is on the respirator. I have to take the flight back to Rome…I cannot leave my daughter alone with my father…he has early signs of Alzheimer," she said amid sobs.

"You don't have anyone else that your daughter could stay with?" I asked.

"Under the COVID quarantine circumstances, absolutely none. Besides, many of my close relatives live in Milan."

"There is no choice then. You must go. When do you plan to leave?

"This evening."

"Don't worry. I will speak to Dr. Mukherjee and the head of infectious diseases. Do call me when you get to Rome."

"Thanks for everything. *Ciao*." She seemed reassured and calmer. She had gone through worse.

In the afternoon I visited Tom Branigan who was in another ICU. I was taken by surprise to see him off the respirator and off the intra-aortic balloon pump. He was sitting in bed waiting to be transferred to the Telemetry Unit. Jacques had saved his life after stenting the acutely occluded coronary artery after suctioning the clot—a consequence of COVID-19. A hypercoagulable state from COVID with clot formation in the lungs and veins was just reported in a British journal.

"You are a lucky man," I said.

"Yes, I know," he said. "You guys saved my life."

"Do you still plan to host the TV program?"

"I'm not sure Doc—COVID-19 has deflated my plans. I have to mull over all that is happening. Healthcare has assumed greater importance now."

"Yes indeed," I said. "Only when illness comes home to roost—a new awakening—the prerogative changes."

"Yes," he responded, looking away from me.

"We were not prepared for the pandemic," I said. "And the the task force formed by Obama was abolished. As a matter of fact, Obama's task force had left a 'Game Plan' for the pandemic, which should have been followed."

Tom kept quiet and did not respond. I sensed some anxiety on his face as his eyelids started twitching. I didn't want to push the button further. It might precipitate a heart arrhythmia.

"Well, I have to leave. You look great and your numbers look good. Probably they will discharge you in a few days."

"I hope so. Have you seen Jacques? He hasn't come around and I haven't heard from my girlfriend either for the last few days. Let me show you her picture."

I saw the picture of a thirtyish, tall, brunette, and wondered what she was doing with this fifty-five-year-old, portly, overweight, cigar smoking man.

"What does she do?"

"She was a Republican pollster. I helped her land a lobbyist job in Washington. She is a young ambitious firebrand. By the way, your wife…is gorgeous."

"Yes, she is," I said. "I'd love to sit and talk, but I have work to do." I immediately thought that the girlfriend was with Tom for visibility and career enhancement. He was her sugar daddy with connections.

It was five in the evening—time to call Fleur. There was no answer. I left a message and decided to go home to see how she was doing. By now she should have recouped from her sour mood. But the rebound could take another day or two. On my way home I dropped by Jacques' apartment. I had called in advance to tell him I was on my way, but he did not pick up the call and the voicemail was full.

The concierge announced me, and Jacques requested to send me up. As Jacques opened the door, the riveting sound of Miles Davis's trumpet playing *So What* permeated the living room. It was as if the music transcended the mood. I was taken by surprise to see a thirtyish woman walk from the bathroom into the living room as Jacques ushered me in.

"This is Carol Johnson, a friend of mine. I took care of her father," he said, introducing her. "And this is Dr. Jeff Anderson, my closest buddy."

I had a mask on and gave Carol an elbow; neither Jacques nor Carol wore masks. Undoubtedly it was Jacques' habit to sleep with his patients daughters. I was about to laugh but controlled myself.

"My friend Jeff is a savior," said Jacques, interrupting my thoughts. "He is in the thick of things—a super infectious diseases specialist saving people with COVID-19."

"Saving people?" I asked. "Well, that's a totally undeserved compliment. We have no treatment for the virus and the patients are dropping like flies." Carol looked at me with a generous smile giving the impression that she was impressed with my honesty and humility.

I noticed the smudged lipstick on her lips, and the uneven blush on her cheeks. I was certain that Jacques was bedding her just before I arrived. No wonder he did not pick up the call.

"Would you like some wine?" asked Jacques.

"Sure," I said. "I'll get it." I saw an open bottle of St. Francis Cabernet, with two empty glasses, one with lipstick stains. I poured myself a generous serving of the wine. The more I looked at Carol I soon realized that I had seen her somewhere before. I scanned my memory trying to place her. And then suddenly I got it. I had seen her photograph a few hours ago. She was Tom's girlfriend—and Jacques was bedding her. He was living it up: wine, jazz, and sex amid all the chaos and death.

"Jacques, I saw Tom a few hours ago. He was asking for you," I said.

"Yes, the house staff called me about him. I'll see him tomorrow morning. We saved the man's life."

I could see that the very mention of Tom unnerved Carol. She got up to leave.

"I have a late-night meeting, with some Republican election Committee members," she said. "Well, goodbye, and nice meeting you." She hugged and kissed Jacques, waved at me and abruptly made her exit.

"Wow Jacques, isn't she Tom's girlfriend?"

"How the fuck do you know?"

"Tom showed me her picture. He said she hadn't answered his calls and hadn't heard from her for several days."

"She's done with him. The man's impotent—diabetic neuropathy."

"My, oh my, how long have you been screwing her? Does Alex know or suspect?"

"The affair has been going on for a couple of months. A rendezvous in San Francisco and in New Orleans. We met again in Frankfurt a couple of weeks before the pandemic hit. She lives in Washington now. She is a Republican lobbyist. Don't give me that look. You know I can't live without sex for more than three days and Alex is in the Hamptons, sunbathing, drinking and who knows what else. Besides, we haven't been sleeping in the same bed for months.

"I gathered."

"I am sure that most couples who are separated because of this COVID thing are having phone sex or FaceTime sex. But that stuff is not for me. I'm no masturbator."

I burst out laughing. Although Jacques knew that I did not approve of his philandering ways, I had no moral right to question him; after all I had sinned last night with Antonina. It seemed that there was a kind of testosterone heedlessness in both of us. But what was the world coming to? Death was everywhere. The only reliable escape from this malady was a moment of love in whatever shape or form. Love, sex, loveless sex—a moment of joy— the sudden release of endorphins—a singular tremolo. Perhaps sex was a myth destined for rupture as soon as it's over, and yet sex was and is apotheosized as a form of rejuvenation in the cycle of death and rebirth. It was and is the very fountain of our existence. The juxtaposition of love and brutality. Wasn't there an element of brutality last night with Antonina? And yet, what an irony: death unexpectedly crept on the old and even the young, when a pandemic finally caught us unprepared after a century. The world was and is in flux: the drum of creation in one hand, the fire of destruction in the other. At the moment destruction has the upper hand.

With all these tragic happenings did infidelity mean anything? Is sin mandated by religion, ordained by a God who doesn't even care have any consequence or meaning? And what about the people dying alone? To be shoved in a freezer! The authority, the finality of death without a decent burial. No, there was no point in guilt when life was hanging by a mere thread. What little pleasures life offered momentarily one had to take it, grab it, savor it for it may never be offered again. And that was what exactly happened with me and Antonina last night and with Jacques and Carol today. Sex—a pleasurable medication, a drug worth its weight in gold, to drown the sorrow all around.

For a moment I wondered about Antonina crossing the vastness of the Atlantic Ocean. Will her mother make it? Will she be able to return to New York to continue with her fellowship in infectious diseases, or will she have to give it all up for now?

On my wat home I called Karen. "How are you doing?" I asked.

"Better," she said. "My oxygenation is good. No fever and the cough is subsiding." I felt reassured.

When I arrived home at about eight-thirty p.m. to visit Fleur, to see how she was doing, I found her asleep. I tiptoed into the bedroom and watched her breathing, and after confirming that she was fine I went to the living room and ordered some Thai food and began watching ECN. It was all about the pandemic showing crowded hospitals, ERs and ICUs, people on respirators and death on a grand scale. I switched on to Netflix, and kept scanning one show after another, one movie after another and finally switched on to HBO and began watching reruns of *Downton Abbey.*

At about ten p.m. Fleur woke up and on the rebound was surprised and even ecstatic to see me. I went over all that had happened: my encounter with Tom, my visit to Jacques and finally that Antonina had to go back to Rome since her mother had COVID-19. I left out the events of last night and Jacques' affair with Carol Johnson.

"I have a headache," she said. "I feel very tired and washed-out."

"I guess it's a hangover with all the drinking you did last night." She looked pale and disheveled.

"It's easy for you to say that. Staying here all by myself with nothing to do is depressing. When is all this going to end?"

"But the heavy drinking. How is it going to solve the problem?"

"It's the only way I can deaden my mind. You know that. Is it so hard for you to understand?"

"Sorry darling," I said. It's best not to contradict her and start another argument.

"When is this damn pandemic going to end?"

"It's just the start, honey," I said. "We have a long way to go. There will be more variants, more mutations of the same virus. It could get worse before it gets better."

"Don't say…more mutations? Isn't this enough?"

"There is going to be a whole lot of depression and anxiety going around. I have decided to come home starting tomorrow. Before I left the hospital, I got myself tested for the virus and for antibodies. I will sleep in the guest room, and it's best we wear masks. I brought a pile of them."

"I'm so happy you are going to come home," she said and hugged me.

We ate the Thai food and went to bed together. We both wanted to make love and we had sex much like married couples did and fell asleep.

I saw her veil tossing and waving in the wind as she took me by the hand zooming into space amid stars and planets speeding by, and the moon so close to the touch. Who was this woman decked in a veil head to foot who took me far beyond the sky at the doorstep of a tunnel? Was it a black hole I was entering? Momentarily I was frightened thinking that I would be trapped in space where even the elusive light cannot get out. And then as suddenly I landed on a surface as if on a distant planet. The land was gullied, eroded and barren. I looked for her who brought me here but found her nowhere to be seen. There was a path of flat smooth rock and in the far-off distance I saw a mote of light. I followed the light gliding into a large space with scattered white light whose source I could not decipher. I had never experienced such illumination, such a white glow before. I saw mummified dead everywhere walking about like pilgrims in a fable swallowed up and lost in the innards of some extraterrestrial planet. It was as if they walked around oblivious of those around them utterly immersed in the glow of white light, as if waiting for resurrection. It felt as if the light sustained some living molecules, some cells awaiting the re-explosion of life. I wondered where I was. What was this place that the veiled woman brought me to and for what purpose? It was then that I saw my father and rushed toward him but tumbled down at dizzying speed into a precipice.

I woke up startled and realized that I was dreaming. It was a REM-dream state, and I remembered the whole dream. I wondered what my father was doing there. It looked as if he had just arrived.

I looked at my watch. It was five in the morning. I got up and went to the bathroom. Sitting in the living room with a cup of coffee, I contemplated on the day ahead of me. I left for work at six in the morning. I had no time to ponder on the dream—I bagged it somewhere in my brain. I had to call my shrink and relate my dreams. It was two nights that I skipped Ambien. Were these nightmares a result of Ambien withdrawal? Were they from all the pressure, the death all around me?

PART 4

My father was left to die alone, at home, without help. We were simply abandoned. No one deserves an end like that.

—Riccardo Munda, a doctor near Bergamo

CHAPTER 15

DEATH FROM NEGLECT

Seated in my academic office, I went over my emails, the New York Times and Yahoo.com for the latest news. I scanned the medical journals for recent developments in the management of COVID-19. I read about the British report on the use of the steroid dexamethasone, the devastating and invariably fatal cytokine release syndrome, a preliminary report that the loss of smell and taste might be the first sign of COVID-19, and a study that raised doubts on the efficacy of hydroxychloroquine. I then called Antonina Bucco at about eight a.m. She told me that her mother was in the ICU on a respirator and that her organs were failing.

"I don't think she will make it," she said. "I don't think I can come back to New York,"

At that moment, I had another call, which I did not pick up and continued speaking with Antonina. I wanted to tell her that it is possible that her mother has the cytokine release syndrome, but what good would that do?

"I am going to test my father and my daughter for COVID today," she said. "I hope they are free of the disease."

"Well, take it one day at a time. Don't make a hasty decision," I said. I surmised that she expected the worst. She was a doctor and had seen an avalanche of death in a short time in New York.

"No matter what—I will have to cancel the fellowship training program in New York, for this year and perhaps for good unless I place my father in a nursing home and bring my daughter with me. Under the circumstances finding a nursing home for my father is impossible—*Che Dio mi aiuti.*"

"Courage, my friend. I'll say a prayer for you," is all I could say.

As soon as I got off the phone with Antonina, I checked my phone for recent calls. It was my mother. I listened to the voicemail: "Please call me as soon as possible. It's an emergency."

I wondered whether she or my father had come down with COVID-19. I immediately called my mother. She gave me shocking news: she told me that she found my father unresponsive. "He is dead," she said, amid sobs. I was stunned. It seemed unreal. As I was recollecting my thoughts, she told me that father was complaining of chest discomfort for two to three days. He thought it was due to indigestion and took Mylanta for it. He had been suffering from acid reflux, but it was well controlled.

"I told him to call you. He said that you must be too busy with the pandemic. I called Dr. Morton Hoffenberg, his primary care. His service said he was not seeing any patients for now because of the COVID situation. He wasn't keen on going to the ER fearful he would catch COVID. You know how stubborn and stoic he was. I was going to call you today for advice." She stopped talking as if she lost the tread of thought. I kept silent, still is a daze.

"He is usually up by six in the morning," she said. "I went to wake him up at about seven. He was unresponsive and cold. I called 911. They were here in three minutes. There was nothing they could do. He must have died several hours before. I called the funeral home. They will be here soon."

We both remained silent, as if our emotions were on tap. Finally, I broke down: "I'm so sorry Mum," I said, and we both sobbed.

"He was so proud of you," she said, in between sobs.

"I feel terrible that I wasn't there for him, Mum. He died of a heart attack in his sleep. I saw him in my dream last night. He is in heaven, Mum."

"He was a good and a kind man. A man of the faith. May his soul rest in peace and heavenly joy."

"Yes Mum, he is rejoicing in heaven. Let me know when the wake is, and the funeral. Anyway, if a flight is available, Fleur and I will come today."

As I hung up the phone, I remembered the dream last night. I had seen my father just arrive on an extraterrestrial planet bathing in a mote of white light. This was not the first time I had an extrasensory perception. Before Martha's sudden death, I had seen her in a dream lying on the street. I had asked her whether she fainted. Before she could answer, I woke up startled from the dream. I didn't think much of it. I wondered whether he died between 4:45 to 5:00 a.m. I felt unsettled, even fearful, not knowing what all of this meant. Are extrasensory perceptions related to the subconscious receptiveness to the subtler and finer messages around us? Or are they just serendipitous?

Seated in my academic office, I called Fleur. "I just spoke to my mother. She found my father unresponsive this morning. He…he is dead, Fleur," I choked as I pronounced these words. She started crying, even sobbing. "I'm sorry, Jeff," she said. I'd love to come with you, but I don't feel well."

"What's wrong, Fleur?"

"The headache hasn't gone. It is weird. I just made myself a coffee, but I cannot smell it. I tried smelling the Thai leftovers. I cannot smell that either."

"Do you have fever? Any cough?"

"No cough. I don't feel feverish… I feel very tired,"

"It is likely that you have COVID-19. I don't think you should come to Ohio with me. Do take some Tylenol. Get into an Uber and come to my office. I will have you tested and come home with you. I will call the funeral home and wait for my mum's phone call to decide when I should go to Ohio. Under the circumstances it is doubtful that there will be a wake."

I called Dr. Mukherjee and informed him that I needed

a few days off and waited for Fleur. I called the funeral home and was informed that there will be no wake and that the funeral will be in two days.

When Fleur came to the hospital her temperature was 97.8 degrees Fahrenheit. The nurse inserted a swab deep inside Fleur's nostrils and then mine for COVID-19 testing. We went back to the apartment, and I asked Fleur to rest. I started her on vitamins, zinc and Tylenol and held off on the drug hydroxychloroquine after reading the article about its inefficacy.

The next day I checked the results of our tests on MyChart. Fleur was positive for COVD, while I was negative.

On my way to Ohio, I thought of my father. He came from a family of conservative Evangelical Christians working on a small family farm inherited from his parents. He had a high school education and married late in life after his parents passed away. He worked hard on the farm; after the family's consumption, whatever was left, he sold to local vendors and large corporate farms. Most small farmers in the area had sold out, but my father refused.

He encouraged me to seek a college education and was proud of me for becoming a doctor but expected me to come back to Cuyahoga County and start a private practice there. He was disappointed to see me settle in

New York, and when he and my mother visited, they were like fish out of water. I enjoyed taking them to Central Park, to the museums and a Broadway musical. However, they couldn't stomach the New York culture scene: the mismatched people on the streets, the noise all around, men with afros blasting their radios and the babble of tongues in Central Park and Columbus Circle. This was not their America.

They were devastated with Martha's death and wondered at my choice of Fleur; however, they were thoroughly impressed with her looks and demeanor after they met her.

I wondered whether my parents were happy together. They were not expressive toward each other. I never saw them hugging or kissing. He was a lowkey man who enjoyed his beer before a home-cooked dinner, his football games on TV; a man who had never travelled beyond his country except for his stint in the South Pacific during World War II. He did not have much of a family except for a sister who lived in California that I had met once when I visited. I gathered he was not close to her.

I suddenly realized how little I knew my father; his ambitions, his wishes, whether he felt accomplished in some way or another. Unfortunately, only after one's death, we wonder about the very person that created and sustained life, our genetic mold; and then we feel at a total loss, hanging onto broken shards of life that we can never recover.

There was no doubt that the pandemic was directly

related to his death. If not for the pandemic, he would have been seen by his primary doctor and had a catheterization and a stent before the fatal heart attack. I wondered how many people are dying at home from heart attacks. Jacques mentioned that hardly anyone with an acute heart attack had come to the hospital for emergent care afraid of acquiring COVID in the hospital. "These people are left alone to die without medical care. This is what the pandemic has wrought," he said.

The funeral was attended by half-a-dozen people mostly nearby neighbors and my mother's close friends. There was no church service, but a pastor's blessing of the grave. The graveyard itself was a surreal deserted wasteland on the side of a hill.

I stayed an extra day with my mother going over her finances and my father's will. I advised her to sell the farm and either buy an apartment or move to an assisted living community. I offered financial help. She promised to think it over. I would have stayed longer had it not been for Fleur. I called her several times a day and was somewhat reassured that she was stable. But the night before my departure, she seemed distant, somewhat withdrawn. I was totally surprised when she asked me what I was doing in Ohio.

Before I took the taxi to the airport my mother and I hugged each other for a long time with heavy hearts.

CHAPTER 16

THE PANDEMIC COMES HOME TO ROOST

When I arrived back home, I found Fleur in a daze—like in a fog—with a blank stare. There was no question she had COVID-19, but I had difficulty understanding what exactly was going on with her. It was as if she had fallen out of life altogether. Her lungs were clear, and her oxygen level was good. I questioned her at length; she mumbled. I took hold of her and made her walk. She buckled and nearly fell. Had she had a stroke? My anxiety surged at the speed of an airplane's takeoff. On my way back from Ohio, I had read on my laptop that Coronavirus disease can increase the risk of acute stroke within the first three days of infection. However, patients who developed strokes from COVID-19 had a higher incidence of high blood pressure, diabetes, high cholesterol, the abnormal heart rhythm known as atrial fibrillation, and heart failure, but Fleur had none of these risk factors. This information was reassuring, but I just couldn't take a chance. I remembered what transpired with my first wife, Martha—I had ignored the warning signs.

I immediately called a neurologist at the medical center and took Fleur to the ER. She was seen by Dr. Morton Bender and had an MRI and MRA examination of the brain, which to my relief, showed no evidence of a stroke. She was admitted to the hospital for observation and placed on the COVID floor. She had lost all sense of smell and taste and was utterly fatigued and drained. Unfortunately, unlike in other diseases, there were no experts for COVID-19, and so Fleur languished on the COVID floor frequently assessed for any improvement or worsening of her condition. For two entire days she remained in a fog and refused any intake of solid foods except liquids to keep her hydrated. Finally on the third day, she felt somewhat stronger and could walk for several feet. I took her home. I stayed with her for the next several days, but we didn't share the bed. I slept in the guest room cum study. My sleep was assisted by Ambien, and the flareups of anxiety by Xanax. To some extent I relished the break from the ICU. Umesh filled me in and updated me of what was going on. I was glad that another infectious disease expert in private practice was called upon to cover me. But my concern for Fleur remained unabated. After a couple of days at home, I was restless, not knowing what to expect. I walked around in the deserted city, on empty streets but the restlessness was unrelenting. Somewhat refreshed after jogging in Riverside Park, my mind was still absorbed with Fleur's condition.

When will she recover?

She had started eating a few morsels of food, most of which she could not taste. What she managed to taste felt spoilt and putrid; she retched and threw up. She complained that she could not smell or taste her favorite espresso or her wines. I ordered spicy Indian food, think-

ing that the strong smell and taste of curry and the spices: saffron, cardamon, cumin, asafetida would make the
difference—but no dice. "It's entirely tasteless," she said.
"More like wood." She was a *connoisseur* of fine wines,
and her father had gifted us a 1982 Chateau Haut Brion
to celebrate our wedding anniversary. Perhaps opening
the bottle and raising a toast would excite her, cheer her
up. Somewhere in the brain the memory must be stored
and if so, could this fine expensive wine rekindle it? I
opened the bottle and after aerating and decanting the
wine poured two glasses. I was no connoisseur of wine
like her, and yet in her company at her prompting I was
able to distinguish the smell of the fruit, of the oak bar-
rel in which it was aged, a berry note, and the hint of
spring flowers. The 1982 Chateau Haut-Brion possessed
a dark, dense ruby/purple color. It was supposed to have
a spectacular aromatic taste of cherry and black current
intertwined in a smoky woody taste of oak, a remarkable
richness, an insinuation of tempered bitterness with faint
echoes of past sweetness of the grapes harvested in the
early dawn. But Fleur could smell nothing and taste nothing. It was a riveting letdown. But what was I thinking
and expecting? How could she rekindle the memory if she
was unable to smell the wine to begin with? I drank half
the bottle to drown my lassitude and sorrow.

It was already a week since she was at home and the

weakness and fatigue persisted. She slept all day and night. She smoked some weed, but that didn't help either. I called the rehab center only to find that they were closed in view of the pandemic. I tried to take her for a walk, but she refused to leave the apartment. She felt dizzy when she got up and her heart quickened. This was something new. I wondered how much of this was psychological and related to depression. I called her shrink and he suggested placing her on Abilifly. I called Dr. Grimes who asked me to check her blood pressure and heart rate when she stood up. Her blood pressure dropped a bit, but her heart rate zoomed to 120. Grimes informed me that she might have Postural Orthostatic Tachycardia Syndrome, a condition when the heart rate quickens on standing. He mentioned that it is possibly secondary to COVID and asked me to make her drink lots of water—at least eighty ounces a day—and increase her intake of salt, a pretzel a day or a couple of salt tablets, in addition to salt in her food for now. "If that doesn't help let me know," he said. "I would be glad to do a Tilt Test, but the labs are closed." I felt somewhat reassured when he mentioned that the heart itself was likely normal. But when will all this end? Nobody seemed to know. This was a new disease with too many unknowns and with no specialists on the horizon to advise and treat the illness. At least her lungs were not involved, and her oxygenation remained good. And yet, I was experiencing the helplessness that patients' relatives must have felt, not knowing what to expect, wondering whether death was just around the corner.

My lips trembled, my vision blurred from a film of tears. Will Fleur have the same fate as Martha? I was gripped by insecurity and an inner fear—an astonishing paralysis of thought.

I remembered when AIDS first appeared on the scene. It was a new disease, an epidemic that felled young men in its killing path. In 1981, cases of a rare lung infection called Pneumocystis carinii pneumonia (PCP) were found in five young, previously healthy gay men in Los Angeles. At the same time, there were reports of a group of men in New York and California with an unusually aggressive cancer called Kaposi's Sarcoma. By the end of the year, there were more than 200 reported cases of severe immune deficiency among gay men of which more than half died. In June 1982, a group of cases among gay men in Southern California suggested that the cause of the immune deficiency was sexual, and the syndrome was initially called gay-related immune deficiency (or GRID). In September, the CDC used the term AIDS (acquired immune deficiency syndrome) for the first time. In April 1984, in a joint conference with the Pasteur Institute, the National Cancer Institute announced that HTLV-III is the likely cause of AIDS. Only in March of 1987, the FDA approved the first antiretroviral drug, zidovudine (AZT), as treatment for HIV. Certainly, things were moving faster with COVID; the virus and its DNA had been identified by the Chinese, and hopefully there will appear some form of treatment and a strong push for vaccines by pharmaceutical companies and the government—*Coronavirus*

Warp-Speed was already in motion. And yet, its symptomatology and its consequences were so variable that it could take months if not years to fully understand this disease. In the meantime, many would suffer, and many would die.

Suddenly, I felt a surge of anxiety and hopelessness. I called my psychiatrist, who advised me to start Lexapro, an antidepressant. He reassured me that my feelings were not unusual; the stress of COVID, the deaths in the ICU, Fleur's situation, the death of my father were all coming to roost.

"There is a lot of depression and anxiety going around. Let me know how you feel in a couple of weeks," he said.

It was more than two weeks that Fleur's loss of sense of smell and taste hadn't returned. She refused food and was sequestered in the bedroom. Sitting at my desk in the guest room, I spend time on the computer, scanning the internet for any information on loss of sense of smell and taste and severe fatigue associated with COVID-19, the duration of the symptoms and ultimate recovery. I found out that in a substantial number of patients it can be the first symptoms of the illness. What was rather heartening was that those who experience smell and taste dysfunction had a milder form of the disease. On the other hand, patients who had normal smell function appeared to have a worse disease course and were more likely to be hospitalized and placed on a ventilator. The virus it seems causes an inflammatory reaction inside the nose that leads to a loss of the smell neurons. In some cases, this was permanent, but in other cases, the neurons would regenerate. What was most disconcerting was that in some, the problem could last for a long time. Exhausted, I ultimately fell asleep.

I was woken up by a scream. I rushed into the bedroom. Fleur was thrashing about with muffled screams. I waited, observing her, and then woke her up. I touched her forehead. She felt feverish. I gave her two Tylenols and made her drink two cups of water.

"You had a nightmare," I said.

"It was horrible," she said. "I was going to die. I was in the process of getting tubed…I asked, begged to spare me from the breathing machine. *I don't need it, I can breathe.* There were robots all around holding me down as the tube was forced down my throat and connected to the machine. I saw you and Jacques among the crowd. You were hooded and in long black robes as if waiting for my death. I was thrashing all about." "You had a nightmare," I said.

"'You will die, if you don't calm down,' you said in a stern voice. It is then that I floated out of my body and observed from above the code that was going on: the robots were shocking my chest repeatedly and injecting drugs into my heart.

"'It's no use,' said Jacques, 'she's dead.'

"'Call the refrigeration service,' someone said."

"Oh my God—what a nightmare! You poor thing," I said.

Now wide awake, sweaty, and in a panic mode, Fleur screamed feeling for her chest. She started hyperventilating, and as she tried to get up from the bed, she felt dizzy. I held her lite body and gave her a double dose of Valium. She lay back on the bed and closed her eyes. Finally, over the course of half-an-hour or so, she calmed down realizing that it was just a nightmare, a horrific dream of death.

I placed my hand on her neck and forehead—it felt warm. Her temperature was 100 degrees Fahrenheit. I checked her oxygen level. It was good. I felt reassured.

"What is the meaning of this nightmare, Jeff? Am I going to die?"

"It's just a nightmare. I assure you… you are not going to die."

I called Jacques the next morning. "We are falling apart. I cannot stay here day and night while doing nothing," I said, describing Fleur's nightmare.

"I am going to Montauk this weekend. Why don't you and Fleur come with me? A change of scenery will be good for you both."

Perhaps it was a good idea, I thought. I remembered what happened to me after Martha passed away. The surges of anxiety could be a sign of oncoming depression. I had felt the same symptoms after Martha's death. I simply could not take a chance.

After Fleur woke up, I suggested we go to Montauk

at Jacques and Alex's home for the weekend. She agreed. Jacques offered to drive us.

CHAPTER 17

MONTAUK

Jacques picked us up in his Lamborghini and once on the Long Island Expressway, we zoomed between eighty and one-hundred miles an hour on an empty highway, something unheard of a few months back. Undoubtedly COVID had thinned out highways into empty waterways to anywhere since most commuters were sitting and working remotely from home and some or many were afraid to venture out. Surprisingly, there were no traffic cops on the Long Island Expressway. We were masked but the nonchalant and aplombish Jacques had his mask sitting on the dashboard.

"Do you guys know Montauk?" asked Jacques.

"I have been to your house before," I said.

"I have never been to Montauk," said Fleur. All I know is that it's at the tip of Long Island. My father was thinking of buying a vacation home in South Hampton or Montauk. I don't know what happened to those plans."

"I think you guys should consider buying something here," said Jacques. "Montauk derives its name from the Montaukett tribe, an Algonquian-speaking tribe who lived in the area. Sometime, as far back as the 17th century the chief of the tribe, Wyan…something, yes, Wyandanch gave the settlers the right to pasture their livestock. After the Long Island Railroad extended its line to Montauk, roads, clubs and houses were built and brought in new people."

"I love it's windswept hills and dunes and views of the ocean and Long Island sound," I said.

"I'm looking forward to see your beach house," said Fleur.

As the car entered the driveway on a rather hot August Saturday, we saw Alex and daughter Belinda in swimming suits all smiles waiving at us. A pair of goldendoodles were jumping around. By their side was a maid with champagne flutes and tall glasses of lemonade.

"I feel happy and even sublime like the crispy blue of the sky," said Fleur, looking upwards at the sky. We made Namaste, with folded hands but Alex and Belinda hugged us anyway. Neither were wearing masks. I assured them that Fleur had already completed the quarantine and had tested negative for COVID-19. I distributed masks to the three of them and suggested they wear them.

Fleur, a champagne buff, like the rest, could not refuse the Moet. For the first time in a long time, I noticed a smile on her face as she intently looked at the view and the house. She drank the champagne in one quick gulp, perhaps fearful of not tasting it and did not comment on its bouquet or taste. I too felt my mood on the rise; perhaps it was the Lexapro; perhaps it was the change in scenery. Or both.

"Come, let me show you the house," said Alex to Fleur.

"I would like to rest a bit," Fleur responded, and was shown to the guest room, while the three of us chatted on Fleur's COVID status. "It's already a little more than two weeks and she still hasn't recovered," I said.

"That's sure depressing," responded Alex.

"She's lost a lot of weight; her cheeks are hollowed," said Jacques.

"She hardly eats and doesn't want to venture out. She feels dizzy and her heart races when she stands up," I said.

After resting for an hour and unpacking, I brought Fleur to the porch near the swimming pool, and Alex and I showed her around. Their summer home on Maple Street was a breathtaking modern house with high triangular ceilings and floor to ceiling glass windows with an inground swimming pool and outdoor jacuzzi with a spectacular view of the ocean and a private elevated wooden walkway to the beach. The house had three large bedrooms with attached bathrooms, a movie theater, a basement with a wine cellar, a pool table, and separate maid quarters.

I left Fleur in the company of Alex and Jacques and went for a dip in the ocean.

After I returned, I went to the guest room to find out how Fleur was doing. I found both Jacques and Alex around the bed and Fleur lying on the bed with eyes closed.

"What's going on?" I asked.

"After the house tour, I enticed Fleur to take a dip in the jacuzzi," said Alex. Fleur opened her eyes and Jacques handed her a drink of Gatorade.

"Sitting in the steaming jacuzzi, I felt great being there: the house, the view…ah…the pool, the open air jacuzzi… my flaccid muscles seemed to come alive, feeling them contracting and relaxing. And momentarily I forgot my troubles," said Fleur, in a shaky voice. I felt encouraged to hear her speak.

"It was my fault," said Alex. I shouldn't have coaxed her into the Jacuzzi."

"When I got out of the jacuzzi, I began feeling dizzy, and then passed out," said Fleur.

"Luckily, I was standing close by savoring a third glass of champagne," said Jacques. "I rushed to her and managed to avert the fall that could have resulted in injuries from the concrete floor. She came out of it quickly and I gathered that it was due to a precipitous fall in blood pressure from vasodilatation of the arteries and veins in response to the hot steaming water."

"Shouldn't we take her to the ER?" asked Alex.

"No way," I said. "I will call Dr. Grimes."

"I'm sorry to have spoiled your weekend," said Fleur. "If you don't mind, I will not come down for lunch."

"We have your favorite: braised branzino with asparagus spears," said Alex. "I will bring it for you."

"I have no appetite, no taste, no smell. Don't bother,"

said Fleur, dejected.

"You have to eat, Fleur—you need calories," said Jacques.

"Okay, I'll try."

I immediately called Dr. Grimes, who again recommended at least eight to ten glasses of fluids per day and plenty of salt.

"The hot jacuzzi was a bad idea," said Grimes. "And no alcohol."

"She refuses food. She wouldn't touch the pretzel or swallow the salt tabs."

"She needs salt. I will call in a prescription for a salt retaining hormone," said Grimes.

I spent most of the afternoon and evening at Fleur's bedside encouraging her to drink Gatorade and tried to coax her to come down for dinner. After the fainting spell, she spent much of the rest of the day in bed, sometimes dosing off, often as if distant, in a fog, and at other times as if in thought.

"What are you thinking?" I had asked.

"I'm reminiscing the past, the future seems rather uncertain and on hold," she said. "I had always wondered about Jacques home in Montauk. He had described it years ago in some detail, perhaps to impress me when I was in the relationship. Now that I'm here, I feel rather strange."

"All of this is temporary Fleur. Believe me, trust me," I said.

"I'm sorry Jeff. The desire for food, for sex is dead buried in an embalmed sarcophagus."

"I fully understand. There is no question it is the result of COVID that has seeped away all desire for life and living. But you will recover, darling."

I wondered if staying in Jacques beach house now, and the memory of their unpalatable distant affair, made her uncomfortable and anxious—a stranger intruding in someone else's domain. I kept on reassuring her that soon she would be back to normal. It was amply clear that besides the COVID, she was depressed. Perhaps the Abilify will help. I promised to take her on a holiday to the French Riviera when the pandemic is over. She listened and shook her head, but I saw that she was not registering.

There was chateaubriand for dinner, another of her favorites with braised broccoli spears. She finally agreed to come down to the dining room. I helped her slowly rise from the bed and gingerly walked with her with my arms around her waist. She ate a few morsels of the chateaubriand. And then suddenly she bursts into tears.

"I cannot taste anything," she said. "I may as well die." She got off the chair and swayed.

I hugged her and held her in my arms. I could see that both Alex and Jacques were upset at the situation, and by the look on Jacques face, his frustration was evident. He simply could not sustain or immerse in such depressive drama. While Alex and I took Fleur to her room, Jacques excused himself to take Belinda to friends for a sleep over and to go to the pharmacy to pick up the prescription for Fleur.

After taking a valium tablet, Fleur calmed down and encouraged me to partake in the company of Alex and Lady K, Alex's friend from Syosset, Long Island who had dropped by for coffee and cake just as we were finishing dinner. She was a fun-loving woman, a party buff who hopped, stepped and jumped three to four parties on a single Sunday evening, now COVID-related home quarantined, she was out for a short spin. Besides, there were no parties any longer, and no one knew when life would blossom again. She joined us at the poolside in shorts and a tank-top, and a rainbow-colored mask, keeping her distance of six-feet. We talked about the pandemic and who had it and who died and who was hanging by a tread. She related that a friend of hers, a famous Indian chef, Floyd Cardoso died in the hospital in a matter of days.

"I'm so sorry to hear that he passed away," I said. I had eaten at his fusion restaurant *Tabla*. The food was delicious, the flavors of the Indian spices were intoxicating."

As the day turned to dusk, a full crimson moon appeared on the horizon, reflecting salmon shades on the ocean waves and the waters of the swimming pool. And Lady K hoped and stepped on the throttle of her BMW bound home.

"Wow! That was zero to sixty mph for Ms. Speed," I remarked to Alex.

It was more than three hours since Jacques left, and we both wondered what was taking him so long. "Why don't you call him?" I said.

"It's no use. I'm sure he is having an affair," she said.

"Here in Montauk? But he hasn't been here for nearly a month."

"I cannot take it any longer, Jeff," she said and began crying. "Jacques' machismo is overbearing. He cannot eat of the same menu; variety is his spice of life."

I hugged her and wiped her hot tears. We remained hugging each other for some time.

"It's over between us. I have contacted my lawyer," she said. "It is you I should have married. I was expecting you to ask me out, but you never did."

"I was going to…the next time you'd come to my office, but Jacques beat me to it."

She poured herself a glass of Chardonnay, drank the whole glass, and poured herself and me another. She drank that rapidly too and took her leave. I felt sorry for her, and angry with Jacques. After all, wealth and fame never translated into happiness. I too was unfaithful to Fleur, but that was an entirely unexpected COVID related one-night stand.

As I sat by the poolside, I remembered one of the pool parties I had attended in this house a few months before Jacques met and married Alex. There were young nurses, pharmaceutical and device reps, nursing students, and models who late at night had taken it all and jumped in the pool, some drunk, others high on weed and cocaine. I was also drunk and slept at Jacques house that night in the company of a nurse, whose name I did not remember and who wasn't around after I woke up at eleven a.m.

The morning after the party, Jacques kept talking about a pilot's license. "Wouldn't it be great if I had my own helicopter, and I could fly from the city to the Hamptons?" Jacques said.

"Yes, that would be swell," I said. "You could commute on a daily basis and land on the hospital's helipad… But have you forgotten the fate of the famous cardiac interventionalist, a pioneer of coronary angioplasty, the German born Andreas Grüntzig who joined the faculty of Emory University in metropolitan Atlanta?"

"Of course, I do. He was and still is my alter-ego. He was made a full professor and director of interventional cardiovascular medicine in the late 1980s, and, classified as a "national treasure," he received automatic U.S. citizenship as he stepped on American soil."

"Wow! I heard he was strikingly handsome, passionate, vibrant, super smart, and technically a dynamo."

"Oh yes, he was described by one of his nurses as an alchemist's version of Clark Gable, Errol Flynn, and Omar Sheriff and some women just threw their clothes off at the sight of him. Not long after, his dedicated German wife of many years was replaced by a young dashing Southern belle—a medical student whom he later married."

"What a fast-paced career climb."

"Deservedly. He was a true pioneer. He developed coronary angioplasty single handedly against all odds. Such men don't come along nowadays. He bought a mansion where he threw lavish parties, a Porsche that he often drove recklessly at high speed, an aircraft Beechcraft Baron that he piloted, and a weekend cottage on St. Simons Island off the Georgia coast."

"He had stepped into the high-flying American Super-Dream of fame and loads of money," I said.

"Not long thereafter, he took off from St. Simons Island with his wife and dogs to attend to a doctor whose coronary artery was re-occluding. His Beechcraft Baron disappeared from the radar caught in hurricane Juan as it approached Atlanta, and that was the end of Dr. Andreas Grüntzig and his Southern belle," said Jacques.

"On second thought, I'm concerned that you might have the same fate. Sometimes you remind me of Andreas. And like him you are handsome, smart, and a dashing Lothario—perhaps not as much as Andreas, but close."

"You flatter me, friend. But I agree with you. On second thought, forget about the helicopter."

"I wouldn't like you to have the same destiny as Andreas."

As I stood up looking at the encroaching night, Jacques appeared.

"Hey buddy, everything under control?" he asked. Before I had a chance to speak, he took me by the arm for a walk and once we were at some distance from the house on the sandy beach, he confessed that he had a rendezvous with Carol Johnson at Burney's. She was on Long Island to meet with some Republican Election Committee members for strategy planning.

"Did you know she would be here? I asked.

"Yes, I did."

"And you planned it all. And Fleur and I were the cover, the distraction?"

"I wouldn't put it that way, my friend," he said. He seemed a tad offended.

Sex to him was an exotic menu like in a fusion restaurant. It was like a kind of medication, an upper for the moment. He believed in a fast-paced life: "live fast and die young with a good-looking corpse," he had once said to me. He had told me that he felt intense pressure stenting the coronary arteries of New York millionaires, the high society clientele, and out-of-state celebrities. They all came to see him and raised the ante: "'Doc, you have been highly recommended. There is only one Jacques Charpentier in the country,' I was told. After the successful an even not-so-successful difficult intervention that nobody else would attempt, he felt an "endorphin high," that demanded an outlet that only sex would provide.

"I plan to enter politics: the Governorship of New York, and I need Carol's and Tom Branigan's help," Jacques said. It was news to me.

"New York is a democratic state. Their support will get you nowhere," I said. "Perhaps you should try for Mayorship of New York City first."

He did not respond. I was surprised and somewhat bewildered, but he was my friend and had come to my aid several times when I needed him most.

"Jacques, you have gone too far," I added. "Alex suspects that you are having an affair. Your marriage is on the brink of a breakup." He did not respond. I wanted to express my anger at his uncanny behavior but held my tongue. Anyway, I had said it all. I knew that Jacques would never change his ways. Besides, I was taken aback with the news that he planned entering politics needing Carol's and Tom's help.

As we went back to the house and sat by the swimming pool, Jacques went inside and returned with a bottle. "I have something very special for you my friend," he said. The holy grail of bourbons—A twenty-five-year-old Pappy Van Winkle!"

"I have heard of it, but never tasted it," I said. "Where did you get it?"

"A gift from a patient."

"Another doctor friend, a Dr. Ribeiro, who has a large clientele of Portuguese immigrants gives me vintage Port, Fleur's favorite after-dinner drink," I said, as I wondered whether the bourbon was a sort of a bribe to keep the rendezvous from spilling over. As I took a large sip of the amber colored liquid cased in full-bodied oak, the rich taste exploded into decadence, with intense flavors of caramel and peppery brown spice.

"Wow. This is something."

"You may take the bottle with you. I have two more in

the city."

"Thanks, buddy," I said.

"What about this pandemic? When will it end?" he asked.

"It will end, but I don't know when," I said. Moreover, viruses mutate, and this one is mutating fast. It may get worse before it gets better. Who knows what the next mutation will bring?"

CHAPTER 18

IT'S AN UPSIDE-DOWN-SIDEWAYS WORLD

Two days later, on Monday evening, we left Montauk for New York City. I had already hired Nadya, a rehab nurse to attend to Fleur. After giving her detailed instructions I was rather contented to go back to work, where I was much needed. Hardly did I step in the COVID-ICU, my phone rang. It was Antonina on the line informing me that her mother passed away that very morning. She was distraught and utterly shaken at not being able to see her and say her goodbye. She already had a breathing tube and was deeply sedated when she arrived in Rome and was not allowed to see her in the hospital. Her mother in a coma, she could only see her on FaceTime from a nurse's phone, but half-a-dozen intravenous tubes blocked the view until the nurse repositioned the camera and brought it closer to see her tubed mouth, her face swollen beyond recognition, her eyes taped shut. She would die all alone like so many others.

"What image of my mother should I hold in my heart?" Antonina asked.

"The last image of her…on FaceTime will linger… for a long, long time," I said, choking on the words. But ultimately, over time…you will remember all those wonderful years you had with her. I didn't know your mother…I'm sure she was a valiant woman." I remembered

Martha lying dead on the street and the paramedics pumping her chest—this image I had held in my mind and in my heart for a long, long time.

"Her body now languishes in a freezer," said Antonina. "I don't know when I will be able to give her a decent burial." There was a long silence between us broken by her gush of tears. She cried relentlessly and I found myself at a loss unable to console her to say something uplifting. But what was there to say after all? Death has a shape, a weight, an ice-cold temperature, an abstract texture, and a very bad depressive taste. The corpse is like a suit, or a dress that is left behind to be buried or cremated; and yet, as Joan Didion said, a single person is missing for you, and the whole world is empty.

When the crying spell subsided, I assured her that I would talk to my boss, the head of infectious diseases and promised to give it all in my power to keep her position open for next year. It was obvious that there was no way for Antonina to continue her training in New York for now.

"Take care of your daughter and your father," I said. "And please call me at any time of the day or night, even if it's just to talk."

There was a long silence and then I heard a child's voice in the background: "*Mamma, mamma, ho fame.*"

"I have to go and feed my daughter," she said.

After I hung up the phone, I went to the recharge room and sat there ruminating on death, which had become so routine in this pandemic. The idea of death, the death of a loved one, however impossible to process, that one's time on earth, one's life, can be a short fleeting moment in this world in decay, in constant change—and the sudden shortness of human life, was impossible to comprehend. It left the mind in a state of incongruous juxtaposition of images of life and death side by side, or one on top of the other like walking over a grave six feet under.

After talking with Antonina, I found myself apprehensive overtaken by anxiety and unease, a dread for my own life, that of Fleur, and the nurses and residents working with me. I had to be careful now, see that I had the right PPE at all times. I had to enforce it on my staff so that they don't get complacent. I called a short meeting of the staff in the recharge room and preached from the pulpit so to speak, regarding the importance of the PPEs, and how to use and discard them.

I then called Nadya who assured me that Fleur was coming along, that she ate buttered toast for breakfast, and that she managed to take her for a short walk. I felt momentarily appeased with Fleur's progress, but the image of Antonina, our unexpected love making in the midst of chaos, destruction and death, and now the tragic demise of her mother, was profoundly unsettling.

Medicine offered me a wonderful opportunity to interact with people when they were sick, in pain, when sad and happy, when they returned to health from illness, and when they were close to dying. But this was entirely different and often hopeless. What hope could I provide to the patient on a respirator suffering from a disease we knew little or nothing about and had no cure for? And what about the imminent or remote appearance of yet another mutation that might affect other organs? How will we deal with these unknowns? The unborn future remained uncertain. Life remained unpredictable. And yet, I felt that I could not give into such depressive thoughts. I had to rise above myself. Doctoring did not afford such privileges under the circumstances. I had to compartmentalize my feelings, bottle up my emotions, and simply keep going. I moved on and rounded on the patients in the ICU with the residents and nursing staff giving orders and talking on the phone with relatives—a most disheartening task under the current circumstances. "At this moment your husband is stable. We are doing our best," is all I could say. At other times, "I'm terribly sorry, your father passed away."

That very afternoon, I received a call from Allain, Fleur's father saying that he had a fever, a relentless coughing spell, and shortness of breath. I asked him to come to the ER right away fearful that he might have acquired COVID-19. I prayed and hoped that it was just the flu. But he turned out to be COVID positive, and the chest X-ray showed pneumonia. He looked sick, but his oxygenation was acceptable, however as the evening progressed it kept on dropping. There were no beds in the ICU, and he lingered in the ER. By eight o'clock another patient died, and Allain got a bed. At twelve o'clock I received a call from the resident doctor. "Dr. Anderson, your father-in-law is gasping for breath. We are going to tube him and hook him to a respirator."

"Sure, please go ahead," I said.

"The anesthesiologist is here. I told him that he is your father-in-law."

I didn't question the on-call resident's decision. I understood that the prognosis was guarded. I had to tell Fleur and wondered how she would take it.

While Fleur slept, I called Allain's wife Victoria who had arrived from Russia about a week back and related to her the situation with Allain. I told her that I had already written a prescription to get her tested for COVID as soon as possible and that I would FaceTime her as soon as I got to work. However, I informed her that it was likely that she wouldn't be able to talk or see him in person. The doctors were doing their best and giving him medications to fight the disease.

"Will he make it?" she asked, in her sleepy voice.

"It's too early to tell. His condition is serious and guarded," I said.

"What will I do if he doesn't make it?"

"Don't worry, we are here for you." And then I went into details of Fleur's COVID-19, and that I was unsure how she would react to her father's illness. She did not respond.

The next morning before I went to work, I told Fleur about her father. I expected her to throw a fit, to cry, to sob hysterically like so many past dramas in response to minor and banal situations. And this one was real—almost tragic—deserving intense emotion. I also expected her to blame Victoria for her father's illness—that she probably gave it to him after returning from Russia. She had even mentioned that she thought Victoria had a boyfriend in Russia, and that was the very reason she went to Moscow on frequent visits. I was flabbergasted when Fleur took his illness rather calmly, asking me questions about his prognosis.

"I saw him in a dream," she said, with a distant faraway look. "He was pale and ashen; he was trying to say something to me, that I couldn't hear or remember. Is it a premonition of death?"

"Well, let's hope for the best," I said, but in my own mind I wondered whether it was indeed a foreboding. It was as if her mind had already accepted the inevitable, and yet the flat unemotional response was so unusual for her. Could it be the COVID affecting her mind? After all it had affected her taste and olfactory nerves.

"I will call you as soon as I see him," I said. "I will pray that he makes it." I left for the hospital and on my way I prayed. I hadn't prayed for some time. I remembered the words of Alfred Lord Tennyson: *More things are wrought by prayer than this world dreams of.*

As soon as I entered the ICU—gowned with an N95

mask and face shield, I rushed to Allain's bedside. Allain was heavily sedated. The respirator was breathing for him eighteen hisses a minute. The monitor showed that he was in normal rhythm and his ECG was abnormal showing a heart rate of 100 beats/minute, and an old heart attack. He was given dexamethasone, and the convalescent plasma was already in. He was also receiving the experimental drug Remdesivir, an anticoagulant, and an antibiotic.

At about eleven o'clock I FaceTimed Victoria and related what was going on. She wore a pink silk blouse, black pants, and stiletto heels. Her outfit brought out her cold self-involved sophistry considering the time of day and the current situation. Her make-up was perfectly applied, with pink lipstick and pink blush on her tight and flawless skin and her straight wheat-colored hair cascaded over her shoulders.

Why was she dressed up? Where was she going? I faced the phone to show Allain. With all the machinery around, I could barely show the silhouette of the bedridden moribund man.

She was suddenly livid seeing him this way. And then I saw her five-foot, seven-inch frame on FaceTime bend down to her knees and in folded hands she uttered indecipherable incantations in Russian with her eyes closed. I gathered she was praying. She stood up and howled, pulling on her hair, and tears rolled down her face together with the mascara. I was much moved at her reaction and felt utterly sorry for her.

"I am pregnant," she said. "I was going to tell him

today. Oh God, oh God, what will I do?”

I was dumbfounded. Her mastery at shifting the conversation on herself, in portraying the victim was unsettling—the forever Communist victim! Pregnant? At her age? She was almost forty-five and she was away for more than a month in Moscow. Was this Allain's child? Could Fleur be right that she has a boyfriend?

“Calm down Victoria,” I said. “Allain is alive and may come out of this.” I now realized that she was dressed up to come to visit Allain in the hospital, but I had already told her last night that she wouldn't be allowed even to enter the hospital, moreover the ICU. Perhaps she planned visiting friends? She was sleeping when I called her; perhaps she did not fully understand what I was saying.

“Please go and get yourself tested,” I said, after she calmed down.

“I was already tested in Russia. I tested negative.”

“Did you get tested after you returned?”

“No, why should I?”

“You traveled. You were on the plane from Moscow with a stopover in Istanbul, where you had to change planes to New York.”

At that moment, the nurse came and told me that there was a new admission in Bed #10, and that the resident doctor was anxious to present her case. I told Victoria that I was wanted and would call her later in the day to report on Allain's progress.

As I entered Room #10, vacated in the early morning hours after its inhabitant an eighty-year-old man, had died, I saw a young woman in her thirties lying comfortably in bed.

"I'll be with you shortly," I said, and left the room. I stayed just outside the room and asked the resident doctor to present her case. In attendance was also Umesh, my fellow Andy Sommer and nurse Sharon who was back on duty after a fourteen-day quarantine.

"Ms. Olivia Smith is a thirty-five-year-old night club performer and singer with nothing much to do, no performing since the pandemic hit New York City, and decided to try internet dating," said the resident. "It's been several weeks she was holed in her apartment phoning and texting with no physical contact with friends. There was a short-lived texting relationship that ended when the man on the other end told her he was getting back with his wife. Then, she had an outdoor date in Central Park, with a guy who made fun of her for asking him to keep his mask on. He wanted to kiss her, but she refused. And that was the end of that. And then she connected with a fellow performer she had met before and with whom she felt more relaxed, and they got intimate. Four days later, she developed slight fever, fatigue, and loss of sense of smell in the beginning and in a day or two she lost sense of taste. She came to the ER, tested positive and despite a good oxygen level, landed in the ICU."

"She seems very comfortable to me," I said. "Why the

ICU? What did the chest x-ray show?"

"The x-ray is normal. No pneumonia."

"By the way John, I liked your detailed personal history on Ms. Smith," I said.

"What is she doing in the ICU?" said Umesh.

"She knows Dr. Vanderbilt in the ER, a family friend. He called the resident on night service and requested a bed at about three in the morning. Since the man occupying the bed had just died, the resident gave her the bed."

I examined her and after looking at her x-ray, decided that she did not belong in the ICU. As a matter of fact, she shouldn't have been admitted to the hospital in the first place. She was better off at home. We immediately transferred her to the COVID ward, with instructions that she should be discharged home depending on her symptoms and oxygen level. We warned her that it was not worth taking risks. Its best she forgets about dating at least for now and possibly till we have a vaccine.

"Sure Doc," she said. "I had some fun, for a stiff price. I can be alone for however long it takes for the vaccine to come through."

As we left her room, Sharon mentioned that despite the pandemic some young people are meeting up, making out and having sex with new partners. "For these people emotional and physical needs supersede safety concerns," she said. "Worse still, some don't even believe in the pandemic—its fake news."

"Recently, I read that the police broke up an eighty-person party at a sex club in Queens," said Umesh.

"And what about the thousands of ultra-Orthodox Jews gathered to celebrate a wedding in Brooklyn's Williamsburg neighborhood?" said Karen. "They were dancing and singing without wearing masks."

"Apparently the organizers will be fined for violating public health restrictions," said Umesh.

"That's totally irresponsible. They should go to jail," said Karen.

"It's a mad, mad world we're living in," I said. I called Dr. Vanderbilt and reprimanded him for soliciting a bed for Ms. Smith. "We have a shortage of beds to begin with for people who need a ventilator. Please don't do this again whether the patient is a friend or a family member."

"My apologies," said Vanderbilt.

After rounding on the ten patients in the ICU including my father-in-law, talking to patients' relatives on Zoom, attending to three codes, and pronouncing two deaths, I sat in the recharge room with dim candlelight and soft relaxing music and munched on a chicken sandwich with a drink of Kombucha. I could not get the people around me off my mind: the recently dead, Antonina, Allain and now Victoria. At least it seemed Fleur was getting better. Somewhat. I had to call Nadya for a report, but fearful of bad news, I delayed the call. It was just too much to handle. But it was Victoria's pregnancy that baffled me. When I met her for the first time, I was taken by surprise at her youth in the company of my aging father-in-law. No doubt she was a trophy wife, and he was her sugar daddy and a fast-paced path to citizenship. I didn't say much to Fleur knowing well what she thought of her.

"My father has gone through a lot. He needs companionship," she had opined. "He has had girlfriends before, but moving from one place to another, the relationships fell apart. There was a wonderful Venezuelan divorcee. She was in her late fifties and ideal for him. She had money and social status. She died in a car accident. My father was distraught. One death of a loved one is more than enough in one lifetime, but two? He is afraid of loneliness. He wanted me near him and that's why he bought this apartment for me. That was before Victoria, however."

I had wondered about Allain's and Victoria's relationship: she was young, and he, an aging man with heart disease. I knew that Allain had problems with erection. I had written prescriptions for Viagra and Cialis, but it seemed that both were ineffective. I had suggested a penile prosthesis after speaking to a urologist at the medical center, but Allain did not follow through.

I now wondered how Fleur would react to Victoria's pregnancy. I decided to keep the information from her at least for the time being.

As I was about to finish the sign-outs for the evening cum night shift, my phone rang. It was the resident on the line: "Dr. Anderson, this is Dr. Sharma, the Chief Resident covering the COVID floor."

"Yes. How is Ms. Smith doing? Are you planning to discharge her tomorrow?"

"Well, it so happened that Ms. Smith saw her boyfriend Domingo Mendoza on the ward. She became totally irrational and berserk and started punching him, accusing him of giving her the virus. We had to call security. She signed out against medical advice."

"Thanks for letting me know. It's an upside-down-sideway world we're living in."

With so much ongoing commotion I had forgotten to call Nadya to find out about Fleur. But no news seemed good news. I saw Allain before leaving for home and I was somewhat encouraged by the numbers. He looked stable and his oxygenation on the respirator was good. Perhaps if things look good over the next several days and there is improvement on the x-ray, we should consider removing the tube. By now a consensus was developing that early intubation was not as judicious as originally thought.

I called Victoria on my way home to report on Allain, but she did not pick up the phone. I left a voicemail informing her that Allain was stable.

CHAPTER 19

FLEUR'S SLOW RECOVERY

Nearly two weeks had passed since Nadya had been attending to Fleur's rehabilitation exercises, and I was pleased with her progress. As I left for home after work, I stopped to buy a bouquet of red roses in the only open flower shop on Madison Avenue. I entered the apartment with trepidation but was surprised to see Fleur all dressed up in a Mosaic Cinched Caftan, a gift from Alex during her stay in Montauk. She was overjoyed with the flower bouquet. But even more impressive was the fact that she together with nurse Nadya managed to prepare a French dinner consisting of *Brie en Croute* as appetizer and *Beef Bourguignon* as the main course. It was apparent that it was mostly prepared by Nadya with Fleur's instructions from her grandmother's recipe book.

I was afraid to ask her if her taste and smell had returned, when she herself told me that she could now smell and taste, not entirely, not as before, but on a scale of one-to-ten, it was more like four or five. At least the putrid smell and the weird taste of the expresso and wine were gone. Also, her heart wasn't racing as before when she went for a walk in Riverside Park. Her IWatch showed a heart rate of around ninety beats per minute rather than the usual one hundred to one hundred and twenty beats per minute. I opened a bottle of Le Grande Rue for the occasion. I had read that the wine's aromatic profile included fruit aromas of red and dark berries, violets, and spices, while the nuances of truffle, hummus, and undergrowth usually appeared with age. Undoubtedly, my interest in French wines and high-end culture including classical music, ballets, and operas was Fleur's influence over and above my Midwestern American culture.

I told Fleur that her father was stable and perhaps out of danger. "The next several days are crucial. He is coming off the respirator tomorrow. If he can breathe on his own, we will remove the tube. Otherwise, he will need a tracheostomy."

"What is that?"

"It is a hole that surgeons make through the front of the neck and into the windpipe. A tube is then placed into the hole to keep it open for breathing."

She gave a guarded smile, and underneath it all I sensed the anxiety; that she was afraid to probe me further about her father.

We asked Nadya to stay for dinner. We were in a restrained silence initially, when Nadya opened up about their day, about their walk in Riverside Park.

"There were a few people jogging," said Nadya.

"It almost felt like the good old days," said Fleur.

"Apparently, some of the people who left the building are returning," I said.

"I hope that this pandemic will end soon," said Nadya.

"I doubt," I said. We just had a mutation—the Delta variant. I'm sure there will be more mutations on the way."

"Yet another mutation," said Nadya.

"Yes," I said. "And the forthcoming one might be even worse. The COVID virus is mutating fast."

I could notice that Fleur's appetite for food and her love of wine had returned. Somewhat. Like dark berries and ripe bananas. Like smoke, salt, and pepper. She ate a few morsels of the *Beef Bourguignon* and drank half-a-glass of wine. And that was encouraging—the process of learning or relearning. Like a baby's first smile, first step, the first word. But what surprised me the most was her calm voice and a demeaner of peace and even an innate sort of a hidden joy as if she were a new person. Had the virus changed her personality? She seemed neither high nor low, but on an even keel, calm like the pristine waters of Lake Erie. Did the virus penetrate her emotional brain? For now, at least the borderline personality trait seemed to have vanished. Only time would tell. But wait a moment could it be the medication—the Abilify that she was taking?

After Nadya left, we made love after more than a month, and even her love making was different, less aggressive, more peaceful, a Zen sort of lovemaking. In the past she took pleasure in pain, made me bite her nipples, so much so that sometimes I was afraid that my teeth would sever one or the other. Yes indeed, a lot had changed.

It's an upside-down-sideway world we were living in.

We lay in each other's arms peacefully, and I wondered whether it was time for us to have children. But what about her fear of amniocentesis? I did not want to broach the issue with her now. It was best to wait until after the pandemic was over and life was back to normal. But what if anther variant appeared on the scene and we were back to square one? Instead of dealing with these abstract thoughts, I felt confident to talk about Victoria and the pregnancy.

"Well, it confirms what I said before, that she has a boyfriend in Russia," she said. My father cannot have children. That's the very reason they adopted me. He doesn't like to talk about it. Perhaps he never discussed the issue with Victoria."

"Or maybe she is not pregnant after all. Maybe she is approaching menopause and has what we call in medical jargon, 'pseudocyesis,'—fake pregnancy!"

"Well, it's possible. Victoria is a drama-queen!"

"It is a mad, mad world we are living in."

"Sweet dreams honey," she said, and we dropped off to sleep in separate rooms.

CHAPTER 20

LIFE LOST, LIFE REGAINED, LOST AGAIN

Some weeks later when I entered the ICU in the morning, I was met with alarming news. Dr. Miles Reinhart the Associate Director of the Emergency Room and his wife Linda were admitted overnight to the ICU. What was of concern was that Linda was pregnant with their first child. It was obvious that Miles was infected in the ER and passed the virus on to his wife. He should have moved out of the apartment or sent his wife to live with her parents in Westchester, like so many doctors in the city had done. However, since she was pregnant, he wanted to be close to her. They had met in Binghamton College in Upstate NY. They began dating during their senior year in college and as soon as Miles graduated from med school, they got married. Linda got her degree in Business Management and worked for a small securities firm in the City, while Miles after receiving his MD, specialized in Critical Care Medicine and worked as a full-time doctor in the ER. This was their first child. It turned out that Linda had a history of asthma and started wheezing and coughing. Inhalers did not work. Three days before she got sick, Miles came down with a slight sore throat. Like most doctors, he insisted on going to work, but ultimately was forced to go home due to a splitting headache. He thought it was a common cold which he often acquired from his patients. He treated Linda at home with nebulizers and steroid inhaler. Over a course of two days both became alarmingly sick, Linda more so, and both came to the ER. They were admitted to the ICU: Miles in Bed #5 and Linda in Bed #6.

Their admission to the ICU had a demoralizing effect on the staff. Miles was a soft spoken, popular physician and both Umesh and I knew him well. Linda was our financial adviser. She was a high-powered, hardworking financial wiz highly knowledgeable in the FANG stocks she had recommended to her clients, which were currently soaring. She was due to assume the position of VP at Goldman Sachs. We had gone out together for dinner several times.

For me it was heartbreaking to see them in the ICU facing death. Even for doctors it is easy to deal with and treat an unknown and unfamiliar face unemotionally, but when it is someone one knows—a friend or family member; someone one cares for—it is a difficult and traumatic proposition consumed with fear of a mistake or many mistakes, particularly when staring at death from an unknown disease such as COVID-19.

Within a couple of days, Linda's condition worsened; she coughed up blood, and her oxygenation was on a free fall. She was rapidly tubed and placed on a respirator. Her lungs showed infiltrates, but neither I nor Umesh nor the pulmonary consultant were sure whether the infiltrates represented pneumonia or blood clots. She went into shock and was emergently submitted to a pulmonary angiogram to visualize the lung arteries. They showed blood clots. She was treated with a powerful intravenous clot dissolving agent: Plasminogen activator (tPA). She bled from the uterus and lost the baby.

Miles on the other hand had a pneumonia restricted to a small segment of one lung and his oxygenation was hovering in the nineties. We administered oxygen with a high flow oxygen mask rather than resorting to a breathing tube. I felt he was improving on dexamethasone, and other drugs but Miles was beside himself. He was guilt ridden and felt responsible for Linda's illness, well aware that she might not make it once she was placed on the respirator.

The next morning, I had to give him the bad news. "Miles, there was a complication," I said. "Linda had a massive pulmonary embolus. We had to give her tPA. She bled from the uterus and lost the baby."

Miles didn't say a word as if what he just heard did not register or he was not listening thinking of something else or nothing at all. Then all of a sudden, he exploded. "I killed her, Jeff! I killed our baby."

"No Miles, you had nothing to do with it."

"That baby was precious. Conceived in a test-tube through sheer luck. And I killed her. There will be no other baby."

"But you have each other."

"She will not forgive me, Jeff. I might as well die."

Miles became totally irrational. He pulled out the IV and the nasal oxygen cannula. I called for help and Miles had to be restrained and sedated. As soon as he woke up after several hours, I called a psychiatrist to see him immediately.

"I can only do a phone visit at this moment," said Dr. Abrams, the psychiatrist. After speaking with Miles, he ordered an anxiolytic. Gradually, Miles calmed down or so it seemed. He wanted to see Linda.

"It's best you don't at this moment," I said.

"Is she alive?"

"Yes, she is alive," I said. "She is undergoing extracorporeal membrane oxygenation (ECMO) at this time."

"Is it that bad?"

"Yes…but there is always hope."

"The baby, the baby, our precious baby," he said, staring at the wall. "We tried having a baby for a long time. She badly wanted a child. She was obsessed about it. I have a low semen count. I blamed myself for the infertility. I lived with depression for a long time. It was all my fault that Linda couldn't get pregnant. We even considered divorce last year and sought marriage counselling." He talked rapidly and then suddenly he stopped as if he had lost the train-of-thought.

"Go on," I said. "I am listening."

"After myriad of tests on Linda, and varicocele ligation in me, and many tries at artificial insemination, we went for in-vitro fertilization. It was an ordeal with bouts of depression and anxiety. The first three attempts did not work. It finally happened. The fourth fertilized ovum seeded her uterus. It was a miracle. We were elated. She was sixteen weeks pregnant. The baby was a girl. She wanted a girl to dote upon. I should have been careful. I should have stayed in a hotel or asked her to go to her parents in Westchester. She was too busy and hyped preparing for her new job." It was rather strange; he wasn't addressing me. He was talking to the wall. And then he started sobbing.

"Don't blame yourself," I said. "You can always adopt. My wife Fleur is adopted."

"We went over adoption, but it wasn't for us," he said. "I had no problem with it, but she objected. It was as if she wanted her smart genes to be accounted for posterity."

"If you love each other, you have each other."

Miles started sobbing. I felt like embracing him, but that was not possible under COVID regulations. Besides, I was in full PPE gear. I placed my hand on his shoulder.

Miles just turned around, exhausted, and after a sedative fell asleep.

A few days later, Linda's condition became critical. I called Fleur and told her that I wouldn't be coming home. I planned to spend the night in the recharge room of the ICU should any eventuality arise with Linda.

After several days, Miles medical condition improved: he was breathing normally and his oxygenation was good. He was ready to be discharged from the ICU to the COVID floor.

The story was diametrically opposite for Linda. She developed the *cytokine release syndrome,* when the body's inflammatory agents are released which causes a cytokine storm that is invariably fatal. In addition to the steroids and the extracorporeal membrane oxygenation, Linda received Tocilizumab—a recombinant humanized anti-human IL-6 receptor monoclonal antibody. She developed kidney failure and required dialysis. Her prognosis was hopeless as hopeless can be.

Before discharge from the ICU, Miles was allowed to see Linda from the hallway accompanied by me and Umesh. I was surprised at Miles flat reaction with no emotion whatsoever. Was it the effect of the anxiolytics or his true state of mind?

As soon as Miles arrived on the COVID floor, he signed himself out. The residents all knew Miles and they reasoned that he was stable and might be better off at home rather than in the hospital environment.

"Sure, Dr. Miles, just sign, and home you go," said Dr. Levine, the medical resident doctor, who didn't bother calling me or Umesh, not that it mattered.

Several days passed and I didn't hear from Miles; my mind was too preoccupied with other sick patients. However, I had been in daily contact with Linda's sister Maureen relaying Linda's condition. On the fourth day I received a call from her asking about both Linda and

Miles. I informed her that I hadn't heard from Miles at all. I expected him to call to inquire about Linda. I found it very odd. Linda's sister confirmed that she hadn't heard from Miles either. We both called Miles, and the calls went to voicemail, which was full. Finally, Linda's sister called Miles brother who went to his apartment on 75th and York. Miles was found dead overdosed on sleeping pills.

The overdose death of Miles Reinhart was shocking and demoralizing to the staff in the ER and in the ICU. I was devastated since I was a friend and had cared for him only a few days back. How and why did it have to happen? —was the question in everyone's mind. Was the degree of his depression underestimated by the psychiatrist who at best only had a phone visit but did not see him personally one on one? After all he had a previous history of depression. Should he have been admitted to the psychiatry ward and had the depression treated? And yet, this very question and his overdose suicidal death would undoubtedly fade from memory as death piled up one on top of the other. Like the piles of emaciated corpses in concentration camps.

A memorial was planned in the hospital, but the date was not set.

The morale of the ICU staff hit the dust. Late in the evening just before the change in shift, both Umesh and I called a meeting in the recharge lounge. I explained all that went on with Miles and called for a minute of silence. I talked at length about depression and mentioned that I found myself depressed and highly anxious at times under the current circumstances. I mentioned how depressed I was after the death of my first wife, Martha.

"It is critical that you're see a psychologist, a bereavement expert," I emphasized. "Depression could hit hard at any moment with so much of death and suffering all around. None of us have gone through a pandemic before. All of this is new to us."

Some were crying; others remained silent in contemplation.

"Please use their services freely," I said.

"I am considering group sessions when staffing and time permits so that the staff can vent their feelings," said Umesh.

"That's a great idea," said Karen.

Immediately after, both Umesh and I had a Zoom conference with the CEO of the hospital and the chairman of the department of medicine. The administration promised that in a couple of days there would be a psychologist, or a psychology nurse practitioner assigned for every ICU.

It was almost six weeks since Linda's condition had become critical. However, slowly but surely, her condition was getting better. Her kidney function showed improvement, she maintained a blood pressure on her own and her chest x-ray and oxygenation improved on the treatment. She came off dialysis and the extracorporeal membrane oxygenation. After nearly five weeks in the ICU, it was decided that she should gradually come off the respirator. She tolerated breathing on her own with oxygen, and the tube in her lungs was removed. Gradually, the sedation was discontinued, and she was awake and responsive, but weak and inattentive, fading off intermittently. The recovery was indeed miraculous and obviously related to the new treatment options—in particular the extracorporeal membrane oxygenation, the powerful anticoagulant tPA, and the Tocilizumab.

Both Karen and I approached her to inform her that she lost the baby. We did not know what her reaction would be and were ready with an injection of a sedative if she became agitated. While Karen held her hand, I went over her acute and serious life-threatening illness and the strong medication we had to use to control it. I wasn't sure whether she was registering. Finally, I said: "Linda, I'm so sorry to tell you that you lost the baby. You bled from the uterus." Surprisingly, she showed no emotion. It was as if she was in a fog. What havoc had the virus wrought on her emotional brain?

After six long touchy weeks it was time to discharge her from the ICU to the COVID floor, and subsequently to vigorous rehabilitation. The day before discharge from the ICU, she was told that Miles did not make it. Umesh and I broke the news together. It was decided that Miles overdosed death should be mentioned only at a later date in the presence of her family. Surprisingly, she did not react to Miles passing away either. It was as if her emotional brain—the cortex with names like the *medial insula and anterior cingulate*, and deeper areas such as the *nucleus accumbens* and parts of the *striatum* that give us emotional feelings—was unreactive or somehow blocked. Perhaps it's a survival phenomenon after so much physical and mental torture.

I felt somewhat relieved yet confounded. I requested the psychiatrist see Linda on a daily basis. He, however, agreed only to a phone or video visit.

"Under the circumstances it is not possible nor advisable to see patients on a personal basis," he said. "It will be a phone or video visit."

I fully understood his reluctance. As a matter of fact, most physicians were seeing patients on "phone or video visits"—particularly after the insurance companies approved payment for such encounters.

I was unsure whether there would be a delayed reaction to the deaths of her baby and husband and what the future held. I had a lengthy phone conversation with her family and stressed the fact that she needed in-person psychiatry care, and if that was not possible then by video.

Her sister assured me that she would take her to her house in Westchester for convalescence, and that she with her mother and father and a brother and another sister would ultimately inform her of Miles overdose death, only after the psychiatrist felt she was ready. I gave her the name of a pulmonologist and an infectious diseases expert in Westchester for follow-up.

CHAPTER 21

STREAKS OF SUNSHINE

As I contemplated on the events of the last few weeks, I remembered the words of Jarod Kintz: *Days turn into weeks, which turn into months, which turn into years, which turn into decades, which turn into cemeteries...* This dictum unfortunately did not hold in this pandemic. Many lives had been shortened into hours, days, and weeks, fallen heroes in a gutless-gunless battle; and in this battle, the old, the poor, the underprivileged, had been in the forefront, foot soldiers mercilessly felled by the virus. The mortuaries and funeral homes were full; the dead discharged to freezer trucks.

In early April of 2020, more than 800 Coronavirus deaths were reported in a single day in New York City; consequently, long term storage was created to ensure that families could lay their loved ones to rest as they saw fit. But this onslaught of death was easing as better treatment appeared on the horizon. What was perplexing was that the virus was affecting people in different ways, stark differences between men and women, old and young, white and non-white, obese and slim, asthmatics and non-asthmatics, and many other factors that remained unknown. And yet, slowly but surely, the ICUs were emptying out; the shortage of beds in New York City and the respirator shortage were easing; rumors abounded fueled by the government that a vaccine was on its way. But viruses are known to mutate often at a rapid rate, and so we didn't know whether a new mutation would be making its appearance any time soon. Was this the calm before the storm?

Allain's condition waxed and waned. He developed an arrhythmia: atrial fibrillation that threw him in heart failure and impacted his oxygenation. He required electrical shocks to get him out of the abnormal heart rhythm. After nearly four weeks on the respirator, his pneumonia was clearing, he was breathing better, and the breathing tube was finally removed. On the morning of the fifth week in the hospital, he was discharged from the ICU to the general medical ward to convalesce.

On the day of his discharge, after nearly six weeks of hospitalization, Victoria was nowhere to be found. I had called her several times at least once a week to report on Allain's condition. She had called me too, but it was nearly a week that I hadn't heard from her. Both I and Fleur left several messages two days before his discharge, and on the day of discharge so that we could coordinate a small homecoming reunion and celebration. But Victoria did not answer her calls and the voicemail was full.

Fleur went to pick up her father and recruited Nadya to care for him, since she had improved significantly from the virus and could function on her own. She no longer felt dizzy, and her heart rate did not zoom as before on standing or walking. She managed to take walks in Central Park and Riverside Park on her own, albeit at a slow pace. The sense of smell and taste had returned but not entirely. Coffee sometimes tasted like tea and red wine had a muddy taste, while white wine tasted like Sprite. Red meat tasted like chicken, while fish had a nasty odor and was tasteless. I reassured her that she was on her way towards recovery, but possibly nothing would smell and taste like before for some time. She now mostly ate salads, cooked vegetables, and fruits.

"Any positive news regarding this damn virus?" Fleur asked as I entered Allain' apartment.

"A vaccine has been approved based on mRNA technology. I'm scheduled to receive the vaccine next week."

"That's some good news but not for those in the hospital with COVID. What about me? When will I get the vaccine?"

"It will be administered first to health care workers and then to nursing home residents," I said. "But who knows—this virus is known to mutate rapidly. We might have a new mutation on the horizon, and if so, the vaccine might not work."

"Don't say…"

I joined in the evening for Allain's welcoming celebration. We opened a bottle of champagne, and toasted Allain for a renewal, a new life. He was one of the lucky ones to be alive, but I did not know what the future held for him. He was weak and fatigued and could barely walk on his own to the bedroom. Overtime he was expected to regain his strength.

There was a note from Victoria on the dining room table that Fleur at the suggestion of her father read aloud:

My dear Allain,

These last few weeks have been very difficult for me living alone here with nobody to talk to and you in a bad shape in the hospital. I simply couldn't bear to look at you on FaceTime. Jeff was kind and encouraging about your progress and prognosis. I love you and thank you for all you have done for me from the bottom of my heart. But as you well know our relationship has not been satisfying for both of us. You will understand this. We come from different cultures and the age difference between us was not helpful. You have your daughter, your son-in-law, your ample friends, and money. But I had no one these last few weeks. I hope you will understand. I am now living with some friends in Brooklyn and hope to go to Russia soon. My lawyer will be in contact with you. I have emptied our joint brokerage account. I hope you don't mind. I need the money for support. You are a kind and generous person and I hope you will understand and don't think bad of me. I don't want to hurt you any further and be a hindrance to your recovery. As you know, I am too emotional and it would be difficult for me to say goodbye in person and so, I decided to write this letter.

Yours, Victoria

There was pin-drop silence in the room after Fleur's reading of the letter. She was right all along, I thought. We had both agreed that we wouldn't mention the pregnancy issue to Allain at least not now.

"Dad, how much money did she take?" Fleur asked.

"I don't know, perhaps half-a-million, perhaps less since the market had tanked, but it doesn't matter. I had a pre-nuptial agreement, and the divorce proceedings will go accordingly."

"I don't think she wrote that letter. Someone wrote it for her," I said.

"Don't worry Dad, I'm here for you," said Fleur. The fridge is stocked up, and Nadya will be here tomorrow at eight in the morning. Anyway, I am going to spend the next few nights here with you."

"Thanks, *mon amour*," said Allain.

"Dad, Victoria told Jeff that she is pregnant with child."

"Fleur..." I said, placing my index finger over my mouth. She was not supposed to raise the pregnancy issue.

"Sorry. It slipped out... Her child, whosever child might claim your inheritance."

"Pregnant? With my child? I cannot have children."

"I know, but does she know that?"

"No, we never discussed it."

"She did not mention it again," I said. "Perhaps it was a false alarm or pseudocyesis."

"What's that?" said Allain.

"False pregnancy," I said. "In this rare clinical syndrome, a nonpregnant woman believes she is pregnant and exhibits signs and symptoms of pregnancy."

"Or perhaps it's a trick to inherit your money—at least part of it—for the child," said Fleur.

"It's not that simple. She will have to prove its mine with genetic testing. And you know the outcome. Don't fret over it, Fleur."

When I left Allain's apartment on the East Side and crossed Central Park on 79th Street to the West Side, I thought of what just transpired. I was totally surprised at Fleur's reaction, her control of the situation, her calm attitude, the lack of anxiety and accompanying drama. It was more than six weeks now that the highs and lows of her personality had not reappeared despite the stress. The virus one way or the other and perhaps mysteriously altered her mind. Was there after all a silver lining to this cloud?

I thought of Allain and the loss of Victoria. I expected some emotion, even a sense of shock while Fleur was reading the letter. But there was none. Perhaps what Allain had gone through was enough of a shock. And to some extent he was relieved that she left. It is said that when marriages are bad, incongruous, despairing, divorce brings about relief and even a feeling of exhilaration. Things were bad between them, and Allain probably sensed that she has a boyfriend.

When I opened the door to the apartment, I looked at my watch. It was 7:30 p.m. and should be around 12:30 a.m. in Rome. I wondered whether I should call Antonina. Would she be awake? She was a late sleeper. I decided to take a chance. She picked up the phone as soon as it rang. She was wide awake, and by the nature of the conversation I gathered she was a tad drunk. She began talking about our lovemaking. I sensed she was touching herself. I could hear her breathing hard. And then she began sobbing. "I want to die," she said and kept on repeating it. I let her vent her emotions. During these emotional outbursts it was best to listen. The poor woman had gone through a lot. She lost her mother and her fellowship training program, and now she has to take care of her demented father and her daughter. After the crying, Antonina calmed down, and thanked me for the call, wishing me good night. "I love you," she said.

"I love you too," I said, after a while and hung up.

I ate the leftovers: a *Cassoulet* of white beans with meat that Fleur had ordered from her favorite French takeout. I was famished and devoured the appetizing dish with the remains of last night's Pinot Noir.

As I retired to bed, I prayed for Fleur, my mother, for Allain, for my dead father, for Antonina, for Victoria and for all the living and the dead and for the living that will die a lonely death. I remembered the words of Mathew Arnold:

And we are here as on a darkling plain

Swept with confused alarms of struggle and flight…

Recently, I feared sleep that was often punctured by nightmares: the distorted faces of my patients huffing and puffing, their bloated warped profiles on respirators, and when it was all over, the dead ashen bodies bagged and inserted in a freezer. I took a Xanax wishing for a sound dreamless sleep.

PART 5

There are no mysteries, no fairy tales, no fables; the giants have been banished, the dragons have been bled, science has found a way to eradicate them, reason has found a way to stifle imagination. There is only one place where the dragons run free—the human brain is the only uncharted land.
—modified from *Vienna Blood* by Frank Tallis

CHAPTER 22

THE AMNESTIC BRAIN FOG

It's been several weeks since Allain's discharge from the hospital. When I visited him, he was coming along slowly gaining muscle tone with the exercises provided by Nadya, and since the pandemic seemed to be somewhat easing, Fleur decided to invite him for dinner to cheer him up. He had just heard from Victoria's lawyer saying that the divorce papers were on their way and that Victoria was claiming half his assets. The lawyer was entirely taken by surprise when Allain mentioned the pre-nuptial agreement and that his lawyer, Mr. David Haines would mail it to him shortly. He expected the divorce proceedings to go according to the pre-nuptial agreement and considering that she had already withdrawn a substantial sum from their joint brokerage account, she would have to forfeit some of the money back to Allain.

When I arrived home after visiting Allain, Fleur raised the dinner issue and mentioned that she would like to invite Jacques and Alex. "They are not together any longer, and as far as I know they are in the process of getting divorced," I said.

"Well, she came back to the city, day before yesterday," said Fleur. "I gather she was bored of the Hamptons, what with no parties, and no cultural gatherings."

"Sure thing. Let's have the dinner this coming

Saturday."

"It's summer again and the flowers are blooming," said Fleur. "A year of this damn pandemic has gone by. People are feeling some hope."

"Oh yes," I said. "It's worth some cautious optimism—that the pandemic could recede to the background. There is the possibility that new mutations of the COVID-19 virus could bring it back however."

"Anyway, time to celebrate," said Fleur. I was encouraged by her optimism.

The next morning when I went to work, I received a call from Alex. "Jeff, it looks like Jacques has COVID."

"Why? What's wrong?"

"He has lost sense of smell."

"Does he have any fever, cough, shortness of breath?"

"No, but he is somewhat detached. Not his usual self."

"What do you mean?"

"He has this kind of an abstract look as if he is in a fog."

"It's possible he has COVID. Do bring him to be tested. And see that he is in isolation with a mask on. And you and Belinda should be masked and stay away from him."

"Sure. We have been sleeping in separate rooms for some time."

That evening when I went home, I told Fleur to cancel the dinner since Jacques and Alex would not be attending.

"Jacques doesn't feel good. He likely has COVID," I said.

"Don't say…COVID again?"

"You can ask your father for dinner. It will be a good distraction for him."

Two days later, when I checked Jacques' computer chart, I found out that he was positive for COVID-19. Late in the evening I called Alex to inform her, but she already knew. I asked her if he had any new symptoms.

"Only loss of sense of smell and appetite," she said.

"Is he more cheerful—the flamboyant Jacques back on his feet?"

"No, not at all," she says. "He is not himself…very tired. He slept most of yesterday. But his breathing and oxygenation are fine."

"Fatigue is a common manifestation of the disease. Does he have any cough or fever?"

"No…I will recheck his temperature this evening."

Two days later when I was busy rounding on the patients in the ICU, Alex called me rather distraught.

"Jacques is totally incoherent," she said. "He doesn't know what day it is nor where he is. He asked me who I was. He was somewhat quiet and detached yesterday. Belinda and I spent most of the evening at my friend Tatiana's place. When we got home at about nine p.m., he was asleep. So unusual for him."

"Can he walk?"

"Yes. He walked to the bathroom and then it was as if he was in a daze, in a fog. He just stood there with the toothbrush in his hand."

"Wow! You mean to tell me he doesn't recognize you and Belinda?"

"Yes, and he does not know who he is!"

"It's that bad! Bring him to the ER right away."

When Jacques arrived in the ER, I hallooed him: "Hi Jacques? How are you feeling?"

"Okay," he responded, with a confused flat expression.

"Do you know who I am?" He did not respond.

"What's my name?" There was a blank expression on his face. He couldn't utter my name.

"I am Jeff, your friend." He had a befuddled look as if he did not know who I was.

"Where are you now?" I asked.

He hesitated and then in a low voice, almost a whisper, he said: "In the hospital ER, by the looks of it."

I asked him what day it was. Who was the mayor of NYC. Who was the president of the US. He did not respond. It was as if he was in a brain fog. He probably felt that something important seemed to be going on, but he couldn't figure out the story. He had obviously fallen out of himself.

Dr. Jacques Charpentier did not exist!

I immediately called the neurologist, Dr. Morton Bender for a consultation. He did not find any focal motor or sensory abnormalities in Jacques except for confusion—*a brain fog with retrograde amnesia.*

His diagnosis: *Encephalopathy of unknown cause, possibly viral.*

He was retested for COVID-19 and a CAT scan, and an MRI of the brain were ordered, and Jacques was admitted to the neurology floor. The CAT scan of the brain was negative. The MRI showed some cortical abnormalities detected as "hyperintensity" areas. An olfactory (smell test) was conducted, which he failed. The test came back positive for COVID. A spinal tap was performed, and the fluid was sent for examination.

A final diagnosis of COVID-19 encephalopathy was stablished. What was mysterious and of considerable interest was that his lungs were not involved, and his oxygenation was entirely normal. I had not seen such a manifestation of COVID-19 in any other patient I had encountered since the pandemic began.

I called Alex and gave her the bad news. "You and Belinda have to come and get tested for COVID-19," I said. "I already set the appointment. Please check MyChart."

"I am afraid for Belinda and for myself."

"Do you have any symptoms?"

"No, none whatsoever. How will Jacques be treated?" she asked in a rather tremulous voice.

"Will let you know as soon as I hear from Dr. Bender, the neurologist. You can also speak to him. I will text you his number."

"What is the prognosis?"

"I have no idea. But considering that he lost sense of

smell, it may take a couple of weeks. Maybe both will recover at the same time. The good news is that his lungs and other organs are not involved. If I have some new information, I will let you know."

"What does all this mean Jeff?"

"It seems that this is a new mutation and unique manifestation of COVID-19—I had predicted. I have a call to Milan and to Wuhan to find out if they have seen anything like this."

I could hear Alex crying. "I don't know Jeff—what if he never recovers and develops dementia? The worst part is that he does not know who he is! I have read all there is on brain fog, and there is hardly anything! *The fog is like a cage without a key.*"

"Let's be optimistic. Hope we find the key."

I called Antonina to find out if they had seen similar manifestations of COVID in Rome and Milan. Not in Rome she said. She would call her cousin in Milan and let me know. She sounded better than the last time I had talked with her. I was pleased to know that she was back working as a resident doctor at the university hospital in Rome and like everybody else, she was assigned to the COVID ICU. I stressed that she better watch out and never work without the proper PPE. She promised to call me tonight or tomorrow when she gets more information.

CHAPTER 23

THE SAINT DYMPHNA BRAIN FOG CENTER

I was entirely taken by surprise when within a couple of weeks, the neurology ward was flooded with patients with amnestic brain fog so much so that the capacity of the ward was nearly overfilled. According to stablished protocol, even before the avalanche of patients, my boss, Dr. Welsh, the chairman of infectious diseases and I had called the head of the Centers for Disease Prevention, Control, and Treatment (CDPCT) informing in detail the novel manifestation of the new mutant of the COVID-19 virus.

In a matter of a few days, the CDPCT stepped in and commanded two top floors of the hospital, which were cordoned off with guards posted at the entrance. The CDPCT took complete control of the newly stablished center including admissions and testing as well as diagnosis and treatment of the patients. New doctors including two clinician scientists—the head, Dr. Peter Fang Zhao, and his assistant Dr. Cornel Jones, as well as technologists, and research fellows and associates were brought in by the CDPCT. However, Umesh, Bender and I were retained and transferred to the newly formed center, named: *The Saint Dymphna Center for Brain Fog*. The name *Dymphna* was chosen, she being the patron saint of mental illness. An 800 number was provided and advertised on the major TV channels for patients to call directly if they manifested any symptoms suggestive of brain fog in association with amnesia. There was an avalanche of calls, and soon an adjacent ward was getting filled to capacity. Patients with *Acute Amnestic Brain Fog* admitted to other hospitals in the city and neighboring counties were transferred to the center at the request of the CDPCT.

The new center was not yet ready for occupancy, with nearly 100 patients waiting in different parts of the hospital; however, they uniformly manifested amnesia with different degrees of severity: most with symptoms of retrograde amnesia like Jacques, while others with difficulty remembering recent events. However, none of the patients had lung involvement, and all had normal oxygen levels.

The doctors taking care of these patients were given the option of staying in the hospital's resident housing or in hotels. Almost all out-of-state personnel elected to stay in the hospital's housing until they found proper abode. This precaution was taken obviously not to infect family members. We were all required to sign a non-disclosure document and were instructed to strictly abide by HIPAA regulations. All management issues had to be cleared with Drs. Zhao and Jones. I was given the charge of infectious issues and the seasoned neurologist Dr. Bender of neurological issues in the center. However, we were not permitted to make management decisions on our own.

Bender and I approached Dr. Zhao and requested

permission to try intravenous immunoglobulin for the possibility of COVID-19 related autoimmune encephalitis. But Zhao vetoed the idea without giving any specific reason.

"What's your hesitation?" I asked. "Please at least let's try it on Dr. Jacques Charpentier. He is a close friend and an important staff member—a top rated coronary interventionalist. Our institution needs his expertise badly. I can get his wife to consent."

"He is the head of intervention cardiology. Without his leadership, the department will be in disarray," added Umesh.

"I'm sorry, I cannot allow you to proceed," said Zhao. "I am waiting for the results of some tests before proceeding further."

"What tests are you waiting for?" I asked.

"Cerebrospinal fluid analysis for quantitative viral load." said Zhao.

"But that could take some time," I said.

"We have time on our hands," he responded.

"What about tracing the contacts?" I asked.

"That's impossible under the circumstances," said Zhao.

"I agree," said Bender. "Memory shot. They don't even remember their contacts. And most don't even recognize their wives and children. Moreover, in the US, nobody has the contact tracing App, unlike in China, South Korea, and Taiwan."

"Has the genome of the virus been identified, and if so,

is it the same as that of COVID-19?" I asked.

"We are looking at it," said Zhao, and abruptly took off.

"One more question Dr. Zhao," I said quickly. "What's your opinion? Do you think we are dealing with a new mutation or a doctored virus?"

"I am in no condition to speculate," said Zhao.

We were instructed not to discuss any treatment options with the patients' relatives. We were directed to say that, "he or she is okay; so far so good, no change in status, and all other organs are fine." The staff members including the doctors, nurses, the research fellows, the technicians, the orderlies were told that they would be summarily dismissed if they did not abide by the rules. I together with Umesh resented these high-handed directives but understood that there was nothing we could do about it.

I called Alex and informed her that Jacques was stable; no new changes, and that he was under close observation. "I will call you if there is a change. We are limited to two outgoing calls per patient per day unless it's an emergency."

"Will you drop by on your way home?"

"Not today. There is too much happening. Perhaps tomorrow or the day after when we know more about this new syndrome."

I called Fleur and informed her of Jacques condition. She attentively listened without any expression of emotion, nor did she ask any questions.

After speaking to Fleur, I approached Bender and asked him to meet me in the doctor's lounge. But when I went there, the place was crowded with CDPCT doctors, nurses, and research technologists. I went into the corridor and called Bender on the cell phone.

"I don't know what is going on here," I said. "The secrecy is mindboggling."

"I agree with you to some extent. I think it's less secrecy and more ignorance. No one knows what's going on," said the tall and lanky Bender. "Viral encephalitis is a sequela of direct viral neuro-invasion and is typically dictated by the receptor binding domain of the virus. Studies in SARS-CoV-1, whose genomic sequence closely resembled SARS-CoV-2 of COVID-19, suggests that the pathology involves a cytokine cascade through angiotensin-converting enzyme 2 receptor binding, which leads to blood-brain barrier breakdown. Angiotensin-converting enzyme 2 is widely expressed in the glial cells and in the brain stem nuclei."

"Thanks for the erudite information," I said. I barely understood his dissertation.

"My concern is the attitude of Dr. Zhao. Besides, I feel that the genome of COVID-19, has either mutated or has been doctored to selectively infect the brain. There is something amiss here the way the CDPCT has taken control."

"Your hypothesis is worth consideration," said Bender, the scholarly cautious neuroscientist. "But I strongly disagree that it is doctored. It is highly likely a new mutation, and I credit the CDPCT for taking prompt action to isolate the patients in one unit with far better resources."

"I guess there is nothing we can do at this stage. What bothers me is that Zhao is against any of our suggestions. We have to find a way to alert the media."

After speaking with Bender, I called Umesh Mukherjee, and freely expressed my concerns.

"I favor a mutation rather than the doctoring idea," said Umesh. "Zhao is a scientist, and he wants to proceed accordingly. I mean evidence-based medicine. Your concern for your friend Jacques wellbeing is obfuscating your thinking process. I am impressed how the CDPCT, and Zhao have acted to contain the virus."

"Mr. Thomson, whom I know well, told me in confidence that they have built a new lab on the annex of the 25th floor, behind the doctor's offices," I said.

"Yes, I know. Zhao told me that he plans to give us a tour of the lab in a few days."

I went back to the neurology ward to round on some of the patients and on Jacques in particular. In about an hour or so, I saw a text message from Dr. Zhao requesting me to come immediately to his office.

When I went to Zhao's office, he warned me against speculation that the virus is a new mutation or that it is doctored to selectively affect the brain.

"You are forbidden to speak to the media," said Zhao rather forcefully.

I got the message. On my way out, I wondered how Zhao came to know about it. Are there spies around? Are conversations being secretly recorded? Are the cell phones tapped?

Within a week or so, we were escorted on a tour of the new lab built on the 25th floor behind the offices of the CDPCT physicians and technical staff. The hastily built facility was a Biosafety Level 3 lab where research on the novel coronavirus responsible for COVID-19, SARS-CoV-II, and the most recent virus causing Amnestic Brain Fog was being conducted. Zhao mentioned that it was critical to decipher the DNA sequence of the presumed newly mutated virus as soon as possible.

I, together with Umesh and Bender among other physicians keenly observed the researchers working on the current enigmatic presumably mutated Amnestic Brain Fog virus in a glass safety cabinet, which they accessed through gloves. They all wore a hooded pressurized suit, fully zipped, that was connected at the small of their back to a hose that pumped in HEPA-filtered air drawn from outside the building. Zhao told us that a negative-pressure air system prevented the escape of anything airborne.

"Can anyone enter the lab?" I asked.

"No," responded Zhao. "The doors are locked. The

lab is accessible only to credentialed personnel who pass through a security barrier that scans their irises."

"That's impressive," I said.

That evening after Zhao's demonstration of the newly constructed Biosafety Level 3 lab, I went to Alex's apartment at about six p.m. to update her on Jacques' condition. The strain of the last few days was visible in her unkempt hair, and she was still in a beige silk nightgown. Much unlike her, she hadn't dressed up and presumably spent the whole day in bed. Her heavily defined cupid lips were pale pinkish flesh unsmeared in her usual bright red or purple lipstick, her favorite colors. Since I first met Alex in the Moroccan desert atop a camel, I had the hots for her but bottled every temptation and opportunity. We hugged each other, and I could sense that she was rather ebullient seeing me. The smell of wine wafted from her breath.

"What will you drink?" she asked, as I took a seat on the leather sofa in the living room.

"A cup of hot tea, and a long shot of scotch," I said. "What brought you to the city?"

"We were in the process of legal separation and divorce proceedings, and I came to the city to meet my lawyer. You do know he is having an affair, don't you?

"Well, yes…sort off." I was caught off-guard.

"Who is she, Jeff?"

"I believe she is a Washington Republican lobbyist."

"Fuck."

"What are you going to do now?"

"I don't know. Anyway, the man doesn't even recognize me."

"He doesn't recognize me either. That makes two of us."

"What is going on Jeff? Is this a new virus?"

"I don't know, and nobody does. For sure it is a new mutation of COVID-19 or an entirely new virus. I even wonder if the virus is doctored to selectively affect the brain. It would be a great biological weapon. Can you imagine if a whole country is in a gaga state? I am totally confounded of how the CDCPT took charge."

"Oh my God, don't say."

"It is possible that they are concerned about the spread and want to contain it? What bothers me the most is that it has mostly affected New York and the area around it. The secrecy is baffling. I haven't heard of similar cases in Wuhan or Milan!"

"Perhaps the government is afraid of a panic situation."

"Yes, that's entirely possible."

"Will Jacques recover?"

"I hope so. It seems that Zhao is working on an antidote in the lab. We are not privy to the information."

"What will happen if Jacques doesn't recover? Spend his days in a nursing home or a mental asylum?"

"Don't even mention."

I got up to leave, and swayed, a bit drunk. I had

consumed a considerable amount of Scotch matter-of-factly; the day having gotten to me in a bad ugly way. Alex rushed and embraced me and began crying. I saw something in her moist eyes—something glistening—that magnified her radiance highlighted by the pale cyan light.

"I will call you tomorrow and update you," I said. I'm sure Jacques will ultimately recover."

I walked to the apartment from Central Park South to West End Avenue. The city streets were deserted except for a handful of cars speeding by. I thought of Jacques, of Alex. I felt that something was about to happen between me and Alex, and I thanked my instincts for leaving when I did. But what did it matter? Our world was unravelling: storms, floods, fires, glaciers melting, dust blanketing cities, graveyards swept into the sea, epidemics and pandemics, families torn apart. People were dying.

The fog of illusion, the fog of confusion was hanging all over the world.

As I crossed Columbus Avenue, I saw homeless people lying on their makeshift beds drinking wine, two urinating on the wall, one defecating on the sidewalk. Other men and women from the Lucerne where the mayor housed the homeless sauntered about aimlessly. They were unkempt and clearly mentally deranged. They belonged in a psychiatry asylum, not on the city streets. One approached me for money. I handed him a five-dollar bill and took off on the run. I entered the apartment. It was in total darkness. I went into the bedroom. Fleur was fast asleep. I found some French onion soup on the kitchen counter. I heated it up in the microwave and ate it with a baguet, and a glass of stale Pinot Noir. I popped an Ambien pill and lay on the bed and fell asleep.

CHAPTER 24

THE HUMAN BOG

When I arrived at the hospital at seven in the morning, I was awestruck to see that finally, the *Saint Dymphna Center for Brain Fog* was ready for occupancy. The engineering department of the hospital together with outside contractors had done a superb job under the circumstances of the pandemic. After identifying myself to the guards at the entrance and using my ID to open the heavy glass door, I entered the center.

The floor housing the patients was arranged like a large dormitory with makeshift see-through Plexiglas enclosed rooms six feet apart with men on one side and women on the other separated by a wall with a nursing station in the middle. What was surprising was that the ratio of men to women was 10:1, and most of the beds allotted to women remained unoccupied. It seemed that the virus had a predilection for the Y-chromosome. Part of the unoccupied women's area was converted into a gym with equipment brought from the hospital's own gym, unused since the pandemic. The equipment consisted of strength training, treadmills, air bikes, rowers, and weight racks.

The patients were identified not by name but by the bed number.

Thus, Jacques Charpentier being the first patient to present with Amnestic Brain Fog, occupied Bed Number

#1, and was identified as Patient #1. Right from the start I, together with Umesh, objected to the numerical identification of patients.

"This methodology seems rather inhumane and ghostly to me—a number without a face!" I said to Zhao.

"I agree," said Umesh.

"I have looked at the name option, but I feel that the numerical choice is superior because of the uniqueness and homogeneity of the symptoms of the Amnestic Brain Fog, which will assure a uniform line of investigation and treatment," said Zhao. "And Bender is with me on this."

"Well, considering the comparable and consistency of the symptoms, the treatment will be similar in all patients when we come up with a protocol. I agree with Zhao. Totally." said Bender.

Although neither I nor Umesh saw eye to eye with Zhao and Bender, we declined further conflict and arguments. Zhao had an unmistakable authority in the center.

"We obviously have a new mutation on our hands," I said to Umesh. "I told you so. This COVID thing is not over."

"I agree," said Umesh. "And there will be many, many more on the way. Ram…Ram, save us!"

As I, together with Umesh surveyed the place from the entrance, the scene looked like a human bog with some patients floating around as they circled their beds aimlessly in an awkward maze-like formation staring into nothingness, zombie-like, while others lay on their beds, heads bobbing, all attired in the same blue scrubs.

Still others wandered around saying: "Hi" to their zombie compatriots, who responded with a "Hi" or a wave of the hand. A few exposed themselves and some were found urinating by their bedside. Nurses, orderlies, and doctors crisscrossed dressed in white scrubs and fully encapsulated in personal protective equipment from head to toe like robots attending to the undead. In this human bog, it was as if life was a movie or a theatrical performance, and in this performance, we were all actors, unable to figure out the story or the parts we were supposed to play or what the plot was.

The patients were instructed to wear masks, but few did; the unmasked were reprimanded and ordered repeatedly to place their masks over their mouths and noses. Their vital signs were registered by nurses, and each patient was examined by neurologists for any improvement or worsening of signs and symptoms, while I examined the lungs and their oxygenation and noted my findings in the computer charts. The patients with comorbidities such as high blood pressure, diabetes and heart disease were attended to by Umesh, and if needed Levy and Grimes were called on consultation.

When I approached #1, I found the bed empty. I went to the nurse's station and was surprised to find Carol Johnson talking to the nurse. "Where am I?" she asked. The Filipino nurse stared at her with her penetrating black eyes.

"You are in the Brain Fog Center," she said, in a soft friendly accent with a tinge of a smile.

"Who am I?"

The nurse looked at the tag on the shirt. "You are #67," she said, in a low subdued voice, probably feeling sorry for her.

I approached wondering whether Carol would recognize me. "Hi Carol," I said. "Do you remember me? We met at Jacques' recently."

She stared at me with her glassy grey watery eyes and did not respond. I noticed her disheveled state; the hair uncombed, the skin below her eyes with its gathers and fussy lines, its smoothness replaced by dark pouches. She seemed confused and irritable.

I turned around and asked the nurse whether she had seen Number 1. At that very instant Jacques approached the nursing station and asked for directions to the bathroom. Both Carol and Jacques were right in front of each other in the line of vision, but neither Jacques nor Carol reacted.

Instead of Jacques going to the bathroom, he circled around and went back to bed, while #67 turned around and opened the door to the women's section. My heart sank into quicksand since neither Jacques nor Carol recognized each other, nor did they recognize me. They had fucked, or call it *made love*, clandestine love, call it *an affair*, slept together, perhaps talked of each other's future plans, each other's accomplishments, drank expensive bottles of wine—the French Chateaus, rendezvousing in expensive hotels in this country and abroad, and now, today, they did not recognize each other like broken engines stuck on the rails parallel to each other leading to nowhere.

I was utterly flummoxed. It occurred to me that the monster virus was fully fleshed in all its mischief and wickedness, like an octopus with its tentacles invading the axons and neurons of brain tissue, the only uncharted land—that rules the human body and mind, the very essence of Man. The body failed to recognize itself, its role, its function; it lost the ability to recognize its domain—confusion and anarchy ruled its world. It was as if these patients were gaga with dementia.

When I contemplated this demented world, initially, I felt lost in this human bog, this dead end, fearful that the virus might own me too, that I suddenly felt a strong desire to bolt away like the desperate fawn chased by the tiger, but soon the doctor in me resurfaced and I felt like a man with a new challenge—absorbed and resolute. My usual inwardness was now thrust outward, as if the essence of my soul had uncoiled in preparation for my life's work. For when one lives at a turning point in history, as I did now, when the world was in flux and dark clouds rushed across the sky, darkening the horizon, and when there were endemics and pandemics that let loose dragons and demons in our lives, it was essential to reimagine and rethink and rewrite in the pursuit of science and human endeavors.

My curiosity on fire, I checked Carol Johnson's computer chart to find out that she was seen half-naked roaming the corridors of the Bierre the day she was brought to the hospital. It was rather obvious that Jacques must have been seeing her at the hotel and I wondered whether she transmitted the virus to him.

I went to see Jacques and sat by his bedside. There was no reaction on his part. I saw urine stains on his pants and took hold of his hand and ushered him towards the staff bathroom and let him pee. In the private staff bathroom, I took off my facemask and shield and wondered whether he would recognize me. He just stared at me as if wondering what was going on and tried to push open the door. I held him back and showed a picture of the five of us on my iPhone: Alex, Jacques, their daughter, and Fleur and me.

"That's me. Hurrah," said Jacques, with a tinge of a smile, as if the photo was something new, something he had never seen before. A virgin discovery. Like when Bartolomeu Dias pointed to Vasco de Gama on his ship's deck observing the sudden appearance of seagulls, that a new land was about to appear—Ahoy India, the Dark Planet—land of the Black spice—the peppercorn!

Jacques did not comment on his wife and daughter. It was obvious he did not recognize them.

"Think, Jacques, think, my friend," I said. "That is your wife and daughter, and that is me, and my wife Fleur."

"Yes, I see the resemblance," he finally spoke, looking at me. My face lit up, momentarily, like a bulb switched on, but soon, I felt a pang of hopelessness—the light switched off.

Suddenly the bathroom door opened. It was a guard.

"What are you two guys doing in the single men's

staff bathroom?" he asked, in a harsh authoritative tone. "Homosexual activity is not permitted here."

"I was only showing #1 the way to the bathroom," I said.

"Well, one never knows. I will let you off the hook this time," he said, with a suspicious look.

"Number 1 was lost. Besides, he is staff—Dr. Jacques Charpentier," I said raising my voice and looking the guard straight in the eye.

When I went back to the ward with Jacques, there was a lot of commotion outside of #10's room. I saw a short stocky balding man who suddenly started a dance characterized by rapid, uncoordinated jerking moments of the face, hands, and feet. Soon, some of the patients followed suit almost in a frenzied imitation. The doctors, nurses and orderlies watched in total amazement and disbelief, wondering what was going on, what prompted such exposition. One nurse went ahead and put a hip-hop song, *Yes Man* on her iPad. Others followed. Several nurses and orderlies joined in the dancing. Some orderlies mixed-in hip-hop dancing steps.

After watching this melee for several minutes, Umesh shouted as if he had made yet another brilliant discovery. "It's a St. Vitus dance!"

A new dance: A variation of the hip-hop? I wondered.

They all gathered around and some of the nurses and

orderlies removed their protective gear except for the face mask and shield and joined the dancing, imitating #10 in the jerky, convoluted, circumvoluted movement. It was a wild scene as more patients joined jerking around in their blue scrubs.

"You are right," I said to Umesh, after much thought. "It's a St. Vitus dance. What does this mean?"

"It is also known as Sydenham chorea. And was seen in rheumatic fever due to the bacteria Streptococcus involvement of the brain. I have seen some cases in India."

"I now remember reading about it in med school. I have never seen a case before," I said. "We need to send blood for anti-streptolysin O titers and start #10 on penicillin."

"Also, he needs to be in isolation," said Umesh. "COVID-19 is bad enough and Streptococcus on top?"

"Could the St. Vitus dance be yet another manifestation of COVID induced Amnestic Brain Fog?" I asked.

"We'll have to wait and see if others develop the same dancing mania," said Bender.

All of a sudden Zhao appeared on the scene with two guards who stopped the dancing and the music and took #10 away. He was sedated and placed in isolation. The nurses and orderlies who partook in the dancing were asked to report to their respective supervisors.

I approached Zhao and expressed my opinion. This time around he agreed and asked me to start #10 on penicillin.

After we left the hospital on this eventful day, Umesh, Bender, and I went for a beer in the Irish pub opposite the hospital. We sat on bar stools and ordered Guinness on tap. There were several nurses sitting at the very end quenching their thirst with beer and munching on potato chips and chicken wings.

"Do you guys want some spicy chicken wings? They make them good here," said Paul, the bartender.

"Can we have three plates," I said. "By the way, how is business?"

"Very slow," he said. "We may have to close down."

"Don't say…You can apply for government funds," said Umesh.

"That dance, I can't get over it," I said. By the way why was it called St. Vitus dance, before Sydenham chorea?"

"The association of the saint and his dance had a long evolution," said Umesh. "Saint Vitus was born during the third century in Sicily. He came from an illustrious family and against their wishes embraced Christianity. He performed numerous miracles. His fame soared when Vitus relieved the son of the emperor Diocletianus of his demons by laying his hands over the boy and praying. These miraculous feats contributed to the making of Vitus' later reputation as the patron saint of neurological disorders. Fearful of his fame and miraculous powers, it was the same Diocletianus who had Vitus put to death."

"Go on, tell me more," I said, as the memory of the wild scene with patients, nurses and orderlies imitating

#10 in a sort of a hypnotic state resurfaced.

"It was as if they were seeking some relief, some fun, some distraction from the tragic illness all around," I said.

"Well, Vitus iconography included many depictions of him inside a boiling cauldron, the symbol of his martyrdom," said Umesh. "His cult grew with the establishment of many chapels to St. Vitus throughout Europe. Veneration of the saint appeared particularly strong among the Germans, Czechs, and Slavs who sought his cure of neurological illnesses."

"Amazing. You know a lot about this St. Vitus," I said, having never witnessed a case before.

"Indeed. For my final medical exam in the Bombay of then and Mumbai of now, I had to write an essay on St. Vitus dance, also known as Sydenham chorea," responded Umesh.

"But how do you remember such details?" I asked.

"I have a great long-term photographic memory," responded Umesh. "The healing power of the relics was believed to be especially efficacious for the sick with movement disorder, also known as *triste mal*."

"Yes," said Bender, who had just joined the discussion. "The mania of Saint Vitus dance is depicted in a well-known print entitled *Procession of the Possessed*."

"I have to look that up," I said.

"In the 17th century, the famous British doctor of the times, Sydenham, clarified the kinetic disturbances and also described rheumatic fever with its joint manifestations, but failed to connect it with the chorea," said Umesh. "It was again the British, Dr. Richard Bright who made the link in the mid-19th Century between rheumatic heart disease and St. Vitus dance, or Sydenham chorea."

After washing down the spicy chicken wings with beer, we left the bar for home.

The following day, the two nurses and two orderlies who removed their entire PPE— including the mask and face shield—recorded on the video camera were recalled to the offices of their respective supervisors and were summarily fired on instruction of Dr. Zhao. Among them was a male nurse, Doug Bommer. The man was so upset and angry at being fired that I saw him struggle and kick one of the guards escorting him out of the hospital. As I followed behind to get a Coke from a vending machine, I saw the security people let him go without calling the police. Anyway, with the ongoing pandemic and defunding of the police, it was likely that the police would take a long time to show up or not show-up at all.

When I was on my way home that day, Doug Bommer approached me. "Hey, Doc," he said. "That son-of-a-bitch, that foreigner—the Chinese motherfucker fired me."

"You mean Dr. Zhao?" I asked. "He is no foreigner. He is an American—born in the USA."

"What's going on there? I bet COVID-19 is a vaccine lobby conspiracy. The virus is made in China and imported to the US and all over to drastically cut down the world population and make money for the vaccine industry."

"Where are you from?" I asked, rather surprised and taken aback as I observed the tattoos on his arms, his neck and upper chest visible through his unbuttoned shirt.

"I am an out-of-towner, a travelling nurse from Oklahoma City, Oklahoma."

"You are far away from home."

"Yah! I came to New York to witness first-hand the COVID conspiracy. Besides, because of shortage of nurses, there is a lot of money to be made—nearly ten grand per week."

"I'm sorry for the firing without a prior warning, and the financial loss" I said. "I'm sure you'll find a job soon. There is a shortage of para-medical personnel in New York since the start of the pandemic."

"Yes. Can I bother you for a reference letter if needed?"

"Sure. But do you really believe that COVID-19 is a conspiracy?"

"Yah! Sure do."

"Don't tell me you belong to QAnon!"

"What's wrong with them—you damn liberal democrats!"

"Look here man…I'm a registered Republican but I don't believe in all the QAnon bullshit! They believe in all sorts of preposterous conspiracy theories including that the democrats are pedophiles led by Hillary Clinton… And that the COVID-19 pandemic is fake news perpetuated by democrats. Anyway, I've got to go home."

I turned around and left. The man's a bigot and a dangerous one at that, I thought. No way, I won't write him a letter of recommendation.

CHAPTER 25

HOUSEKEEPING

When I arrived home, I was surprised to find Alex, Allain, and Fleur sitting in the living room, drinking wine, and Fleur and Alex sharing a joint and conversing. I was glad to see that they were all masked excepting when sipping wine. I bend down with folded hands and made 'Namaste' to them all. After a quick shower and dumping all my clothes into the washing machine—a daily ritual since the pandemic—I went to the bedroom to change into casual clothes. Fleur approached and mentioned that Allain was expected for dinner, but Alex dropped in without advance notice, so unusual for her. It was obvious to me that Fleur and Alex had no time alone for themselves. I joined them in the living room.

"They can't locate Victoria," said Allain. "Her lawyer called saying that her phone was disconnected. And his email bounced back."

"I'm not surprised," said Fleur. "Did her lawyer speak to her about the Pre-Nuptial agreement?"

"Yes, he did," said Allain.

"Figures," I said. "She flew the coup with the money."

"How much did she take?" asked Alex.

"She owes me around two to three hundred grand," said Allain.

"Sorry Dad, she took you for a ride," said Fleur.

"My lawyer is dealing with it, and my bank has notified other banks and the FBI."

We sat for a meal of *soupe à l'oignon*, *Boeuf bourguignon*, and for dessert, chocolate soufflé Fleur ordered from her favorite French takeout. Since the COVID infection, Fleur had lost interest in her grandmother's French recipes, and mostly ordered out. We had barely started eating, when the conversation turned to the pandemic, something that I wanted to avoid talking about, bound by HIPAA regulations and the non-disclosure document. But what else was there to talk about if not the pandemic?

"So, tell me Jeff," said Alex, "how many patients do you have with the Amnestic Brain Fog?"

"Sorry Alex, I am not permitted to discuss numbers."

"But surely, you can tell us more or less: ten, twenty, fifty, a hundred?" asked Fleur.

"Closer to the top number. Well…I guess no harm done in telling you guys what happened today rather unexpectedly,"—and I described the St. Vitus dance that afflicted one of the patients and how some of the patients and the paramedical personnel joined in.

"Actually, I'm not supposed to tell you according to HIPAA rules, but everyone does it," I said.

They all burst out laughing except for Alex.

"I don't get it, Jeff," said Alex. "How come the press is not reporting on the Amnestic Brain Fog Syndrome? Is the government keeping tabs on it not to cause panic? I have half a mind to call ACN and the New York News."

"Any progress with Jacques?" asked Fleur. "Did he join

in the dance?"

"Well, Jacques no dancer," said Alex. "He does a few Johnny Carson's phantom golf swings after he stents a closed coronary artery in sheer triumph, though." We all laughed.

"Jacques is more or less the same," I said. But he was able to recognize that the man in the photo and I were one and the same person."

"Isn't that considered an improvement?" asked Allain.

"Perhaps. But that ability was not at all tested in the beginning," I said.

"Did he recognize me and Belinda in the photo?" asked Alex.

"No, he did not. I'm sorry Alex."

"Is he getting any treatment?" asked Fleur.

"There is no treatment at this juncture. We are planning to start rehabilitation and brain stimulation soon, and Dr. Zhao is working on an antiviral pill."

Perhaps thinking that I was not entirely honest and forthright, a flush appeared on Alex's tanned face; she kept on rubbing her hands and gulped down a whole glass of wine. I could see that she was viscerally upset.

"I can't take this damn secrecy on your part Jeff," she said. "After all, Jacques is still my husband." She got up from the table to leave. I immediately stood up and placed my arm around her shoulders, and apologetically told her that I would speak to her in private after dinner. She calmed down and sat back down to eat.

We ate the French delicacies and finished a bottle of

Chateau Greysac. But Fleur only ate the soupe à l'oignon, and a few morsels of the Boeuf bourguignon.

"What is the status of the divorce?" Fleur asked Alex, as we were about to leave the table.

"It's on hold," she said. "Until…I don't know what or when."

I took Alex to the guest bedroom and explained what was going on with Jacques, and about the rehabilitation we were about to start. I repeated all that I had already mentioned before since there was no new information to divulge. To give her some hope, I again mentioned that we were working on an antiviral pill and hopefully would start the study soon. I sensed that Alex was high and hardly listening. I asked Allain to drive her home.

After they all left, Fleur and I lay on the bed with lights off. But it was obvious that neither one of us could fall asleep.

"Be honest with me," said Fleur. "I have a feeling you are hiding something—some bad news. What is going on with Jacques? Will he regain his senses?"

"Truthfully, I really don't know," I said. "We don't even know how to approach the condition or how to treat it. The center has hired rehabilitation specialists to start exercises related to sensory and motor function to stimulate the brain. This is again new territory—a desert with mirages, like when the alpha and the delta variants made their appearance; but we will persevere. At least we hope to. We also plan to start Repetitive Transcranial Magnetic Stimulation. The method has shown some promise for depression, addiction, and memory loss."

"What about a drug to kill the virus?"

"I believe the head of research, Dr. Zhao, and his group are working on it. But that may take some time. He gave us a tour of the newly constructed Biosafety Level 3 lab. On the other hand, it took you several weeks to regain your taste and smell function. It may take Jacques several more weeks as well."

"I hope so. Losing one's sense of taste and smell is one thing but losing one's mind, not being able to recognize one's wife and daughter and oneself is altogether catastrophic. I am afraid for you. What if you come down with the Amnestic Brain Fog?"

"I am very careful. Besides, this new virus doesn't seem as infectious as the previous variants. We haven't had new admissions to the center for the last two weeks. And as far as I know none of the medical and paramedical personnel have come down with the Amnestic Brain Fog."

"But what about you, Fleur? I notice a degree of emotional flatness, almost a lack of interest since the COVID."

"You are right. The emotional ups and downs are gone. I don't feel passionate about anything. What is strange is that I have lost interest in cooking, singing, dressing, make up, and sex. I don't have much appetite for food either. I don't cry any longer."

"I noticed that. The pangs of crying, the sudden torrential tears have evaporated. Besides, we haven't had sex for a long time." I went close to her, coddled her face, and kissed her.

"Not tonight," she said and turned around. "I cannot stomach all that is going on. It has drained the life out of me like an unstoppable hemorrhage."

I lay in bed wide awake wishing for the old Fleur I was so used to: the passionate, the dramatic—even, at times, the absurd Fleur. COVID-19 had killed it—her emotional brain. I got out of bed, popped an Ambien pill, and waited for sleep. I was supposed to take Xanax and not Ambien. I badly needed sleep to rest my tired sensorium.

I found myself in a sort of dream-like twilight state, cognizant of the world around me, the world of my patients: some coughing, others on respirators, and still others walking around zombie-like transforming into vampires feasting on the blood of those tied down to the respirators. These blood-soaked bloated vampires fell on the ground too heavy to fly around. I ran toward them in my cast iron protective gear like a medieval knight, but with a submachine gun and shot at them and the blood siphoned out in pulsating fountains and like a wave, splashed on the walls of the corridors, seeping down the stairs onto the street—a river of black blood. I slipped on the sticky, slippery floor, and some of the vampires still alive searching for prey, pinned me down, removed the head gear and sucked blood from my jugular vein. It was then that I woke up startled moving my arms frantically and kicking with my legs. I touched my neck, feeling for vampire tooth marks, until I realized it was only a nightmare. An Ambien induced nightmare? This will be the last time I will take an Ambien pill. These black Kafkian nightmares were a blending of the real and the surreal—the supernatural and the natural.

I looked at my iWatch. It was five in the morning. I drank a tall glass of water and went back to bed, somewhat invigorated from the six hours of sleep, despite the horrible nightmare. I couldn't fall asleep, again. Anyway, I had to get up by six.

I began to ruminate on all that was going on, seeking solutions to the problems of my patients in the Brain Fog Center. But at this moment in time, I found myself on a dead-end street, and yet I couldn't give up hope. At least the patients I was caring for were not dying like flies in the ICUs. I felt they would recover over time. I turned around and glanced at Fleur. She was still fast asleep, her breathing a hissing snore, but it was her naked back I found myself staring at, the narrow waist now narrower, giving way to a bottom that had somewhat lost its rounded contour. I much wanted to make love last night, to release some of the pent-up energy, to feel entirely fatigued and yet relaxed—sex did that to me—but she had brushed me off. This was not the Fleur I knew—that Fleur died, killed by the virus. And yet, I felt in my bones that this wasn't unrequited love or a bad marriage. It was all temporary like the water lily that blooms and closes its petals overnight to bloom again in the sunlight. True, there were times when I wished for a calmer, controlled, less dramatic Fleur without her ups and downs and flare ups and copious tears like the waves produced by a sea faring monster, but there was always a price to be paid on the ebb and flow of things. Everything in life seemed to be uncoupled from its shoring, sustained by a gasp.

I turned to look at her again. Now fully formed as I marveled at sleaves of her flesh untangling in the bed sheets, I felt like taking her. I moved closer to her and embraced her. In deep slumber, she did not react to my caresses. I walked into the bathroom for a hot shower and masturbated fantasizing about Antonina. I felt relaxed when I stepped out of the shower.

On my way to the hospital, I texted my shrink requesting him to prescribe a new drug for sleep.

CHAPTER 26

THE SPECULATIVE TREATMENTS

It was nearly three weeks since the formation of the Brain Fog Center. During this time period, patients were encouraged to use the gym; however, consumed by lethargy, they did not indulge in any physical activity. Consequently, the three of us—Umesh, Bender, and I—suggested that twenty patients at a time had to attend supervised gym activity for at least a twenty-minute period before breakfast consisting of treadmill and air bikes. For fear of injury other activity was not permitted. But as of yet no specific treatments were administered to the patients; albeit we were busy devising protocols.

Finally, I was excited when I went to work on a Monday morning on the first day of the beginning of the fourth week. That day, the motor-sensory program was due to start by the rehabilitation experts supervised by myself, Umesh, and Bender from the Uptown Medical Center, and Jones and Conrad from the CDCPT, while Zhao, the consummate scientist remained occupied in his lab deciphering the mysteries of the Amnestic Brain Fog virus.

For the supervised motor-sensory program, the patients were instructed to touch themselves and touch each other in alternate pairs in the recreation center. Men among men and women among women consisting of groups of twenty for a ten-to fifteen-minute period. I intently observed Jacques with #3, a doctor himself, a dermatologist in private practice. At the request of the head rehabilitation nurse practitioner, Maria Bradford, they touched each other's face, hands, arms, and in particular, the palms and soles of the feet while lying down, according to established protocol for all patients.

Within a few days, because of interpersonal issues such as: some refusing to touch each other, others banging into each other, and still others getting into a fight, the partnering element of the program was discontinued, and the patients were instructed only to touch themselves.

After a break of about an hour, slow music was played and the patients were asked to dance first by themselves and then with each other following the steps of the instructors for a ten-to fifteen-minute period. This too resulted in a haphazard and disorganized movement with some following the instructors while others went on their own. Ultimately, only dancing by themselves following the steps of the instructors was permitted. After an hour from ten to eleven in the morning of the motor-sensory program, the patients were asked to rest, and the program was repeated in the evening from four to five.

The motor-sensory program yielded vastly different results. Some cooperated, others refused any contact whatsoever, still others among men sought sexual contact and gratification (#2 with #8, #7 with #20, #34 with # 74, among others), characterized mostly by touching and masturbatory activity, which was summarily stopped by the supervisors. Some, including numbers #9, 11, 24, 38, 52, 77 and 97, turned violent and started kicking their respective partners.

Among the violent ones, I was surprised to see Doug Bommer (Number 97) in the center. I asked him what he was doing in the Brain Fog Center. He told me that he had COVID, and because of mental confusion and disorientation, he was transferred to the Brain Fog Center from the County of Queens Hospital where he worked in the ER. To me he didn't seem confused or disorientated and I wondered whether there was another ulterior motive for him being here. I spoke to Bender to perform a through neurological evaluation. He concluded that Doug Bommer did not have Retrograde Amnesia, but some elements of Brain Fog such as confusion and a déjà-vu effect. He let him stay in the center for enrollment in the Brain Stimulation Study.

I was disillusioned with the motor-sensory program and did not hesitate to express my opinion to Drs. Zhao and Jones. It was becoming amply clear to me that however well intentioned, we were grasping at straws.

After a week of the motor-sensory program, at my suggestion, Dr. Zhao convened a staff meeting to decide whether to continue or discontinue the program. A heated discussion ensued between the neurologist Bender and Maria Bradford, the head of rehab.

"I reviewed the data on the motor-sensory program," said Bender. "The program has not had any impact on the Amnestic Brain Fog."

"The program has had a positive effect on the patient's movement and muscle tone," opined Maria Bradford.

"The primary purpose of the treatment is amelioration or cure of the Amnestic Brain Fog," I said. "Improvement in movement and muscle tone are secondary outcomes."

"Let's take a vote," said Zhao. "Those for the program to continue raise their hands." Continuation of the program won the day for its benefit on muscle tone and movement.

"Since the program had no effect on Amnestic Brain Fog, I believe we should start Repetitive Transcranial Magnetic Stimulation right away rather than wait three weeks after the motor-sensory program has ended," said Bender.

"I agree," I said.

"What is Repetitive Transcranial Magnetic Stimulation?" asked Umesh.

"It is a noninvasive form of brain stimulation in which a magnetic field is used to induce an electrical current at a specific area of the brain through electromagnetic induction. An electric stimulator is connected to a magnetic coil which is connected to the scalp," said Bender. "There is some evidence that memory recall is enhanced during and after treatment."

"For now, let's take a vote," said Zhao. The vote was unanimous in favor. Both Bender and I were delighted.

Over the course of three weeks since the center became functional another twenty-one patients developed the St. Vitus dance including one female patient, Carol Johnson, #67. It turned out that this unusual manifestation was indeed related to the virus itself that produced the Amnestic Brain Fog rather than the bacteria Streptococcus. Initially, these patients were not included in the motor-sensory program, nor the Repetitive Transcranial Magnetic Stimulation study for fear of precipitating the St. Vitus dance.

Not uncommon during the St. Vitus dance, some, but not all, at times, but not always, lost their bladder control and wet their pants. The nurses and orderlies who attended to these patients complained that their pee had a somewhat rotten-sweet and pungent smell usually noted after eating asparagus spears in some individuals. Obviously, since the patients themselves had lost all sense of smell, they were unaware of the smell of their urine, while some of the orderlies and nurses made faces and shut their noses in sheer disgust. Some, but not all of the nursing staff and orderlies complained to their supervisors and refused to attend to these patients. After promises of hefty bonuses, they readily went on with their job. It was of considerable interest and even mindboggling that a couple of nurses and orderlies did not complain, and after questioning, they secretly confessed to me and to Umesh that they were not at all bothered with the smell, and actually liked its sweet-pungent order. Umesh, the quintessential interpreter mentioned to me about Florentino Ariza, the main character in Gabriel Garcia Marquez's novel *Love in the Time of Cholera* who consumed loads of asparagus for the very heady, intoxicating aroma of his pee that he much enjoyed.

"It is one of Gabo's best novels," said Umesh, an avid reader of fiction. I was utterly perplexed and found the information rather intriguing and ordered the novel on Amazon intending to go home and read it.

All the doctors including myself and Umesh were simply flabbergasted at this new observation and had no explanation whatsoever until Bender hypothesized that the virus was producing sulfur byproducts, and it was likely dependent on the viral load in the brain. He further theorized that possibly only those who had a very high viral load in the cerebrospinal fluid exhibited the abnormal movements and the 'asparagus pee-smell.' Zhao agreed with Bender, and both were lauded and congratulated when the results of the cerebrospinal fluid analysis showed the highest count of virus particles in patients exhibiting the St. Vitus dance. Bender and Conrad were ecstatic and planned to report their findings in the *Journal of the American Medical Association* or the British *Lancet*. However, the balloon popped when I, after investigating the diet of these patients found out that both asparagus and broccoli were standard vegetables in the diet, and those that exhibited the 'asparagus pee-smell,' indulged in eating these vegetables with much gusto. I agreed that it was the sulfur byproducts from the asparagus and broccoli but had nothing to do with the virus itself. Furthermore, I found out that both asparagus and broccoli were added to the lunch and dinner menu in copious amounts by the PhD nutritionist, Preeta P. Patel, a co-author on a paper that showed that these vegetables had a positive effect on memory in rats. And so, hoping for a positive effect on mine, and particularly Fleur's memory, I bought loads of asparagus and broccoli on my way home from a Chinese vegetable stand only to find that my urine and Fleur's as well, were odorless. After googling the issue, I came to know that some people lack the ability to detect the joys of asparagus because of genetic variation in the degradation of sulfur byproducts. Yes, the gene, the very essence of life and disease. Nevertheless, I enforced upon Fleur the importance of eating the vegetable to improve her memory somewhat dimmed after the COVID infection.

Finally, at the suggestion of Bender and the CDCPT neurologist Dr. Conrad, who after much deliberation considered the St. Vitus dance as a form of "seizure disorder," particularly when stressed, the patients were placed on the antiseizure drug Keppra, which entirely controlled these awkward movements, to the benefit of the patients and the relief of the doctors and nurses caring for them. And so, not to deprive them from the possible benefit of the Transcranial Magnetic Stimulation, they were enrolled into the study.

About eighty percent of the patients consented for

the experimental treatment—Transcranial Magnetic Stimulation—while others, fearful of the equipment and the large magnetic coil over the head, bolted out of the laboratory in utter fear. Many of these patients suffered panic attacks, which were looked on in a positive light for the simple reason that they were reacting. Although the patients were informed that half would get the actual treatment while others would get no treatment falling into the placebo group selected by a lottery system, I felt that most did not clearly understand what exactly constituted the double-blind protocol.

Finally, after a lot of convincing by Dr. Zhao's research associate, Dr. Susan Wu, and Bender's and my intersession explaining that it was possibly the one and only last hope to get better from the Amnestic Brain Fog, the remaining twenty percent signed the consent to our satisfaction. Fearful of panic attacks during the procedure, the patients were mildly sedated with Valium.

CHAPTER 27

THE LIGHTING BOLT

To our utter disappointment, the first two weeks of Transcranial Magnetic Stimulation yielded no results after thirty minutes of treatment on different days. I was personally devastated seeing no alternative to my friend Jacques and the other patients in the center. Furthermore, Zhao announced that animal experiments regarding dosage, efficacy and toxicity of the antiviral pill were not yet complete and could possibly take several more weeks.

However, we were all in for a surprise. Suddenly, at the completion of the third week of stimulation, #13 started singing:

Nur wer die Sehnsucht kennt
Weiss, was ich leide!
Allein und abgetrennt
Von aller Freude...

The technician and the doctors including myself, Umesh, Bender and Conrad, supervising the procedure looked at #13 in utter amazement and fascination. The tenor voice of this tall, bald, and barrel-chested man was remarkable and was heard throughout the Center. I found out that he was a rather famous Russian émigré who, before the pandemic, sang opera at the New York

Metropolitan, the Royal Opera House in London, Semper Opera House in Dresden, and the Wiener Staatsoper in Vienna, Austria among others around the globe.

An afficionado of Opera ala Fleur, I was spellbound with his singing and another man, a research assistant, a German émigré, was kind enough to explain that #13 sang the composition of the Russian composer Pyotr Tchaikovsky, and even went so far as to provide a translation from the German:

> *Only he who knows longing,*
> *knows what I suffer.*
> *Alone, cut off from all joy,*
> *I gaze at the firmament,*
> *in that direction..........*
> *Only he who knows longing,*
> *knows what I suffer.*

Zhao and Jones appeared on the scene and were applauded by the technicians, the nurses, and the doctors in particular those that came from the CDPCT. However, it was the idea of the seasoned neurologist, Dr. Bender who came up with Transcranial Magnetic Stimulation in the first place after a conversation with his close friend a psychiatrist from the Mayo Clinic in Rochester, Minnesota. The fact that the Transcranial Magnetic Stimulation could induce such a response was highly encouraging. Subsequently, every time #13 was subjected to the stimulation, he kept on singing arias from famous operas including:

La Traviata, La Bohéme, The Marriage of Figaro etc. What was of additional interest was that he commanded a large audience of patients, doctors and nurses who listened to him in pin-drop silence and utter concentration, and after he finished, they clapped, and uttered bravos. In this regard #13 provided much needed entertainment to these unfortunate human beings, a sort of an awakening, and some were seen smiling and even crying for the first time since their internment in the center.

"That is what music does: it improves sleep quality, mood, mental alertness and memory," explained Bender to me. I in turn congratulated him, tapping him vigorously on the back.

I immediately suggested to Zhao that it might be wise and therapeutic to have speakers in the center playing music. Zhao agreed but mentioned that, under the current circumstances of the pandemic it would take weeks and possibly months to get a stereo system installed. However, he assured me that he would place a request to the CDCPT for funding for a speaker system. I was encouraged with Zhao's response and noticed some softening toward me. When I went home that evening, I discussed with Fleur any suggestions regarding the type of music to be played in the center. She suggested classical music of Chopin and Mozart to begin with. Obviously, I came up with this idea after hearing #13 sing opera, and the interest and awareness it created among most of the patients. Moreover, Fleur and I, together with our friends Jacques and Alex had spent a holiday in Italy where we visited a vineyard *Il*

Paradiso di Frassina in the hills of Montalcino in Tuscany where Mozart's music was played for the grapevines from speakers installed in the vineyards, day and night. The owner of the vineyard claimed a faster growth of the grapes and attributed the very texture of the famous Brunello wine to the music. I hoped that music would indeed awake a memory in my friend Jacques, albeit he was not fond of opera, or for that matter, classical music, having walked out during intermission of the last Opera, *Cosi fan tutte* performed at the Metropolitan Opera House in New York, that we, together with him and Alex had attended.

When it was #4's turn to undergo Transcranial Magnetic Stimulation, rather surprisingly, the sixty-year-old tall, husky, bearded African American was reluctant to be strapped into the chair, having forgotten that he underwent the treatment several times before. Only after the technologist, a woman named Sandy sat in the chair and underwent a sham stimulation, the man agreed to be strapped in. After finishing the stimulation, he started preaching in a loud baritone voice: "We are living in the end times!" he said. "The pandemic, this COVID virus that has afflicted us all…the chaos and confusion going on in the world…you may have wondered why you all sinners—it is an act of Almighty God—the end times are here. But while God's Word encourages us to be ready for

Jesus's return, it also reminds us that '*concerning that day and hour no one knows, not even the angels of heaven, nor the Son, but the Father only.*' (Matthew 24:36).

He continued with eyes closed in a dramatic recitation moving his hands and stepping forward:

"I am the priest of God's flame.
Executioner of Gods will.
Before Jesus returns,
In this Temple of Flames-
The non-believers shall burn.
And when the Son of God returns,
wrong shall be righted,
Justice shall prevail,
Under Christ, Our Lord
Amen!

I, a onetime Evangelical Christian, together with some of the nurses and technicians in attendance, echoed: *Amen!* And then, a sudden fear gripped me, and I saw a similar dread on the faces of the nurse and technologist in attendance. I gather like me, they too wondered whether it was the end times.

Subsequently, #4 would continue preaching the Gospel every time he underwent the stimulation.

When Carol Johnson, #67 completed her third week of Transcranial Magnetic Stimulation, at first, she mumbled and then in a rather loud and forceful voice talked about her lobbying job in Washington and how she was friendly with Kevin Jokes and Mitch Bundy. And then she proclaimed that she would be appointed Chief of Staff in the next Republican administration. Subsequently, she began relating her affair with Jacques, actually using his professional name: Dr. Jacques Charpentier, the very best cardiac interventionalist in New York. As she was going into some sordid details of their recent encounter at the Bierre, the female technologist, Wendy Thurman, who was administering the treatment abruptly and prematurely took her away, giving her no wind to speak her mind. When Zhao heard about it, he reprimanded Wendy with a warning. "If this happens again, you will be suspended," he said. Because of a break in the protocol, #67 had to be removed from the study.

I was flabbergasted listening to the boastful descriptions of Carol with much braggadocio, and like Zhao, regretted stopping her oration prematurely.

"Why did you stop #67 from speaking her mind?" I asked Wendy.

"Well, you know that I run the Cardiac Rehabilitation Center in the hospital and Jacques is the main referral of heart attack patients to the Center," she said. "He is a great guy. I did not want to hear her describing publicly her concocted intimate scandalous relationship with Jacques."

"I understand," I said. I wondered whether she had had a relationship with Jacques as well. Was it an expression of jealousy that made her cutoff #67?

It was now clear to me that the Transcranial Magnetic Stimulation was stimulating memory cells. Similarly, my colleague the neurologist Bender—who was a co-principal investigator in the study—opined that the treatment was indeed working, but the long-term results still remained unknown. I pondered, rather amazed at the reaction of Carol who had failed to recognize Jacques a few weeks ago and waited in great anticipation and at the same time a degree of angst, on the response of Jacques to the stimulation. What if Jacques does not react? What then? What else was left for my friend? And how will I face Alex?

When Jacques was submitted to Transcranial Magnetic Stimulation there was no reaction after three weeks of treatments; whereas #13 continued his singing, and several others began relating their stories as the treatment continued over a three-week period. Similarly, when #17 was subjected to his third week of Magnetic Stimulation, he started singing a rap song and began dancing while humming the tune.

I was utterly let down with the negative response in Jacques, but I did not give up. Perhaps another week of treatment would do it I thought. "Patience," I said to myself and remembered my pastor saying: *"Ten Fuerza, Fé e Paciencia."*

Number 41, a short balding bespectacled elderly man stood out among the rest for his political admonition. He went on a diatribe against what he referred to as the 'Communist virus' calling it a cabal hatched by the democrats in collaboration with China to cause havoc in the American economy and bring about the downfall of our great President comparing him to George Washington. "Wait and see," he said, "He will win the upcoming election, and make America great again. He will win—God willing. If he loses, it's a fraud perpetuated by the democrats and the communists." Waiving his hands rather wildly, he went on to say in a shrill voice like that of a cat in heat: "And soon the Antifa people and Black Lives Matter—all Communists—will come for your homes, my friends. Beware!"

As I looked at #41 rather flabbergasted wondering whether I had heard such a tirade amounting to a long jeremiad before, the next man—#43 waiting in line for his treatment to start, an obvious liberal or a democrat or an independent—hearing #41's political admonitions charged at the man. There was a scuffle between #41 and #43, and the large magnetic coil fell on the floor with a bang like a gun going off. The technologist administering the treatment pressed a button and two security guards appeared right away and separated the two. Both were sedated and removed from the study for the time being, awaiting a decision by Zhao and Jones. Luckily, the slightly dented magnetic coil did not suffer any functional damage. However, a replacement was readily available.

Although the pronunciations and even the interaction between these two men of opposing political views were considered highly positive findings, in the sense that action was met with reaction, hours after the treatment they seemed to fall back into their Amnestic Brain Fog. Nonetheless, significant improvements were observed after the fourth treatment in both #41and #43. After much thought and memory refreshment, I wondered whether he was a lookalike to a past politician of the city of New York—*one of the great cities of our civilization, it is, like that civilization, in peril from above, from below and on the flank,* in the words Normal Mailer pronounced as far back as 1986.

However, when I checked the man's computer chart, it turned out that he was a sanitation worker from the county of Queens. Another Archie Bunker.

When the bearded #55 with long curly sidelocks and a Yarmulka was submitted to his fourth week of Transcranial Magnetic Stimulation, it was as if he had a revelation: "The Messiah is coming!" he shouted. "Rebbe Menachem Mendel Schneerson is not dead. He is not dead. He resurrected from the death bed, as he was dying! The Messiah is coming... The Messiah is coming," he continued repeating with eyes closed, bobbing his head, as if shuckling at the Wailing Wall in Jerusalem. Unfortunately, the stimulation was stopped because of the artifact created by the movement of his head and body, and the restraint of the equipment used for Transcranial Magnetic Stimulation. However, I recommended to continue subsequent treatments under stronger sedation.

Needless to say, both I and Umesh were surprised by #55's pronunciations. Bender explained that as Rebbe Menachem Mendel Schneerson of the Chabad movement of the Lubavitcher Sect lay dying in New York's Mount Sinai Hospital, Hasidim signed petitions to God to permit their Rebbe to rise from his deathbed and lead Jewry to the messianic age. They carried beepers set to go off and signal them when he revealed himself as the Messiah. They debated how he would lead them to the Promised Land of Israel. But after an extended code due to cardiac arrest, the doctors pronounced him dead. It seemed the prophecy had failed like the end of the world Mayan prophecy of 2012 and the End Times of Nostradamus.

"Wow," I said. "Also, many are waiting for the Apocalypse, and the coming of Christ."

"They'll wait forever," said Umesh.

"Irrespective of what is said and what is believed," said Bender, "it is clear that the Transcranial Magnetic Stimulation is activating memory cells akin to what is observed during stimulation of the brain while performing neurosurgical procedures."

Both Umesh and I agreed.

CHAPTER 28

ALL FOR ONE AND ONE FOR ALL?

After the fourth week of stimulation, I requested a meeting and proposed that the double-blind protocol should be abandoned. I asserted that the treatment be made available to all the patients in view of the seriousness of the condition with no other treatment in the foreseeable future.

In the meeting held in the conference room around an oblong table, I opined that those who did not react to stimulation were obviously in the placebo group and accounted for nearly 50% of the patients.

"How did you come with the 50% number?" asked Zhao.

"It's a rough guess," I responded.

"Rough guesses are not science," said Zhao, and I was abruptly silenced. Zhao, the consummate scientist had killed my argument. There was an acrimonious dialogue calling for a vote for or against my proposal. Umesh seconded my call for a vote, while several of Zhao's research associates rejected a vote call. Zhao's silence implied that he did not agree or was pretending a neutral stand.

"Well," said the erudite Bender, perhaps not to sound undemocratic. "Let's have a vote on Jeff's proposal."

"I agree," said Conrad seconding the vote. I was

pleasantly surprised.

But before the vote, Zhao and Jones announced that they should be ready to start a pill in collaboration with a pharmaceutical company they were not currently privy to disclose but would do so when the study starts. The pharmaceutical company had come up with a dose and the results in mice, rabbits and canines were positive without any significant side effects. Thus, they argued that only a double-blind study could reliably prove the scientific efficacy of the brain stimulation or the pill.

A vote was held. The double-blind protocol won the day. Unfortunate for me, my bosom buddy, Jacques would stay in the placebo group, if in fact he was in the placebo group. It was also decided by Zhao that the Transcranial Magnetic Stimulation will continue for a total of thirty sessions for each patient after which the study would be terminated and the results accessed.

Since most of us including Bender felt that the stimulation procedure was having positive effects, I then proposed that the statisticians should blindly revue the results, and if significantly positive, then the study should be terminated, and the treatment made available to all the patients. A vote was held. And my proposal won by an eighty percent margin. I was elated. All was not lost.

CHAPTER 29

THE CASE OF JACQUES CHARPENTIER (#1)

During the motor-sensory protocol on day twenty-five, the angry, heavy-set tattooed Doug Bommer, #97, who was next to Jacques, suddenly grabbed and pushed him hard and was met with a kick in his groin. Bommer doubled up in pain, after which he unhooked a left-handed jab on Jacques' face. The blow was so powerful that Jacques fell to the floor. On his trajectory to the hard ceramic floor, he hit his head on the handle of a metal chair and blacked out. A gash on the back of Jacques head seeped blood.

"I accidentally stepped on that man's foot. And despite my apology, the man grabbed me and pushed me hard, and I almost fell on the ground," explained Jacques.

A surgical consultation was called, and Jacques's wound was sutured by the surgical resident on call. I requested a CAT Scan of the head to rule out any internal bleeding, but my request required approval from a neurologist. Bender having taken the day off, the neurologist, Dr. Conrad from the CDCPT, examined Jacques who was awake after the concussion and responsive with normal reflexes.

"At this moment, he is fully conscious with no neurological deficit," said Conrad. "I would hold off on a CAT Scan."

I was not entirely surprised since the medical staff

was instructed not to pursue unneeded investigation in view of a lack of personnel in the hospital's radiology department due to COVID.

When I went to see Jacques after about three hours, I found him confused in a semi-comatose state, with an abnormal breathing pattern involving a period of fast, shallow breathing followed by a slow, heavier breathing and moments without any breathing at all referred to as apnea. This breathing pattern was originally described by a British physician, John Cheyne, and an Irish physician, William Stokes in the 19th century and goes by their names 'Cheyne-Stokes breathing.' After keenly observing Jacques, I immediately called Dr. Conrad who finally ordered a stat CAT scan, stat, which showed a large collection of blood known as a 'subdural hematoma' with midline shift that needed to be evacuated urgently, since there were signs of a rise in intracranial pressure resulting in the Cheyne-Stokes breathing.

I called Alex at about six in the evening, explained the acute situation and she gave verbal consent to Dr. Allan Whitmore, the Chief of Neurosurgery to procced with a craniotomy to evacuate the clot and stop the bleeding.

Jacques was taken to the neurosurgical operating room and placed under general anesthesia. The spotlights were blinding as the assistant surgeon, the anesthesiologist, the nurses and technicians, all masked in their sterile gowns, moved around, talking among themselves, preparing for the craniotomy and awaiting the head surgeon.

Dr. Whitmore, well known for his speed, creativity, and calm under duress, stood beside the sink just outside the OR, all masked and hatted, and stretched out his hands under the gushing tap as he rubbed them vigorously with a sponge full of antiseptic, over and over again for several minutes. He entered the operating room with his hands apart like a priest about to give a blessing. He wiped his hands with a sterile towel when Kyung, the head nurse handed him a light blue sterile gown the color of the sky. She opened the gloves with her hands, and he inserted his own, and the gloves snapped around the right hand and then the left.

With a scalpel and an electrical perforator and a craniotome, Whitmore created a temporary flap in the skull bone. The blood collection—the hematoma—was gently removed using suction and irrigation and the bleeding vein was cauterized.

Umesh and I attended the procedure, and I requested Dr. Whitmore to electrically stimulate Jacques' brain after the bleeding was stopped as Whitmore was about to close the craniotomy.

Whitmore, the current President of The American College of Neurosurgeons, and an expert in the technique, had carried out deep brain stimulation in several patients with severe Parkinson's disease.

"It's a great idea," he said to me and his assistant, Dr. Shah. "But we did not obtain consent. Neither has the procedure been approved for COVID related Amnestic Brain Fog."

"Dr. Zhao, the head of the center, could get us all fired," said Umesh.

"He has no jurisdiction over me," said Whitmore in an angry tone of voice.

"Look, Jacques Charpentier is one of New York's prime interventionalists. I take responsibility. I will seek emergency approval for the procedure from the chairman of medicine."

"Actually, it is I who will have to seek permission from the chairman of surgery, and not you," said Whitmore. He instructed the OR nurse to call the hospital operator to get Dr. Jackman, the chairman of surgery on the phone right away. The operator informed the nurse that Dr. Jackman was unavailable.

"We have no choice. It is our only chance," I said. "It is nearly 8:30 p.m., and I'm sure that the chairman of medicine is not available either. These chairmen unlike us, small potatoes, have a 9 to 5 job! And because of the pandemic most work from home."

After much contemplation, standing aloft in telescopic glasses with his gloved hands folded, as if in prayer, the highly religious tall and lanky Whitmore, a conservative Catholic, a member of the *Opus-Dei*, and an anti-Pope Francis for his liberal views, suddenly called out like a forthcoming revelation by the Holy Spirit: "Okay, let's proceed. Wake him up," he said to the weary, half-asleep anesthesiologist, Dr. Kim, who had spent most of his previous night running around in his PPE gear intubating and extubating patients from one ICU to another. Whitmore's tone of voice was a command like when Yahweh met Moses at Mount Sinai and Dr. Kim went about stopping the anesthesia.

"It was my suggestion," I said. "I take full responsibility for the procedure."

"Please obtain verbal consent from his wife," said Whitmore. I went immediately to the OR lounge, called Alex and recorded a verbal consent for the experimental procedure on her husband.

Two patch electrodes were inserted superficially and positioned over the Frontal and Temporal lobes of the brain and the electrical stimulation began when Jacques was wide awake. After nearly twenty minutes of stimulation, when the operating staff including Whitmore, Umesh and I were sitting on stools waiting in anticipation, it was as if Jacques woke up from the Amnestic Brain Fog.

"What am I doing here?" he asked.

"Do you know who you are?" asked Whitmore.

"I am Dr. Jacques Charpentier, head of intervention cardiology." A broad smile crossed my face.

"What am I doing here in the OR?" asked Jacques.

"You had a fall and a large subdural. I just evacuated the blood."

"Swell. Where did I fall? Was it a car accident? Are

my wife Alex and my daughter Belinda, okay? Is my Lamborghini totaled?"

"You fell in the hospital."

"While doing an intervention?"

"Oh, no. Jeff will explain it all, soon."

"Is my friend Jeff here in the OR?"

"I'm here buddy," I said. "Welcome back Jacques."

It was a Eureka moment. Umesh and I high fived.

The procedure over, Whitmore unscrubbed and left his assistant, Dr. Shah, to close the craniotomy with titanium plates and screws.

I just couldn't wait to inform Alex and Fleur. At the same time, as I pondered, I felt it was best not to be too optimistic. Let's wait a couple of days and see what gives, I thought. I went to the OR lounge and called Alex and gave her the news of the events in the OR. I told her not to be too optimistic. "It's best we wait and see."

"I want to hear the details. Can you come over on your way home?"

At about the same time, Bender entered the OR lounge. "What's going on Jeff?" he asked. "I heard about Jacques fall and subdural from Conrad and came here on the run."

"I'll call you later," I said to Alex.

"Why the broad smile?" asked Bender.

I explained what went on. "You are a genius," said Bender.

"First thing tomorrow morning, I have to see the chairman of medicine."

After closing the craniotomy, Jacques was transferred

to the neurosurgery unit under the care of Whitmore and his team, far away from the *Saint Dymphna Center for Brain Fog.* From now on he would be Jacques Charpentier, and no longer #1.

Doug Bommer was placed in isolation, sedated, and under guard for his violent behavior. He was re-evaluated by Bender and Conrad the following morning. They reported their findings to Zhao, who recommended that he be discharged from the center since he did not have Amnestic Brain Fog, tested negative for COVID, and refused Transcranial Magnetic Stimulation.

In the beginning, he adamantly refused discharge, until Zhao and Bender appeared on the scene and ordered the guard to escort Bommer out of the unit. I was pleased to see him go.

The next morning, Umesh, Whitmore and I raced to the chairman of medicine, Dr. Noam Friedlander. Normally, an appointment was necessary, but after I explained the urgency of the situation, the head administrative secretary, Cassandra Cross—whom I had once dated some years ago—waved us in after speaking to the chairman.

We entered the large, spacious office of the chairman, it's walls decorated with certificates, plaques and memberships of prestigious organizations around the globe that Dr. Friedlander belonged to, proclaiming his many accomplishments. He was sitting behind the large mahogany desk reading the *New York Times*.

"Come in," he said, getting off his chair and pointing to the sitting area around a glass table. With a serious stare, the short, balding and aging Friedlander, asked: "So what is going on in the Brain Fog Center?" I explained in some detail about the goings-on at the center, something I was not supposed to disclose, and subsequently narrated the brain stimulation on #1 to make my point.

"What?" said Friedlander. "Who the hell is #1?"

"Dr. Jacques Charpentier," I said. "The patients in the center are known by numbers rather than names."

"Don't say. That is preposterous. Jacques Charpentier intervened on my coronary artery a couple of years ago."

"I'm glad you know the great Dr. Jacques Charpentier."

"Why didn't you call me from the OR? I would have given verbal consent before the procedure," said Friedlander.

"Well, I was in scrubs and did not have the presence of mind to call you. Besides, it was late and I'm sure you had left for the day."

"I couldn't get in touch with the chairman of surgery either. Furthermore, I could not keep him under general anesthesia any longer. It was our only chance," added Whitmore.

"Why don't you guys wait outside in the reception area," said Friedlander. I will call you as soon as I speak to the CEO.

"Thanks a million Dr. Friedlander," I said.

"Cassandra, can you get these gentlemen some coffee

and doughnuts," ordered Friedlander. We sat in the waiting lounge rather anxious not knowing Friedlander's and the CEO's decision regarding the matter at hand. In the meanwhile, at the coaxing and insistence of Cassandra the three of us munched on chocolate glazed donuts.

Hardly had we finished drinking the hot steaming coffee, we were called in after about fifteen minutes and informed that both Friedlander and the CEO would support the stimulation procedure done on Jacques. Friedlander requested me and Whitmore to write a letter addressed to him and the CEO outlining the circumstances.

"Don't forget to mention that there was no time to inform me, and that it was of the utmost importance that you proceed without wasting any time, since the craniotomy had to be closed, and the patient could not continue under general anesthesia any longer."

"Sure, Sir. Will do," I responded.

"I tried contacting Dr. Jackman, but he wasn't around," said Whitmore.

"Please add that you tried to contact Dr. Jackman before the procedure, but that he was unavailable. I believe he is out-of-town on holiday."

"Will do," said Whitmore.

"The Department of Medicine and the Institution will protect you against any liability," said Friedlander. "I will speak to Jackman when he returns. But I cannot speak for Dr. Zhao. He is not under my jurisdiction."

"Thanks much," I said, and we left.

CHAPTER 30

THE AFTERMATH

As I was about to go home at about six o'clock in the evening, Alex called requesting me to drop by.

"So much secrecy surrounding the center," she said. "I don't understand what's really going on."

"I'll come over and we'll talk," I said.

I called Fleur and briefly related the events of the day and told her that Alex wanted me to come over to better explain the situation with Jacques.

"Sure," said Fleur. "Alex is very anxious. She called me this morning, crying. It's best you go and spend some time with her."

When I, rather tired but upbeat entered Alex's apartment, she hugged me and began crying. I could smell the scent of wine on her breath.

"Where is Belinda? How is she taking Jacques' absence? It's already been several weeks."

"She is spending the night at friends. I told her that her dad is sick in the hospital with COVID. You do know that she is not very attached to him. How can she be? The man is not around and unlike you, he travels all over the world lecturing."

"I don't know how he does it."

"Every other week he flies to Frankfurt to do research with his friend Dr. Helmut Schein on new devices. They apparently line up cases for him. Granted, he makes a lot of Euros. At least the COVID situation has put an end to these travels, but now the Amnestic Brain Fog."

"We maybe at the cusp of a cure at least for Jacques." I explained in detail what went on.

"I'm sorry. I didn't even offer you a drink. Do you want wine or scotch?"

"A tall scotch, straight up with no ice."

"Single Malt or Johnny Walker Black?" I eyed a half-a-bottle of Caskers-Glenfarcia resting on the mini-bar.

"That one there," I said.

"I hope Jacques makes it in one piece. That way I won't feel guilty. Otherwise, it will look as if I am abandoning him."

"We will know tomorrow. At least have an idea of the future."

"How are things with you and Fleur?"

"She has changed after COVID. Her emotional brain is shot!"

"What do you mean?"

"There are structures deep within the brain with names such as Hypothalamus, Amygdala, the Limbic system etc. known as 'emotional brain' that is responsible for behavioral and emotional reactions including sexual responses."

"I'm sorry to hear that. I'm sure she will recover."

"I hope so."

On my way home I felt a rush of adrenaline—that I am on the threshold of something big. My idea of stimulating Jacques' brain was reportable, and certainly, I would be a coauthor with Whitmore since it was my idea to begin with. Why not—*The New England Journal of Medicine* or *The Journal of the American Medical Association* or the British *Lancet* in that order. My ticket to fame.

Fleur was watching TV when I arrived home. "Tell me, tell me about your day," she said.

"It's a long story," I said.

"It was a day to celebrate or a day to die." I told her the whole amazing story.

"Wow," she said. "That's exciting. What if he comes out of the Amnestic Brain Fog tomorrow?"

"And what if he doesn't? I'm probably not going to fall asleep tonight and I don't want to take an Ambien and suffer nightmares."

"You look tired. Why not get some sleep?" I wished she would ask whether I wanted to make love.

"Yes, honey," I said. "I will do just that. A double dose of Xanax."

As I lay down to sleep, part euphoric, even energetic despite the tiring day, my blood infused with a shot of testosterone and adrenaline, I met Fleur's insouciance with frustration, and the virus with bitterness and exasperation, as my mind gradually dulled into sleep.

CHAPTER 31

THE REVELATIONS

The next morning my anxiety surged precipitating the rapid heartbeat—the Supra Ventricular Tachycardia—as I entered the Neurosurgical ICU. I tried coughing, then straining, then splashed ice cold water on my face in the kitchenette of the ICU, but to no avail. I called Dr. Grimes, who came on the double. He took me to the cardiac electrophysiology labs, now empty deserted rooms with x-ray machines and their large control rooms with three-dimensional mapping systems and an array of computers more advanced than in the *Millennium Falcon* of *Star Wars* now idling with blank dark screens. He hooked me to an ECG machine, and administered an intravenous drug that immediately, miraculously, terminated the rapid rhythm.

"You have what we rhythm experts call A-V Nodal Re-entrant Tachycardia," he said. To me it sounded like a mile long circuitous track in the heart. Noticing a bewildered look on my face, he took a sheet of paper, drew a diagram of the heart, and went about explaining the electrical circuit that was causing it. I looked at the drawings and for the first time understood my problem.

"These are stressful and anxious times, Jeff," said Grimes. "It's best you take Metoprolol 50mg on a daily basis. And once the pandemic is over, you should have an ablation. In the meanwhile, I will send an e-prescription to the pharmacy."

I immediately left for the Neuro-ICU, anxious to find out if Jacques had recovered from the Amnestic Brain Fog. Still heavily sedated, Jacques was unable to talk to me yesterday. But today was the day. When I entered his room, I found him asleep. The head of the unit, Dr. Menezes, requested me not to wake him up.

"Sure," I said. "Will you call me when he wakes up?"

As I entered the Brain Fog Center, I found Zhao talking to Umesh. As soon as he saw me, he turned around and told me that he wanted to see me in his office at eleven a.m. and left the unit. I asked Umesh what they were talking about.

"He knows all about the brain stimulation performed on Jacques after the surgery on the subdural hematoma. He wants to see me at 10:30 a.m. I have a feeling he is going to fire us both."

"I don't give a damn," I said. "I'm certain we can go back to our previous jobs, you as head of the ICU, and I, as infectious diseases attending. Most importantly, both Friedlander and the CEO are supportive."

As I was rounding on the patients in the center, I received a call from the Neurosurgical ICU that Jacques was awake. I immediately called Whitmore, and we both went to the Unit to see him. His head was bandaged, there was an IV in his arm, and he was sitting in a chair staring at the palms of his hands and kneading his fingers as if he was inserting a catheter in the heart. He recognized me right away, but when Whitmore asked him questions such as the time, the day, the year, the president, and vice-president of our great exceptional USA that was totally unprepared for the pandemic, he gave some incorrect answers. He got the year, the month, and the president right, but could not name the vice-president. He said he was a doctor, a cardiologist, but when asked about his super specialty, he seemed a tad confused. He said he was married and had a daughter, Belinda, but when asked the name of his wife, he struggled and ultimately to my embarrassment, said Fleur.

The three of us, including Whitmore and Menezes, went into conference and concluded that there were some positive signs. But that Jacques had a long way to go. We agreed to proceed to occupational therapy and assign a neuropsychologist for the task. Both Whitmore and Menezes recommended that when feasible in a few days, he be taken to the catheterization laboratory to witness an intervention. Whitmore suggested continuing Transcranial Magnetic Stimulation. I mentioned that it was impossible since Jacques was likely in the placebo or sham group, and Zhao would not go along with it. We agreed that Jacques should not be sent to the Brain Fog Center, but rather transferred to the neurology floor.

At eleven o'clock I entered Zhao's office. Even before I sat down, he immediately mentioned that he knew what went on, and that I had to seek permission from him to proceed with the brain stimulation during neurosurgery.

"Since Jacques was already in the double-blind study he

should not have been subjected to another experimental protocol without consent of the patient and without approval of the head of the center," he said rather curtly.

"There was no time for all that," I said.

"I was in my office. You have my number."

"As I understand, we did not need your permission, Sir. Whitmore called the chairman of surgery to seek permission to use 'novel therapy cum technology' on an emergent basis. But he was not available, neither was the chairman of medicine. We have their full support and that of the CEO of the Hospital."

"By the way, where is #1?" Zhao asked moving forward in his chair and staring straight at me.

"He is in the neurosurgery unit. Can he be removed from the study and allowed to undergo Transcranial Magnetic Stimulation?"

"Absolutely not. He is already part of the study. I want him transferred back to the center."

"No way," I said, elevating my voice a tad. Number 1 is negative for COVID, and he will be better cared for on the neurology service. Do keep in mind that he is post-neurosurgery." I noticed an angry reddish flush on Zhao's face.

"It has been agreed by all, including his neurosurgeon and the chairman of medicine that Jacques, your Number 1, should be cared for in the neurology unit," I said with an element of finality.

"You are fired," said Zhao pointing and looking straight at me. The guards will escort you to your office in the center, and wait outside till you pack your things, and usher you out."

"Sure," I said. "With pleasure." I wanted to tell him to wait till he hears from the news media but managed to hold my tongue.

As I left Zhao's office, there was a text message from Umesh informing me that he was also fired. We agreed to meet for a drink in the evening on our way home.

I immediately called Dr. Noam Friedlander and informed him that both Umesh and I were fired. I also mentioned that it was agreed upon that when Jacques was stable, he would be transferred to the neurology service rather than the Brain Fog Center of Dr. Zhao.

"I am not at all surprised. Zhao has a tight rope around the center. But don't you guys worry. You and Umesh have your old jobs back. It makes a lot of sense to assign Jacques a private bed on the neurology floor. You have my full support in this. I will visit Jacques today."

I felt entirely reassured. Friedlander's and the CEO's support meant a lot to me. On my way to the Neurosurgical ICU, I received a text from Ms. Aguilar, a neuropsychologist, assigned to Jacques's case by Whitmore. She requested a meeting with me that afternoon. She also needed to meet with Alex and asked for her number. After lunch I met with Ms. Aguilar and related in great detail Jacques Charpentier's professional and personal life history. I also called Alex and told her to expect a call from Ms. Aguilar and also told her that I would call her later to discuss Jacques's condition.

I met Umesh in the nearly empty Irish Pub opposite the hospital and we both ordered Guinness on tap. A few nurses at the other end of the bar, high on Irish whisky were cackling away about their experiences. Hardly were we seated on bar stools at the far end of the bar when Bender appeared. We discussed at length Jacques' condition and that of other patients in the center. Bender informed us that nearly 40% of the patients undergoing Transcranial Magnetic Stimulation were showing significant improvement in the Amnestic Brain Fog. "It is highly likely," he said, "that those not showing any improvement are possibly in the placebo group, although the groups haven't been divulged."

"Yes, both Umesh and I concur," I said.

"I raised the issue about breaking the Code with Dr. Conrad from the CDCPT," said Bender with a flourish. I asked him to take it up with Zhao and Jones."

"And..."

"I don't have an answer yet."

"I googled Dr. Zhao this morning at your suggestion," said Umesh. "He is a graduate of MIT, where he got his PhD in microbiology, and med school and residencies at Harvard, and subsequently he worked at Chapel Hill in the department of virology. About two years ago he joined the CDCPT.”

“Any information whether he was involved in gain-of-function viral studies?” I asked.

“No idea,” said Umesh.

“What about at Chapel Hill?”

“His name was not on the paper published in 2015. It is possible he was already abroad, perhaps in China at the time and possibly doing research there.”

“He must have been vetted to work for the CDCPT,” said Bender.

“Why?” said Umesh. “The viral research at the Wuhan Lab was supported in part by the NIH.”

“I know an FBI agent who perhaps can find out more,” I said.

It is then that our eyes shifted to ‘Breaking News’ on ACN.

“We have information from a reliable source that there are patients with COVID related Amnestic Brain Fog cloistered by the CDCPT at the Uptown Medical Center in New York City, and according to reliable sources are undergoing experimentation. This apparently is a novel COVID related syndrome affecting solely the brain and no other organs. Doctors’ familiar with the condition are apparently sworn to secrecy. Questions have been raised whether the unusual COVID -19 virus has been doctored to selectively infect the brain. We will have a follow-up once we get more information from Dr. Zhao, head of the Center. We called the Center to speak to Dr. Zhao, but he has not returned our call as of yet."

"I'm sure it's Alex, Jacques' wife who must have spoken to the reporter from ACN," I said. I immediately called Alex and left a message to call me back.

"I hope she has not incriminated you," said Umesh.

"I'm concerned. I feel somewhat betrayed. But it's doubtful that ACN will disclose its source," I said.

"I don't think you should feel betrayed. After all her husband is in the center. And all that you were doing is relaying his progress. She has the right to know," said Umesh.

"It has been a long day. I am going home."

"Me too," said Umesh. "What a relief—at least tomorrow I don't have to go back to the Brain Fog Center, and all the madness going on in there."

"Yes, that's some respite," I said. "See you at seven in the ICU."

"I will keep you guys informed of what's going on in the center," added Bender.

As we were leaving the bar, I received a text from Alex. "I don't want to talk on the phone. Can you come over?"

"I'm very tired; about to go home. Can you come to the apartment after eight? And we'll talk," I texted back.

"Will try if I can find a babysitter on such short notice," she texted back.

"If not, bring Belinda with you." I responded.

At about nine o'clock, as Fleur and I were finishing eating our ordered French Bean Thai Duck curry with Green Papaya salad, the doorbell rang. It was Alex and Belinda. I immediately noticed that Belinda had gained height and weight and resembled so much her mother. Fleur hugged her and holding her by the hand took her to the playground on 60th Street and West End Avenue so that Alex and I could have some quality time discussing Jacques' condition and the Breaking News on ACN. We sat on the living room couch, and I handed her a glass of Merlot and poured for myself a shot of the golden-brown Pappy Van Winkle Bourbon, a gift from Jacques. I related to her that Jacques had regained some retrograde memory, but that he was not out of the woods as of yet. He would undergo occupational therapy.

"Do expect a call from Ms. Aguilar, his occupational therapist," I said.

"She already called," she said. "I have an appointment with her tomorrow. I would also like to see him."

"That's a great idea but the timing is important. Discuss it with Ms. Aguilar. By the way, did you spill the beans to a reporter from ACN?"

"Yes, I did. There has to be accountability. The public has to know what's going on."

"You shouldn't have…without discussing with me first…Did you mention my name as your informant?"

"Absolutely not. I mentioned that my husband was interned in the center, and I did not know what exactly was going on." She looked somewhat distressed.

"Look Jeff, you are my friend, and more so a close friend of Jacques. You only informed me of his progress and nothing else!" She said after some time. "If I hurt your feelings or you feel that I was disloyal to you or compromised you in some way, I'm terribly sorry."

"It's Okay…after all you have the right to complain."

"Apparently, it's not only me. Other family members have also approached the news media."

CHAPTER 32

A DOCTORED COVID VIRUS?

The next morning Umesh and I reported to the cardiac ICU, and the attending doctors temporarily transferred there went back to their respective positions. The number of sick COVID-19 patients on respirators was down by around 50%, and the cardiac ICU was getting back to its original status with cardiac patients with heart attacks, heart transplants, and heart rhythm abnormalities. Over 80% of the COVID-19 patients who were on respirators in the ICU for weeks—locked alone in uncharted destinies, moved towards their deaths. And death was relentless. Bodies remained in freezers parked outside the hospital awaiting ground burial or cremation. After all, isn't our world partly run on invisible things like viruses and bacteria? Aren't we living beings feeble and dispensable and live under the shadow of the ultimate darkness—the terminal oblivion—the eternal rest—the egg from where we sprout and the death toward which we move?

My services as an infectious diseases expert were no longer needed except as a consultant for a specific patient, and so I went back to my academic office in the infectious diseases department and waited for consultations. In the meanwhile, I scanned the newspapers and the medical literature for any new information on COVID related

Amnestic Brain Fog. I found some new articles where some young patients with COVID-19 reported late symptoms of fatigue, weakness, and heart palpitations weeks after the initial illness. And a new syndrome: *Late COVID* was coined. Some of these patients did describe, "brain fog" characterized by intermittent episodes of "mental blankness" or "absent-mindedness," and even a "déjà vu" effect, but none reported retrograde amnesia. Surprisingly, the majority of these patients were young women who had COVID-19 months before, unlike the patients in the Brain Fog Center who were mostly and predominantly male.

As I was on the computer reading several reports on the subject, my phone rang. It was Donald Rudin, the FBI agent and one time my patient.

"Hey, Don. How are you and family? Hope you are keeping safe," I said.

"Yeah, we are fine. I am tired staying home. The wife and kids get on one's nerves," said Don.

"I understand. It's not easy for an active person like yourself to be suddenly locked up at home. Any information for me?"

"I did locate Zhao's file. Apparently, your man was at Chapel Hill, but then the trail went dead. He seems to have disappeared for two whole years. In his application for the job at CDCPT, he mentioned that he had gone to the Far East to visit virology labs, and to familiarize with their research, as well as spend time with his family in Hong Kong."

"Where in the Far East I wonder? Is there any mention of the Wuhan Lab in China?"

"No, none whatsoever."

"Did you find any letters of recommendation?"

"Yes, there were several praiseworthy letters that mentioned that your man is a wiz at genetic manipulation of viruses."

"Thanks Don. Thanks a million," I said. "The information is certainly helpful."

After the conversation with Don, the information that Zhao was a wiz at genetic manipulation of viruses, struck a major chord—a loud C major. It occurred to me that what we were dealing with in the Brain Fog Center, was possibly a doctored COVID virus. I felt that my mission was to unearth the mystery.

I called Bender seeking any new information, but Bender did not answer and his voicemail was full. I called Umesh to find out if he had any new particulars. He told me that by chance he met the hospital pharmacy director, Dr. Robert Sinclair, who told him that Zhao and Jones were about to start a double-blind study on a new pill: AC#476984001.

"Who is going to dispense the drug and placebo?" I asked.

"The hospital pharmacy," said Umesh.

"Can you ask him the label on the placebo and the real pill?"

"I'll try. But why?"

"I need the real pill for Jacques. Since he is not in the

center, he will not be part of the study."

"I doubt Sinclair will cooperate."

"I am convinced that what we have on our hands is more likely a doctored virus."

"You may be right. We have to knuckle down."

With nothing much to do, I left the hospital at three in the afternoon for the first time in a long, long time. I walked through Central Park to the West Side. It was the end of spring and the beginning of summer. The sunshine, the cool breeze, the ruffling leaves, the black-capped chickadee, and the red-winged blackbirds chirping away, and the blooming summer flowers added a feeling of renewal, of belonging, of joy, that no matter what, life endured.

When I got home Fleur was not there. I called her on her cell. She answered my call and told me that she was with her father; that he was not feeling well.

"What's wrong with Allain?"

"Why don't you speak with him?" She handed the phone to Allain.

"I feel weak and tired," he said. "I have a slight headache."

"Any fever?"

"No."

"Perhaps it just a common cold. Take two Tylenols. And to be on the safe side come over tomorrow for a

COVID swab."

"I think I'll spend the night here," said Fleur.

"Sure," I said. "Please wear a mask at all times and keep your distance from Allain."

After I hung up, I felt unsettled. "Not again," I uttered to myself, concerned that Allain might have come down with a COVID recurrence. It was known to happen. I poured a generous shot of scotch, and began sipping the golden-brown liquid, hoping for its calming and its soothing effect on the mind.

As I took a second sip, the phone rang. It was Antonina. She told me that she had spoken to the infectious diseases doctors in Milan and Rome. They hadn't seen any cases similar to the ones I described.

"You have a new syndrome on your hands," said Antonina. "You better write it up soon. It's your ticket to fame and fortune." I sensed optimism in her voice unlike in the past long-distance conversations.

"That's not possible, Antonina," I said. I had to sign a non-disclosure document. Besides, I was fired from the center." I went on to describe what transpired.

"I have news for you, *mio amico*," she said. "I have been accepted for a fellowship in infectious diseases at the University of Milan, and I have a new boyfriend. A doctor. He is specializing in cardiology. We are getting engaged. We plan to marry next year after he finishes his training. He would like to spend a year learning coronary artery intervention with your friend Jacques. And if that is not feasible, perhaps a few months as an observer?" I could sense the excitement in her rapid-fire voice.

"I am happy for you Antonina," I said. "That's great news! I hope he is Italian or European and not a Middle Easterner. Well… Just kidding! As far as Jacques is concerned, he is out of commission with COVID related Amnestic Brain Fog. I don't know what the future holds for him. Don't even know whether he will completely recover."

"*Merda, questo COVID*," she said. "By the way, my boyfriend is Italian, a true Roman!"

"I was only joking."

"I know, *mio amico*."

"I don't know what the world is coming to, everything seems to be falling apart, melting like butter."

Suddenly, I broke down. I couldn't continue. I hadn't choked up this way before.

There was a long silence at the other end. "I'm sorry, Antonina," I said after I took hold of myself. "It's been hard on me dealing with the patients, my wife, my father-in-law, and now Jacques…one after the other with COVID related issues; besides, I was fired, and it's not over. My wife, Fleur—her emotional brain is shot. She has lost interest in music, in food and in sex. Besides, there is a lot going on in the medical center that I don't understand and don't have a hold on…and that creates a lot of insecurity and fear."

"You'll be fine. I'll pray for you."

"Thanks, *Ciao*."

The rather unexpected unravelling and the confession

to Antonina provided some relief to my turbulent mind. I called my mother in Ohio and was reassured that she was safe and sound. She told me that she could take care of herself and prefered to stay at home. I apologized for not visiting her, but promised to do so as soon as things get back to normal, or near normal. In the meanwhile I asked her to come to New York for a visit.

CHAPTER 33

THE ROAD TO RECOVERY

The retrograde memory recollection turned out to be a long and tedious process for Jacques. Ms. Aguiar spent an hour each day going over details of his past life and at the same time probing his memory with photographs provided by Alex and me. To some extent it seemed at times as if Jacques did not want to remember the past.

We finally took him to the catheterization lab to witness a stent intervention procedure on the coronary arteries. In the beginning it seemed that Jacques's problem was a lack of concentration, but all of a sudden, he was mesmerized just before the stent was deployed in the coronary artery and exclaimed: "I can do all that." He began advising the operator, Dr. Swami how to proceed with the rigid calcified right coronary artery with an atherectomy before deploying the stent and went into historical details of cleaning the coronary arteries of calcium.

"It seems that the stent procedure triggered a memory in his brain cells," said Ms. Aguilar.

I wanted to pursue further questioning, but Ms. Aguilar stopped me cold.

"Let's not push the envelope," she said.

I was encouraged with the outcome and felt that it was time to bring Alex and Belinda for an encounter.

The day was set for Jacques to meet his family. Alex wore a blue pant suit and Belinda a beige and brown checkered dress. Jacques was sitting in a chair in his room in hospital clothes when Ms. Aguilar ushered them in. I stood behind them. Their visit was kept a surprise.

"Look who is here to see you," said Ms. Aguilar.

"Hi Dad," said Belinda, and she went and embraced him. Jacques seemed startled and confused at first, but soon hugged her tight. "My daughter, my sweet, sugar plum Belinda," he said.

"And you know who this lady is?" I asked. Jacques looked at her intently, and then it happened. "She is my lovely wife, Alexandra," he said, and the three of them hugged each other. Ms. Aguilar and I left the room and let the three of them reconnect.

After about half-an-hour, Alex and Belinda said their goodbyes and met with me and Ms. Aguilar. Alex told us that Jacques questioned her at length of how they had managed during the pandemic and his absence. She told us that he related the most recent events: the emergency room visit, the admission to the center, the fall, the surgery, his stay in the Neurology ICU and now the ward. He also spoke excitedly about his trip to the lab, and how he was anxious to go there again. He mentioned that at times he felt that he knew how to deploy stents while at other times he needed to make an effort to refresh his memory. At the end he expressed a desire to come home. All of these observations were signs that he was in the recovery phase of the retrograde amnesia. However, both Bender and I felt that the recovery would be faster if he would be a part of the pill study to kill the virus. Bender however informed me that the study had been postponed for several weeks since Zhao wanted definitive results on the Transcranial Magnetic Stimulation study before proceeding with the pill study.

Over a month had gone by since the Brain Fog Center was established and the improvement in patients brain fog varied substantially from patient to patient. However, nearly 50% of patients in the center who recovered after the stimulation treatment were discharged from the hospital.

During a Board meeting, chaired by Zhao, Bender told me that he announced that those who did not recover or those who were demonstrating a slow recovery and those that developed the St. Vitus dance had a higher viral load in their cerebrospinal fluid. Of these patients, those with the St. Vitus dance had the highest viral load, and all twenty-one had a negative Streptolysin O-titer implying that their symptoms were indeed related to the virus and not to the bacteria Streptococcus. Bender also mentioned that Jacques fell into the high viral load group. Zhao suggested changing the name of the dance to *"the COVID-19 dance"* rather than the St. Vitus dance. Bender agreed.

Finally, I pushed Umesh to speak with Dr. Sinclair, the head of the pharmacy. A meeting was arranged for the three of us. Umesh felt that since I was a close friend of Jacques, I could make a stronger case for Jacques receiving the antiviral pill: AC#476984001. Surprisingly, I did not have to convince Sinclair. He too had been a patient of Jacques who had intervened on his coronary artery and the heart bypass graft about a year ago that got rid of his angina.

"Because of Jacques, I can live a normal life, walk around the trails, ride a horse, go hiking in the Tetons and have sex," he said.

"You made my day," I said, and shook hands with him and patted him on the back.

"There will be five red capsules to be given every day for five days after breakfast. The transaction will occur between you and me near the Irish pub at seven in the evening next week on Friday. I will hand you a Matchbox, and it is both our responsibility that no one is looking our way. Since the packet is so small, I'm sure no notice will be taken."

"Swell," I said. "I promise that this is just between the three of us."

"Here," he said, and removed a Bible from the bookshelf. All three of us placed our hands on the Bible and swore that the secret will not be disclosed even under duress. Umesh was a Hindu, but since Hindus tolerated all religions and a multitude of gods including even some Christian deities, he had no problem swearing on the

Bible.

"One last question: Do you know when Zhao plans to start the study?"

"Within a week I believe. But in the past, he has promptly postponed the start, and it might happen again."

Mission accomplished, we went for a beer at the Irish pub.

Within a few days Jacques was discharged from the hospital and Alex seemed outwardly contended that he was home. However, I could sense anxiety in her: the way she was acting, darting about in the apartment, pouring me a glass of wine, a snifter of brandy and handing me both at the same time. In the beginning it almost seemed to me that she was conflicted at having Jacques at home; perhaps unsure, unclear how to deal with the illness or their personal relationship.

Fleur and I visited Jacques regularly and tried to involve him in a spirited conversation about his intervention in famous New York personalities, his lecturing abroad, his frequent visits to Frankfurt, but found Jacques just listening. However, sometimes he shook his head, while at other times, he seemed rather oblivious. On the other hand, slowly but surely, he was able to carry on his ablutions and walks in Central Park with Alex. She expressed her opinion that the improvement in Jacques was slow going, unsettling and anxiety provoking. She was uncertain about their future. She decided to hold on the divorce proceedings for now. We made it a point to assure her that we are there for her as well and to confide in us any misgivings.

When the women were not around, I asked Jacques whether he remembered meeting Carol Johnson at the Bierre Hotel, and whether he remembered anything unusual about the food or drink or whether he had met anyone else there. After a long silence he shook his head. "I don't recollect meeting anyone else there. But wait a second, I do remember both of us feeling a bit dizzy and nauseous after a scotch and soda, so much so that we skipped dinner, and hit the sack."

"Anything unusual about the waiter?"

"I don't remember. But the Amnestic Brain Fog developed about three days later."

PART 6

Plot is no more than footprints left in the snow after your characters have run by on their way to incredible destinations.

—Ray Bradbury, *Zen in the Art of Writing*

CHAPTER 34

THE FIRST PLOT

That evening as I put on the TV, I switched on to ACN. I was taken by surprise to see Dr. Zhao on a Zoom interview. "The virus in question is indeed a variant of COVID-19," he said. "Preliminary genetic studies show that it is a new mutant derived from the Delta variant that was first seen in India. We have decoded the genetics of the virus but await collaborative confirmatory genetic studies from Wuhan Laboratory in China, the Louis-Pasteur Institute in Paris, and Cambridge University in England, before going public with the information." He mentioned that he did not know where the virus originated; however, since it was initially noted in New York, it likely originated in New York City itself.

"We do know that the father of one of the patients with the virus was highly immunocompromised and ultimately passed away," he said. "It is possible that the virus mutated in this unfortunate man, and then he passed it on to his son."

"Would you like to elaborate?" asked the anchorman.

"The virus unlike other variants selectively affects the brain, and the route of transmission is via the nasal passages," said Dr. Zhao. "The unique relationship between nasal cavity and the brain tissues makes possible intranasal delivery to the brain. The olfactory nerve is right there sampling air; but it is also at risk for bacteria and viruses."

He went on to speculate that a certain enzyme in the lung tissue could potentially prevent the Amnestic Brain Fog virus from infecting the lung, unlike the previous variants. "My group at the center is looking into this," he said.

The anchorman asked about rumors of viral experimentation and manipulation at the Brain Fog Center. Dr. Zhao glared at the reporter as if he was an unruly, aggressive man on the attack and said, "The center was established to keep the patients from far and wide interned in the center, to keep the virus from spreading, and to provide specific protocol-based treatment on a sound scientific basis that fits all. These objectives were attained."

"Are you satisfied that the virus is contained and not spreading?"

"Yes, absolutely. The virus has been contained," he said with emphasis, and a sort of self-congratulatory smile. He further mentioned that this was indeed a serious and damaging virus to the brain cells; however, it was less infectious than the previous mutations including the Delta variant.

"What about treatment, Doc?"

"Several treatment options are being carried out according to current scientific standards and some are showing signs of significant improvement."

"Can you elaborate?"

"At this time, I cannot discuss which treatment is showing positive results. However, a study on an antiviral pill developed in collaboration with a pharmaceutic company is about to begin within a few weeks."

"Some sources have specifically accused you of secrecy. Can you address this issue?"

"It is preposterous to suggest that the center is tightly controlled and under secrecy. All precautions are taken so that the virus does not spread beyond the confined area."

"Since the start of the pandemic, we've seen a number of prominent variants, including Alpha, Beta, and Delta. Have you named this new variant?"

"I have named the newly mutated virus *Pi*, from the Greek alphabet," he said, pointing to himself with a broad smile as if he was patting himself on the back.

The ACN anchorman praised Dr. Zhao's candidness and forthrightness, calling it the *Pi virus of Dr. Zhao.*

The following evening all three of us: Umesh, Bender and I met at the Irish pub for a drink to discuss the events in the center and to debate Zhao's statement to the media.

I was not entirely satisfied with Zhao's detailed explanation. "He is certainly very smart and a smooth talker," I said. "But to deny that the center is not tightly controlled and guarded and not under secrecy is preposterous."

"I thought he was brilliant," said Bender.

"He came across as an honest, well-grounded scientist," said Umesh.

"With his sweet talk the man has conned the news

media and the government, and now the country," I said. Was he telling the truth?"

"He did a good job explaining the situation with the new variant," said Bender. "Moreover, he squashed any speculation of a doctored virus, by asserting that it originated from the Delta variant."

"The government supports his version of the events, and expressed total faith in the man," said Umesh.

"We have to get access to his office," I said.

"But how?" asked Umesh.

"You guys leave me out of this," said Bender. I still work at the center, and I want to see the results of the double-blind Transcranial Magnetic Stimulation study. I am a co-principal investigator with the CDCPT neurologist, Conrad. Do you guys mind if I leave? I don't want to hear about your plots."

"Sure, I understand," I said.

After Bender left, Umesh commented that he is a frightened puppy. "On the other hand, he still works at the center and is compromised."

"Could he be a spy for Dr. Zhao?" I asked. "How did Zhao know about our conversation the other day, and all the details about Jacques surgery and brain stimulation?"

"Well, if he is a snitch wouldn't he want to hear our plans?" asked Umesh.

"Perhaps yes, perhaps not; perhaps he is guilt ridden," I said. "Anyway, we should watch out for him."

"What's your plan anyway?" asked Umesh.

"The only way we can get access to Zhao's office is if

we bribe the night cleaning lady. Her name is Claudia Martinez, and to make some extra money, she used to clean our apartment once every two weeks before the start of the pandemic. Several weeks ago, when I was here late, I saw her entering the CDCPT offices. She possibly has the code to Zhao's office."

"That's a great idea," said Umesh, tapping me on the back.

"I have her number. I'll call her and ask her to meet me."

As I left the hospital, I saw Doug Bommer loitering around on the street opposite the hospital entrance. He was smoking a cigarette and talking to another man. I wondered whether they were plotting something. I thought of reporting him to hospital security; but hanging around the hospital outside did not constitute a crime. Besides, he might be there to visit a sick friend or reapply for a new position.

On my way home, I received a call from the Chairman of Medicine, Dr. Friedlander: "I have some good news and some bad news for you," he said. "The credentials committee has approved your promotion to associate professor with Tenure. Besides, I am going to appoint you as interim chairman of the department of infectious diseases."

"Swell and thanks, Dr. Friedlander," I said. "And the

bad news?'

"Your boss, Dr. Welsh has come down with pancreatic cancer and is stepping down as chairman.

"I am so sorry about Welsh. I hadn't seen him in the hospital or spoken to him recently. I'll give him a call. And thank you for the promotion and your trust in me," I said.

As soon as I got off the phone with the chairman, I called Welsh. He did not pick up the phone and the voice mail was full.

When I got home, I enthusiastically related to Fleur about the promotion. "I expected the associate professorship but did not even dream of interim chairmanship."

"Wow," said Fleur. "You are climbing up the ladder fast."

"I think my decision to proceed with brain stimulation on Jacques impressed Dr. Friedlander. It showed Leadership. And that is what a chairman needs!"

"Will you automatically become chairman?"

"No, not at all. A search committee will be formed. I will obviously be one of the candidates. Because of COVID and the disruptions in academia, I don't see many out-of-towners applying for the position."

After we ate dinner, I called Ms. Martinez and requested a meeting. She agreed to come over to the apartment right away. She told me that she cleaned the offices of Dr. Zhao and the other doctors on Tuesdays and Fridays. She had the code to enter the CDCPT offices but not the lab, which was behind the offices. She also had the code to Dr. Zhao's office, and the other doctors, but that most of the other doctors did not usually lock their doors. She told me that the security guard leaves at six o'clock.

I explained the importance of getting into Zhao's office to look at some documents pertaining to the virus. I went into genetic details of mutation, gain-of-function, and doctoring of the virus. Yet by the expression on Ms. Martinez's face, I fully understood that she did not have the vaguest idea of what I was talking. But anyway, I went into details to impress Ms. Martinez the importance of my request and quest. Finally, I told her that Zhao was experimenting on people and hiding important information that could save lives.

"You are a Christian like me," I said. "It is your God given duty to help humanity." Her face turned serious as she made the sign of the cross. I heard her whisper: "*Que Dios me ayude.*"

"I am an Evangelical Christian, and our pastor tells us that they are using fetal tissue to develop the vaccine against this virus," she said. "Is that Chinese head doctor involved in such research?"

"I doubt it… but who knows?" I said. I felt guilty for not vehemently denying my response to her question.

"I will do anything you say, Dr. Jeff. *Que Dios me ayude.*"

I scored a homerun. Now the icing on the cake.

"There is money in it for you," I said. "Five hundred dollars."

A broad smile crossed Ms. Martinez's face. "Come to the lab at about eight-thirty sharp and tap on the door three times and I will let you in," she said. "Zhao usually leaves the office by eight o'clock, but sometimes he is there way after ten p.m. You have to check his schedule so that we can fix a date and time."

After Ms. Martinez left, I poured a double scotch and went to bed. Another reward awaited me: Big Love? It was Vanilla Sex better than no sex. And sound sleep. Sex had always been better than Ambien for my periodic insomnia. I wondered if Fleur was rewarding me for the promotion.

CHAPTER 35

THE EXECUTION OF THE PLOTS

The handing of the pill, AC#476984001, by Sinclair went smoothly. I immediately went to Jacques' apartment and handed the matchbox with the pills to Alex, instructing her to give Jacques one pill a day after breakfast for five days. I also told her to wait until I give her the go ahead.

"Do you know whether these pills work?" asked Alex. "Any side effects?"

"I have no idea whatsoever. I am sure they were tested in the animal model."

"Isn't that of concern?"

"Yes, to some extent. As far as I know Jacques will be the first human to receive the drug. How is he doing by the way?"

"The improvement is slow. He doesn't talk much, but watches the news and the shows on TV, has an improving appetite for food, and enjoys his walks in Central Park. Obviously, I accompany him at all times. Besides, Ms. Aguilar comes three times a week and spends an hour with him."

"That's good news on the whole. Has he expressed a desire to go back to work?"

"No. Do you really think he needs the pill? Maybe he will completely recover over time."

"Well, to tell you the truth, I don't really know. But the Amnestic Brain Fog is related to viral infection of the brain. Apparently, he fell into the group with a high viral load. The antiviral pill could kill any residual virus. Without the pill he might even relapse."

"Okay. But I don't want to take responsibility considering the possibility of divorce. It's best that you speak with him."

"Sure, I understand. I will speak to him."

I went to Jacques room where he was watching the news and informed him about the pill. He readily agreed to take the pill. Not at all surprising. Most doctors are happy pill poppers and treat themselves. *Physician, heal thyself!*

On my way out I informed Alex that nobody should know about the pill and especially Ms. Aguilar. Furthermore, since Ms. Aguilar is blinded about the pill, she would be in a great position to judge any memory improvement in Jacques.

"One more observation I need to mention: Your problem with Jacques has been his infidelity partly or fully related to sexual addiction. But all of this might change. He might even loose interest in sex altogether."

"You mentioned that it had happened to Fleur. Killed the emotional brain, right?"

"Yes."

"What are you getting at, Jeff?"

"I mean the divorce. Shouldn't you reconsider?"

"I have made up my mind. No more wait and see. This damn virus has played havoc in our lives."

The day arrived for the clandestine operation: a visit to Zhao's office in search of any documents that might shed light on the origin of the virus. Bender had informed me during a casual conversation that Zhao was to leave for Washington to debrief the task force on the Amnestic Brain Fog endemic on Friday morning and would return on Sunday evening. He also mentioned that Jones would be in charge of the center during his absence, and he, Bender, would be in charge of the Neurology Service.

Both Umesh and I now felt that Bender was Zhao's confidant and protegee.

On Friday evening, at around eight fifteen, Umesh and I entered the hospital separately. It was agreed in advance that Umesh would stay in his office, while I would enter the office of Zhao and Jones by myself. If I needed his help for any unforeseen eventuality, I would text him.

Since there was no security, it was easy going for me as I tapped on the glass door three times, following which Ms. Martinez let me in. I was anxious as I stepped in, fearful that I might accidentally trigger an alarm and get caught in the process. The rush of adrenaline despite the beta-blocker I took at six o'clock, did not do the job and my heart started racing and I started feeling dizzy. I sat on a chair and strained as if I was constipated, but nothing happened. I pressed on the neck first on the right side then on the left. I could sense anxiety and nervousness on

Ms. Martinez when I asked her to get some ice from the refrigerator in the kitchenette. I thought of calling Umesh and took out the phone from my pocket when suddenly I coughed hard, and the rapid heartbeat stopped. At that moment I thanked God and promised myself to have the ablation procedure when all this was over.

"It's okay, I am fine now," I told Ms. Martinez as she came running with a bucket of ice.

"What happened, Doc?" she asked. "You looked pale."

"We'll talk about it some other time. Please open the door to Zhao's office."

As I entered Zhao's office, the first thing I noticed were his PhD and MD diplomas, as well as scientific awards from University of Peking, University of Nippon, and Chapel Hill on the wall. But there were no photographs on the bookshelves which were mostly empty except for a few books. I found that rather unusual. Most academic doctors in charge like politicians usually have a family photograph lying on the desk. Perhaps Zhao was unmarried; perhaps he was a loner. The desk was spotless clean, and except for some printed manuscripts from the *New England Journal of Medicine, Science, Nature* and the journals of Virology and Infectious Diseases, I found no documents or protocols on the desk. The drawers were unlocked; but for some pens and pencils and plenty of Swiss and Belgian chocolates, they were empty.

I soon surmised that all the information, study protocols and documents must be in the computer, but I did not know the password to login. I tried several probable passwords including COVID and Zhao's initials. No dice.

In contrast to Zhao's office, Jones' desk was more cluttered, and a photo of his wife and two kids rested on the desk. But here again except for recent manuscripts from journals I found no documents or protocols. I decided that there was no point in probing further and fearful of some untoward mishap, I told Ms. Martinez that I was leaving and thanked her. I did not visit Bender's office that was by the side of Jones' office.

"Did you find what you were looking for?" Ms. Martinez asked. I just shook my head and handed her a packet with money.

On my way to meet Umesh, I called Alex and gave her the go ahead with the pill. I called Dr. Welsh again and this time he picked up the phone.

"I'm terribly sorry about the cancer," I said. "Is there anything I can do?"

"It's no good Jeff," he said. "I am due to start chemo, but it's on hold because of the COVID situation. I am waiting to hear from the oncologist. I have asked Margaret to hand over all documents and correspondence to you."

"If there is anything I can do, please don't hesitate to call."

"Sure…your prayers."

I then met Umesh in his office and informed him that the effort was a failure.

"I'm not entirely surprised. Everyone keeps documents in the computer or in iCloud these days."

"I still keep a folder with all my documents, and a separate folder with my research protocols, as well as in my computer."

"Well, Jeff—you are a bit old fashioned! Besides you have nothing to hide."

"What if the computer crashes?"

"That's why there is the Cloud. Satya Nadella, my countryman—the CEO of Microsoft— introduced it to the company and the stock took off. By the way, if you don't have it in your portfolio, you should buy Microsoft stock, plus Apple, plus Google, plus Amazon."

"I have them all. Linda stashed my portfolio with technology stocks. Gosh—I have to find out how Linda is doing."

After contemplating with a rather serious and thoughtful look, Umesh said: "I got it man. *Vande Mataram*! We have to hack Zhao's computer."

"But how?"

"Leave that to me, my friend. I know a lot of Indian IT computer wizards. I'll find someone to hack his computer. We Indians are aces in computer technology. Did you know that we invented the zero in the fifth century AD?"

"No, I didn't know that."

A week later, Umesh and I met at the Irish pub. Over

a tall beer mug of Guinness, Umesh informed me that he had found the right man to hack Zhao's computer. All that the man needed were Zhao's email and a PDF attachment that he was bound to open. "It is best that we select a most recent article on COVID-19 (pathogenesis or treatment) from either the *New England Journal of Medicine* or the British *Lancet* or *Nature*."

"I favor *Nature* or the *New England Journal of Medicine*," I said.

"How much do we have to pay your man?"

"Leave that to me. You took care of Mrs. Martinez."

"Okay, friend," I said.

"Can you select a most recent article as soon as possible and email it to me as a PDF attachment and I will also do my own research. It is important that Zhao open the attachment. If he doesn't then all bets are off."

"Should we use his work email?"

"Absolutely. My contact plans to send the email early Sunday morning, say two-three a.m. He says that the odds are good that the recipient will open it on Monday morning when he comes to work and checks his email first."

"Makes sense."

A couple of days later, as I was leaving the hospital, I met Bender in the corridor. I asked him about any new developments in the Brain Fog Centre. He told me that there was significant improvement in most of the patients undergoing Transcranial Magnetic Stimulation. "The double-blind study is due to be terminated prematurely," he said. "The preliminary results are encouraging. The statisticians are looking at the results and we should have a p value soon. If the results are significant, then the antiviral pill study maybe postponed. I credit Zhao for continuing the double-blind protocol."

"That's great news," I said. "Thanks for the information."

I proceeded to see Jacques at his apartment with some trepidation but found him asleep. Alex told me that he had some strange movements such as twisting of his body, sudden flinging of his arms, some restlessness of his legs. Sometimes he seemed to be out of it. All these unusual symptoms occurred from the third to the fifth day of taking the pill; additionally, he complained of nausea and hardly ate any food during the first two days. Also, he couldn't sleep much, was awakened by nightmares, and often kept pacing the floor most of the night. But over the last few days the side effects have subsided, and he slept well. This morning he was more cheerful and for the first time expressed a desire to go back to work.

"Perhaps you should talk to him," said Alex.

"I don't want to wake him up, particularly since he had problems sleeping. Whatever it is, it seems that the pill had neurological effects. And that is a positive sign for better or for worse. Do let me know how he is doing."

A few days later, on a Friday, I heard from Alex that Jacques was coming along fine. She told me that he spent a lot of time on the internet reading about the COVID-19 pandemic. He relentlessly searched for information about the *Pi* variant causing the Amnestic Brain Fog but was disappointed that he couldn't find any particulars. She told me that he wanted to talk to me about it.

"Although he wasn't his ebullient self, he talked a lot about his experience over the last month or so in the Brain Fog Center, about the Transcranial Magnetic Stimulation that did not work for him…the events that led to the development of the subdural hematoma…and how you had cured him by suggesting stimulation of the brain during the neurosurgery…and how you were instrumental in transferring him to the neurology floor and ultimately sending him home."

"Well, what are friends for?"

"He said that your commitment and your genius was amply displayed in your leadership and decision-making processes. He was flabbergasted and surprised how you had obtained the antiviral pill that he now believed had made a big difference in his recovery. He said that you are his one true friend."

"Both of you had done a lot for me after Martha's death and Fleur's depression after the miscarriage." I said.

"Finally, he apologized for putting me through so much: the lies, the deceptions, and the many affairs, and he began crying, something I had never seen him do before," she said. Amid an outpouring of tears, he said: "'I love you Alex, please don't leave me.'"

"Wow! Coming from Jacques, that's something. A *mea culpa*."

"I am confused, unsure whether I should proceed with the divorce," she said. "A part of me says that I should go ahead. A part of me is crushed with guilt."

"There is no need for you to feel guilty. He has been unfaithful to you. But give it some time Alex. Don't make hasty decisions. Both you and Jacques have gone through a lot."

"I am planning a picnic in Central Park this coming Sunday. Will you and Fleur come?"

"That's wonderful. I'll speak with Fleur and let you know."

CHAPTER 36

THE PICNIC IN CENTRAL PARK

We spent Sunday afternoon and most of the evening picnicking in Central Park on the great lawn. We sat on reclining lawn chairs and lay on Moroccan quilts and pillows surrounded by the towering skyline around us aflame in the midday sun. We could hear red-winged blackbirds and American robins chirruping in the mellow evening sunlight. I remembered the last time Fleur and I walked on the great lawn at night after Jacques' birthday celebration and the flock of birds that appeared singing wildly, the red fox and the white-tailed deer we saw. Then it seemed they owned the park and perhaps their reign, their freedom, would soon come to an end.

There weren't many people in the Park like in the past, most still under the penumbral shadow of the pandemic. But for us it was sort of a celebration, a rekindling of our friendship, a coming out, as if we were entering into a new world, running away from an old. Today, near the end of summer, it seemed like a day to celebrate freedom all over again with champagne, chicken and chutney sandwiches, foie gras, devilled eggs and eggs with caviar, and plenty of strawberries. We felt at home under this sky, our abode.

While Belinda ran around the park playing with her friend Darina, and Fleur and Alex went for a walk to the lakeside, Jacques and I sat sipping wine and talking.

Jacques asked me a whole lot of questions about the *Pi* virus and what I knew about it. His questions to my surprise were very provocative particularly regarding the origin of the virus, whether it was a mutation or a doctored virus to selectively affect the brain. I told him that I did not know the answer but like him had my own suspicions. In my own mind, I knew that tomorrow was the day when the hack of Zhao's computer would occur and finally Umesh and I would have the answer one way or the other.

At about five in the evening a drizzle sends us homeward bound. Fleur and I spent a quite evening watching and laughing at the reruns of *Better Call Saul.*

With all the anticipation mixed with apprehension, foreboding, and misgivings waiting for me tomorrow morning—the day of the hack—I couldn't fall asleep. Would I be dumbfounded, overwhelmed, and thunder-struck if my theory of a doctored virus held up and the mystery solved? Or would I be disappointed, deflated? And if my hunch was right what would I do with the in-formation? Take it to the media? Would I be opening a Pandora's Box? Am I running too fast with it all? I began focusing my mind on my deep breathing exercise I had recently started and ultimately fell asleep.

CHAPTER 37

THE RECKONING

The next morning, I quickly drank an expresso at home, picked up a chocolate croissant and another cup of coffee from the street cart vendor and arrived at my hospital at seven in the morning. I sat in my academic office, and proudly placed the new plaque on my desk by the side of Fleur's photograph. The plaque read:

Dr. Jeffrey Anderson, MD, FIDSA
Associate Professor of Medicine
Interim Chairman, Infectious Diseases.

This was the big day—the D day. I waited anxiously for a coded phone message from Umesh: *Manuscript accepted* (for successful hack); *Manuscript, revision requested* (for no news yet); *Manuscript rejected* (for unsuccessful hack). In the meanwhile, I scanned the Internet for news.

Rather restless, I decided to visit Bender who had informed me that he would have the final results of the Transcranial Brain Stimulation study and was anxious to begin writing the manuscript. And so, at about 7:25 a.m., I left for the physician offices above the Brain Fog Center to meet Bender. As I got off the elevator and approached the door to the doctor's offices, I was shocked to see the guard in a pool of blood and the glass door shattered. As I hurriedly tried to enter the office area in an attempt to avoid the blood and the shattered glass on the floor, I heard rapid pop-pop-pop-pop shots from a gun. Instinctively sensing danger, I ran away to the stairwell and called security. "I heard gunshots coming from the doctor's offices in the Brain Fog Center on the 26th floor," I said. "Please send security right away."

"Sure Doc," said the security officer.

It was then that I called Umesh who did not pick up the call and I presumed he was in his car on his way to the hospital. I left a message to call me right away. I took the elevator to my academic office and sat at my desk in utter shock and bewilderment.

As I was nervously and apprehensively looking at my iPhone, at about eight in the morning, a message appeared on *BreakingSmartNews*, which read: "There has been a mass shooting in the newly established Brain Fog Center at the Uptown Hospital in New York City. Several people have been killed!"

I called Umesh immediately and asked whether he had heard the news. As I was about to tell him what I saw, he asked me whether it was real or fake news. I told him what I had witnessed.

"Oh my God—Ram, Ram," he said. "You could have gotten yourself killed my friend! Why don't you come to the ICU recharge lounge? We can watch the TV news channels."

I together with Umesh and several nurses and residents watched the shocking news on the TV channels which mostly showed the front of the hospital, and a reporter announcing that there had been a mass shooting in the Brain Fog Center. He mentioned that preliminary reports suggested that several people had been killed including the head of the center, several guards, and several patients, including the gunman. He also mentioned that the area had been cordoned off by the police and the FBI.

"The identity of the gunman remains unknown," he said.

Many of the nurses couldn't stop crying and we embraced each other in an attempt to console one another. I began praying and uttered aloud the Our Father. It was yet another immense tragedy on top of the deaths piled up from COVID-19.

In the meanwhile, all non-critical staff were ordered to vacate the hospital premises immediately. The place was teeming with police officers with dogs sniffing for bombs and FBI agents. One FBI agent after carefully examining our IDs questioned us at length whether we had seen or knew of anything pertinent to the mass killing. I mentioned that I had seen the dead guard in a pool of blood and heard gunshots coming from inside the offices of the Brain Fog Center, and immediately called security. The officer took my detailed statement.

After explaining to the FBI agent that we were needed in the ICU to manage sick and critical patients, he let us go about our work. And so, Umesh and I stayed in the ICU, rounding, treating patients, and intermittently scanning the TV channels for further news of the unfolding tragedy and further orders. I called Fleur and Alex and gave them the shocking news and told them that I was fine and unharmed. I did not mention what I saw. Fleur was relieved. Alex thanked me for saving Jacques' life.

"It was you who was instrumental in keeping him away from the Brain Fog Center, as well as influencing his discharge from the hospital, if not Jacques could be dead too."

It was a harrowing day, a tragic day and yet, a too familiar day in our country with guns galore and mass murders—the monsters fully fleshed in their finery of assault weapons with steel bullets, spattering blood and eviscerating flesh.

I left the hospital at five o'clock in the evening. On my way home, I wondered if the unidentified gunman was indeed Doug Bommer. And what would have happened if I confronted him? He knew me rather well; we had conversed twice. Would I be able to stop the carnage, or would I be met with a hail of bullets? Most certainly I would have been killed. Had total insanity possessed the man? A desire for blood and death on a large scale. The very thought was chilling—the sudden, unexpected dwindling of precious life. I tried to drive these thoughts away, to block my misfiring neurons, but they kept coming back.

After I got home, Fleur embraced me, and we remained

locked in each other's arms for a long time. I poured myself a stiff brandy snifter and we watched TV for the latest updates on the tragic incident.

At about eight p.m., the New York Police Commissioner. Mr. Dudley Murphy gave a news conference. He stated that the head of the center, Dr. Zhao, the assistant chief, Dr. Jones, and the neurologist, Dr. Bender were killed together with two guards, as well as another five patients and two nurses. Several additional patients suffered injuries. The center, he said: "was a river of blood, seeping down the corridor." He mentioned that the gunman used a submachine gun. He did not mention the type or make of the gun.

"He killed the guard and entered the CDCPT offices first, where the offices of Drs. Zhao, Jones and Bender were located. He shot them in their offices. Luckily, because it was 7:30 a.m., most of the other doctors and technologists and researchers hadn't yet arrived; otherwise, the toll would have been higher. The gunman proceeded one floor down, and after killing the guard, went into the center and randomly shot to death the patients, some still sleeping on their beds and the nurses who had just come for the day shift. As the gunman was exiting the center, the security officers alerted by a doctor, whose name I am not privy to disclose at this time, saw the gunman running out with a submachine gun and shot the man dead. If not for the quick action and presence of mind of this doctor, more people might have been killed.

"The gunman was identified as a disgruntled nurse

employee, Mr. Doug Bommer, who was initially fired from the center by orders of Dr. Zhao. He was readmitted to the center with COVID related brain fog, and because of a violent altercation with one of the patients, he was discharged from the center. We are investigating further details regarding the gunman and whether he had any accomplices as well as affiliations with right wing groups and para-military organizations."

He went on to mention that there was the possibility the gunman had an inside accomplice who helped him hide in the hospital overnight and bring in the gun. Review of security cameras have identified the gunman entering the hospital at eleven p.m. last night. The man did not carry any bag suggesting that the gun was brought in by someone else or it was already hidden in the hospital.

"Was the shooting connected to the experimental procedures going on in the center?" asked the reporter from the *New York News*.

"I don't have an answer to your question at this time."

"Did you procure any documents from Dr. Zhao's or Jones' computer pertaining to the center, since there was a lot of speculation regarding the origin of the virus?" asked the reporter from *Daily News*.

"Unfortunately, no," said the commissioner. "In the shooting the computer was destroyed. However, the damaged hard drive and Dr. Zhao's and Jones' cell phones have been impounded by the FBI."

"Currently, how many patients remain in the center?" asked the reporter from ACN.

"Ten, I believe. They are transferred elsewhere in the hospital. The center has been closed. The names of the victims have been disclosed to the closest of kin and should be announced to the public tomorrow. There is an 800 number set up: 1-800-1299887 for any information regarding the gunman and his possible accomplice."

"What about the gun?"

"We are looking into it. Most likely it was purchased out-of-state."

"I am terribly sorry that we had to go through yet another tragedy in addition to the pandemic. Thank you very much and goodnight."

A reporter went on interviewing people on the street—the onlookers asking the same questions after a mass killing and receiving the same answers of shock and dismay. And then the camera shifted to Oklahoma City, Oklahoma showing a ranch house, with some neighbors around.

"I am surprised and shocked," said one tall heavily built neighbor. "Doug Bommer was a great guy, a church-going man, a true American. We went hunting together."

"He believed in all sorts of conspiracy theories, and strongly felt that our government was controlled by Jews and foreigners," said another neighbor. "He had a short fuse, but I find it hard to believe he did this."

After a long pause, the reporter continued: "His ex-wife who refused to appear on camera, confirmed a rather violent streak in the man."

"It's all over," I said. "Finally. Tragically. It seems we will never know the truth!"

"I am so sorry for all those dead people."

"I was the doctor the Police Commissioner referred to," I said. "I saw the guard in a pool of blood…As I was about to enter the doctor's office area, I heard gunshots."

"My God…you could have been killed," she said, and embraced me.

It was the fiery end of an enduring, outlandish chapter in the Coronavirus landscape.

EPILOGUE

Life is the tragedy, she said bitterly. You know how they categorize Shakespeare's plays, right? If it ends with a wedding, it's a comedy. And if it ends with a funeral, it's a tragedy. So, we're all living tragedies, because we all end the same way, and it isn't with a goddamn wedding.

—Robyn Schneider, *The Beginning of Everything*

The ten patients that survived the carnage and those previously discharged received the antiviral pill, and ultimately recovered from the Amnestic Brain Fog.

An obituary in the New York News praised Dr. Zhao to the hilt for containing the *Pi* virus and preventing its spread. A memorial was held at the hospital for the dead where Umesh and I spoke. Referring to Dr. Zhao, I said: "We disagreed on some issues, but Dr. Zhao was a great scientist who not only discovered and isolated the Pi virus, but also contained it, preventing its spread. The science of virology will sorely miss Dr. Zhao."

The FBI concluded their investigation of Bommer and maintained that he was a lone disgruntled gunman with no links to any right wing or other organizations or any conspiracies. They maintained that he acted alone and had no accomplice. The conclusion was not dissimilar to the previous mass killings in the country.

I managed to access the results of the Brain Stimulation Study from Bender's office. I was deeply distressed and saddened at his premature death. He was a great, smart and a seasoned neurologist who had cared for my friend Jacques and my wife Fleur. He had the data analyzed by the biostatisticians and was writing the manuscript when he was shot. The data showed that the brain stimulation study was highly effective with a significant statistical p value of <.0001. I also found the cerebrospinal viral data in patients with severe retrograde amnesia versus those with mild amnesia for recent events and in those who developed the St. Vitus dance. I re-named it as *the Pi Virus dance of Dr. Zhao*. We would publish the results of these studies as co-authors together with Conrad and Zhao's and Bender's name mentioned posthumously. Together with Whitmore and Umesh, I also published the case report on direst brain stimulation on Jacques Charpentier.

Among other things, the publications of the above-mentioned articles earned me the chairmanship of the department of infectious diseases and Dr. Umesh Mukherjee the directorship of the Department of Intensive Care. Also, I was conferred the Bronze Medal by the mayor of New York City for alerting the security services of the hospital that prevented additional deaths.

It turned out that not all was bad at least for the majority that survived the pandemic. But some young women were devastated by long COVID months after the episode. For the families of those that succumbed to the virus, their hearts were broken to see their loved ones suddenly disappear without even a goodbye—their lives a profound emptiness without closure like a well without a bottom. Many of these unfortunate human beings would seek seers and fortune tellers to connect with the afterlife. In this regard, it reminded me of the *Famadihana*, or the "Turning of the Bones," a festival for the dead held in the highlands of Madagascar. Every five to seven years, people honor their ancestors by exhuming them from the family tomb and wrapping them in fresh shrouds. It's a joyful event, with music, hog roasts, rum, and dancing.

My friend Jacques completely recovered from the Amnestic Brain Fog, but he metamorphosed into a kindler, softer, contemplative human being who lost interest in high-powered coronary intervention in New York celebrities. He continued to work part-time as a consultant cardiologist at the medical center, and also joined a Medicaid clinic in Harlem once a week to serve the poor and underprivileged. Disillusioned with the Christian Right for their diehard anti-abortion ban, he ultimately abandoned the Christian faith and joined the Zen Center of New York—Fire Lotus Temple—where he attained the art of peaceful meditation. He sold his Lamborghini and donated the proceeds to the temple. During his free time, he was often seen walking around in Central Park in saffron robes.

His sexual appetite, his highfalutin talk, and his Don Juan forays were somehow killed by the virus. His wife Alex, despite Fleur's and my advice to the contrary, ultimately filed for divorce. However, the divorce being rather amicable, they continued seeing each other and had joint custody of their daughter Belinda.

As soon as the pandemic waned, I had a catheter ablation performed by Grimes and Levy of one of the razor-thin electrical pathways they referred to as the *slow pathway* as one of the limbs that caused the tachycardia. I simply marveled at their technical prowess as they went about identifying the electrical circuit in the heart and zapping it. I went home the following day completely cured. I was told that in the past I might have had to resort to open heart surgery.

After the mass shooting, our personal lives, that of Fleur and mine, would change to focus on ourselves. Fleur did not entirely recover from the viral devastation of her emotional brain; however, this very fact resolved many of her emotional issues for the better. She would take up yoga and her fear of amniocentesis dissipated. She became pregnant and delivered a beautiful baby boy attributing it to the Kamasutra position of Om, called *Padmasana* or Lotus in the original *Kama Sutra* text.

After a year or so, she became pregnant again and delivered a girl. She would wholeheartedly indulge in motherhood, but ultimately pursue her career as a substitute Metszzo-soprano in small operas, and a consultant chef in a New York Michelin French restaurant. The uptick in her professional life seemed to have also made a difference. It was as if we found each other again and fell in love; but our love was different: a love of familiarity, a love of understanding, a love of respect for each other's ways and idiosyncrasies, a love that celebrates that despite all odds and the angst of COVID-19, we survived.

In all of this, I remained totally absorbed in building up the infectious diseases department, by hiring additional staff and revamping the Fellowship Training Program. Due to my academic success, I began delivering lectures all over the country and was sought after by drug companies as consultant. My monograph on *The Corona Viruses: Genetics, Pathophysiology, and Management* was a bestseller. I was also hired by one of the popular TV channels as an expert on COVID-19 and the various vaccines floating around, their efficacy and possible side effects. I was offered to sit on the boards of several pharmaceutical companies and asked to become a spokesman for the vaccine industry, which I turned down. It was rather ironic that I, the soft-spoken, contemplative physician would take the place of the one-time high powered testosterone heady friend Jacques.

A lot happened during this pandemic—it exposed the weaknesses in the country: its preparedness for the pandemic—shattering the *terra firma* and leaving deep fault lines.

Despite the introduction of COVID vaccines—some based on novel mRNA technology, many in the country refused to get vaccinated. With so much going on: the death of George Floyd at the hands of the police, the election of a new President, and the storming of the House of Representatives on January 6th, the news cycle spun around at a rapid dizzying pace, and the *Pi* virus of Dr. Zhao was soon forgotten. Some months thereafter, when things were settling down and the economy was bouncing back, yet another more infectious, but less dangerous mutation—the Omicron variant, appeared out of South Africa, and the panic button was punched again as it spread throughout the world at a rapid pace.

What was perplexing is the disorder and fragmentation of our times under the duress of the pandemic. Doctors and nurses were threatened for dispensing COVID vaccines, and school board members were assailed for supporting mask mandates. Sometimes it was hard not to feel that we were living through another surreal and dangerous iteration of Didion's America, where "disorder was its own point." Our times reminded me of a Yeats poem, *The Second Coming*:

> *Turning and turning in the widening gyre*
> *The falcon cannot hear the falconer;*
> *Things fall apart; the center cannot hold,*
> *Mere anarchy is loosed upon the world;*
> *The blood-dimmed tide is loosed,*

I hope as the saying goes: *After every storm, there is a rainbow.*

As of this writing, the pandemic is over; however, it is possible that the virus will ultimately become endemic and seasonal like the flu and even the common cold. I was repeatedly asked to address this very question. I went on to elaborate that there are two possible ends to the pandemic: first and foremost is the medical end when the incidence of infection and hospitalization and death rates plummet. This is undoubtedly the best scenario. The second scenario is the social, when the epidemic of fear about the disease wanes, and people decide to go on with their lives, to live with the disease, vaccinated or not. This second element is determined by sociopolitical processes such as opening of the economy and challenging and lifting mask and vaccine mandates as has already happened in most quarters of the country.

"I am sure," I said, repeatedly, "there will be ups and downs, and new mutations will appear in the future. We are near the end until a new virus makes its appearance."

GLOSSARY

Abaya: a long, black, shapeless garment that covers women from their throats to their feet. It is worn over the womens clothing.

Amniocentesis: the sampling of amniotic fluid using a hollow needle inserted into the uterus, to screen for developmental abnormalities in the fetus.

Amnesia: a partial or total loss of memory.

Anticoagulant: a drug that thins the blood so that it doesn't clot readily.

Atherectomy: an invasive technique for removing atherosclerotic and calcified plaques from blood vessels in this case the coronary arteries.

Cath lab: a laboratory where heart catheterization procedures are performed, which mostly consist in measuring pressures inside the heart and injecting dye in the arteries of the heart (coronary arteries) and if necessary, opening the arteries by dilating them (angioplasty) and stenting them.

Cardiac Interventionalist: a medical doctor, a cardiologist who specializes in heart procedures such as insertion of stents in diseased arteries of the heart and diseased valves.

Cardiopulmonary resuscitation: a medical procedure involving repeated compression of a patients chest, performed in an attempt to restore the blood circulation and breathing of a person who has suffered cardiac arrest.

Chimera: In Greek mythology it represents a fire-breathing female monster with a lion's head, a goat's body, and a serpent's tail. In medicine, Chimera is a living object, in this instance a virus composed of two genetically distinct cell types.

Cytokine release syndrome: seen in COVID-19, happens when the immune system responds to infection aggressively with the release of inflammatory agents and can be fatal if not treated aggressively.

Downing and doffing: refers to changing into and out of work clothes, gear or equipment. To don means to put on work clothes, gear or equipment. To doff means to take off work clothes, gear or equipment.

Down syndrome: a genetic disorder caused when abnormal cell division results in an extra full or partial copy of chromosome 21. This extra genetic material causes the developmental changes and physical features of Down syndrome characterized by low muscle tone, short stature, a flat nasal bridge, and a protruding tongue.

Encephalitis: infection of the brain (viral or bacterial)

Encephalopathy: a disease that effects the brain leading to an altered mental state.

ER: Emergency Room.

Extracorporeal membrane oxygenation (ECMO): The method allows the blood to bypass the heart and lungs It is used in critical care situations when the heart and lungs need help so that they can heal. It is used in severe cases of COVID-19.

Gain-of-function: involves medical research that genetically alters an organism, in this case a virus that may enhance its biological function making it more lethal, more infectious, and more resistant to vaccines.

Heart-lung machine: a machine that bypasses the heart and adds oxygen to the blood before it is pumped throughout the body.

Hijab: head coverings worn by Muslim women.

HIPAA: The Health Insurance Portability and Accountability Act of 1996 is a federal law that required the creation of national standards to protect sensitive patient health information from being disclosed without the patients consent or knowledge.

Immunocompromised: an individual whose immune system is weekend.

Infectious diseases: Medical specialty dealing with infections such as bacteria, viruses etc.

Intubation: insertion of a breathing tube that is connected to a respiratory machine.

Intra-aortic balloon: a device that is inserted in the aorta, the major artery of the body that helps the weakened heart pump blood.

Long QT Syndrome: a genetic heart signaling disorder that can cause fast, chaotic heartbeats (arrhythmias) and sudden death.

Monitored unit: where a patient's heart rate is constantly monitored. It is also referred as a step-down unit.

MRI: Magnetic resonance imaging is a noninvasive test that produces detailed images of organs of the body. MRI scanners use a large magnet and radio waves.

MRA: Magnetic resonance angiography is a test used

to visualize the blood vessels in the brain.

N95 masks: respiratory protective devices designed to achieve a very close facial fit and very efficient filtration of airborne particles.

Namaste: a customary Hindu non-contact greeting.

Negative pressurization: The air pressure inside the room is lower than the air pressure outside the room, which means that when the door is opened potentially contaminated air inside the room will not flow outside into non-contaminated areas.

Parkinson's disease: a debilitating disorder of the central nervous system that affects movement, often including tremors.

Placebo group: this group consist of patients in whom a dummy pill is administered.

p value: a calculated statistical value showing whether the intervention in a study is significant when compared to controls. The lower the p value, the greater the statistical significance of the observed difference.

Re-occluding: occurs when a heart artery is opened with a balloon known as balloon angioplasty and begins blocking again.

Supraventricular Tachycardia: a rapid heart rhythm originating in the upper chambers of the heart.

Sleep Apnea: a common disorder that causes breathing to stop or get shallow for seconds to minutes. It is seen commonly in obesity.

Telemetry Unit: a step-down unit where patients in the CCU or ICU go for monitoring after recovery from the acute illness.

The code: in this case "team 700" is called when a patient's heart stops beating, or the patient has stopped breathing. A team of doctors arrive and start resuscitating the patient.

Transcranial Repetitive Magnetic Stimulation: a non-invasive form of brain stimulation in which a magnetic field is used to induce an electrical current at a specific area of the brain through electromagnetic induction. An electric stimulator is connected to a magnetic coil which is connected to the scalp.

Tilt Test: a test that is commonly done in patients who faint. The patient is placed on a table that tilts the head up to about 70 degrees and the heart rate and blood pressure is monitored. Many patients with syncope or black out spells do faint during the test when the heart rate and blood pressure falls precipitously.

Tracheostomy: a surgically created hole in the windpipe that provides an alternate airway for breathing. A tracheostomy tube is inserted through the hole and secured in place with a strap around the neck.

Vasovagal attack: strong stimulation of the vagus nerve to the heart causes marked slowing of the heart rate and fall in blood pressure resulting in fainting episodes. It is often seen in dehydrated individuals and is precipitated by severe pain, nausea, and vomiting, and unanticipated bad news such as a death of a loved one. Usually It is a benign condition, however it can result in trauma due to falls.

ACKNOWLEDGMENTS

I would like to express my gratitude to my wife Margarita Mikhno for being there, to Dr. Gidwani for filling me with some details of what went on in the ICUs during the COVID pandemic, my friends Grace Schulman and Linda Thorson for their consistent encouragement and suggestions, to the Two Bridges Writers Workshop for their revision advice, and specially to Stephanie Dickinson for her advice, encouragement and support.

ANTÓNIO GOMES, aka J. Anthony Gomes is a prominent physician, and a professor of cardiology at the Mount Sinai Medical Center, NYC. He has been listed in *The Best Doctors in New York, Top Doctors*, and *Best Doctors in America* for several years.

He has published articles in the humanities in anthologies, books, newspapers, and magazines. In addition, he has published two books of poetry entitled *Visions from Grimes Hill* (Turn of River Press, Stanford, Connecticut, USA, 1994) and *Mirrored Reflections* (GOA 1556 and *Fundacão* Oriente, 2013); and three novels, *The Sting of Peppercorns* (GOA, 1556 & Broadway Books, 2010); 2nd edition, Amaryllis, New Delhi, India, 2017), *Nas Garras Do Destino*, (Chiado Editora, Brake Media, Lisbon, Portugal and Brazil, 2019), and Have A Heart (Serving House Books, Copenhagen, Denmark and South Orange, NJ, 2020)

His publications in medicine include more than 180 scientific articles and three textbooks in cardiology: *Signal Averaged Electrocardiography: Basic Concepts Methods and Application* (Kluwer Academic Press, London/Amsterdam, 1993), *Heart Rhythm Disorders: History, Mechanisms and Treatment Perspectives* (Springer-Nature, 2020) and *Rhythms of Broken Hearts* (Springer-Nature, 2021).